"It's not ... ...
F... ...**promise.**

Faith felt hot all over, and ice-cold deep inside. She knew that feeling, and she knew she couldn't keep it in check for long. Especially if Walter went on the way he was going. One more wrong word out of him and she might have to commit murder. And the only attorney she knew who could get her off would be the one surrounded by police chalk lines.

She stormed out of his office, not so blindingly angry that she didn't notice Walter failed to call after her.

Murder is *always an option,* she thought, seething. Nothing, nobody, was going to talk her out of having this baby!

Dear Reader,

I love small Southern towns, as you might have guessed if you've read some of my earlier books. I've found a new town I hope you'll like as much as I do.

About two years ago, my husband and I visited Hot Springs, Virginia. The town and a grand spa resort grew up around the hot springs. It was gracious and quaint and one of those places where your soul feels peaceful right away.

Baby Boom is the first of a series of books about the people of a similar town—Hope Springs, Virginia, a town whose motto is You'll Need No Other Medicine But Hope. Each book will be about people who face a crisis and turn their lives around, people who heal their lives with the help of the warm-hearted people in Hope Springs.

I hope you'll enjoy Faith O'Dare and her friends and will hang around for the next HOPE SPRINGS book, which will be out this fall.

Happy reading!

Peg Sutherland

Books by Peg Sutherland

HARLEQUIN SUPERROMANCE
673—DOUBLE WEDDING RING (3 WEDDINGS & A SECRET)
675—ADDY'S ANGELS (3 WEDDINGS & A SECRET)
679—QUEEN OF THE DIXIE DRIVE-IN (3 WEDDINGS & A SECRET)
734—AMY (SISTERS Trilogy)
754—ONLY YOU (with Leigh Greenwood)

Don't miss any of our special offers. Write to us at the following address for information on our newest releases.

Harlequin Reader Service
U.S.: 3010 Walden Ave., P.O. Box 1325, Buffalo, NY 14269
Canadian: P.O. Box 609, Fort Erie, Ont. L2A 5X3

BABY BOOM
Peg Sutherland

Harlequin Books

TORONTO • NEW YORK • LONDON
AMSTERDAM • PARIS • SYDNEY • HAMBURG
STOCKHOLM • ATHENS • TOKYO • MILAN
MADRID • WARSAW • BUDAPEST • AUCKLAND

If you purchased this book without a cover you should be aware that this book is stolen property. It was reported as "unsold and destroyed" to the publisher, and neither the author nor the publisher has received any payment for this "stripped book."

With much gratitude to Anne Lowry, for sharing her personal and her professional experience

ISBN 0-373-70780-0

BABY BOOM

Copyright © 1998 by Peg Robarchek.

All rights reserved. Except for use in any review, the reproduction or utilization of this work in whole or in part in any form by any electronic, mechanical or other means, now known or hereafter invented, including xerography, photocopying and recording, or in any information storage or retrieval system, is forbidden without the written permission of the publisher, Harlequin Enterprises Limited, 225 Duncan Mill Road, Don Mills, Ontario, Canada M3B 3K9.

All characters in this book have no existence outside the imagination of the author and have no relation whatsoever to anyone bearing the same name or names. They are not even distantly inspired by any individual known or unknown to the author, and all incidents are pure invention.

This edition published by arrangement with Harlequin Books S.A.

® and TM are trademarks of the publisher. Trademarks indicated with ® are registered in the United States Patent and Trademark Office, the Canadian Trade Marks Office and in other countries.

Printed in U.S.A.

BABY BOOM

CHAPTER ONE

THE WHOLE BLASTED TOWN saw it coming before I did.

Actually only three people in town even knew Faith O'Dare's news. But all three of them seemed to know better than she did how Walter would react. And that was enough to keep her fuming all the way back up the mountain to Hope Springs.

First to know—and issue a warning—was Doc Sarah of course. But Faith O'Dare and Sarah Biggers had climbed trees and made themselves sick on peanut-butter cupcakes more than once when they were growing up together on Timber Gap Lane. So Faith didn't always give the proper weight to her old friend's advice, medical or otherwise.

"I take it this means you're happy with the news," Sarah had said when Faith finished twirling her around the worn wooden floor in the old examining room.

Drawing a deep shaky breath, Faith had pressed her palms to her cheeks, which were flushed and warm with excitement. "I'm not happy. I'm..." But her heart was so full she couldn't come up with a single word to express the joy she felt. So she launched herself at her friend once again, hugged Sarah tightly enough to leave the imprint of the stethoscope on her chest and said, "Oh, Sarah, what do you call it when it's ten times happy?"

Sarah's soft laugh drew her back to earth and Faith looked at her friend. Sarah was composed to Faith's emotional, tall and sturdy to Faith's petite and lithe, dark to Faith's fair. Faith's eyes filled; she was so grateful to be sharing this moment with her oldest friend.

"A baby," she sighed, trying to capture some of the thoughts and emotions whirling through her. A baby with Walter's eyes. Or hers? His brains or her exuberance? A boy? A girl? "Oh, Sarah, a baby. Can you imagine anything more perfect?"

That was when she saw the doubt flicker across Sarah's heart-shaped face.

"What?" Alarm filled her. "What is it? Something's wrong, isn't it?"

"No, no." Sarah put her hands on Faith's shoulders and guided her into a chair. "Not a sign of anything wrong. It's just... What about Walter?"

Now it was Faith's turn to laugh. "Walter? You mean because we're not married? Yet."

Sarah shook her head. "Faith, that's been your problem. You don't always see things the way they really are. You see things the way *you* are—you expect everyone to be as open and eager and straightforward as you."

"Not everyone," Faith said, her heart still dancing a happy jig. "Just Walter. You'll see. Walter is going to be the proudest papa-to-be you've ever seen."

A half hour later she'd repeated the same words to Donna and Kelsy, her partners at Times Square

Crafts. Their skepticism had been less restrained—and harder to dispel—than Sarah's.

"Darlin', I know men." Donna Wilson, who was only a few years older than Faith but sometimes acted as if she were the mother of the world, had sliced through the corrugated top of a box full of tubes of paint. "Men need a little warming up before they're thrilled about babies. Especially men who haven't even walked down the aisle yet."

Kelsy nodded in agreement.

Faith shook her head. "Donna, we're talking about *Walter.* Solid, dependable, family-values poster-boy Walter."

Donna rolled her chocolate brown eyes. "All I'm saying is, spring this one easy."

"Come on, Donna. Do you know how long we've been seeing each other?" Faith glanced at her watch, too hyper at the moment to help prep the store for opening. The doors didn't open for another twenty-five minutes, which gave her plenty of time to call Walter with the news.

"About a year and a half." Kelsy Beattie, younger than both of them at barely thirty and looking younger still thanks to an abundance of freckles and springy carrot-colored hair, began shelving the paints as Donna unpacked. "It was right after I broke my engagement to Freddie, but just before I met Steve."

"I thought Freddie was the fiancé before Hank," Donna said. "Didn't Freddie come before Hank, Faith?"

"No," Faith said. "First came Jim. That was right after we opened the shop. Then came Hank. She almost made it to the altar with Hank. He was the one who wore glasses, remember? And she started worrying about having children who would have to wear glasses before they were out of diapers."

"It's something to think about," Kelsy said.

Faith ignored her. "*Then* came Freddie. Freddie was my personal favorite."

Donna shook her head. "For my money, Steve was the one. That boy's gonna be rich. Win a couple of golf tournaments, make a hole-in-one and get himself a Cadillac. You made a mistake there, girl."

Kelsy frowned. "Life on the road? I don't think so."

"You're just chicken," Donna said.

"Maybe I'm just not the marrying type," Kelsy countered.

"Well, Walter is," Faith said. "And I'm calling him right now."

She reached for the phone, but Donna put her hand out to cover it. "You're joshing, right? Faith, you can't tell a man something like this over the phone."

True enough. Besides, Faith realized she wanted to see the look in Walter's eyes when he heard the news. "Okay. You win. I'm driving into Richmond right now just to prove how wrong you both are."

"Now, Faith, don't get mad." Donna grabbed her by the sleeve. Kelsy snatched her car keys out of her hand.

"You'll know when I get mad," Faith said, although she could feel the telltale surge of energy tightening her chest. A fit of temper might be coming on. How could her best friends doubt Walter?

"Darlin', you're rushing into this without thinking. This kind of thing needs a little candlelight, a little wine."

"I've had a lot of fiancés," Kelsy said, "and I wouldn't have surprised any of them with this kind of news without softening them up first. And Walter's not even your fiancé."

"I trust Walter."

"You trust everybody," Kelsy said, and it sounded like an indictment.

"Pop always said people live up or down to whatever you expect of them." Faith had pried her keys out of Kelsy's long potter's fingers and backed toward the door. "Hold the fort, ladies. I'm going to Richmond to make Walter the happiest man alive."

Excitement had bubbled up in her all the way down the mountain in her dilapidated station wagon. She was like that, her emotions always close to the surface and impossible to contain.

But her bright balloon of optimism had deflated somewhat the minute she breezed past Walter's protesting administrative assistant and burst into his office without knocking. Something unfamiliar flickered in his piercing blue eyes, a shadow of fear, a whisper of irritation. Things Faith had never seen there before. And suddenly she questioned the wisdom of driving the hour-plus to Walter's office—a place she'd never been before—to spring her good news on him.

"Faith." There it was again. The way Walter said her name as he stood and adjusted his conservative silk necktie told her something was askew besides his Windsor knot. "What a surprise."

She let out the breath she'd been holding, but her tension rose, instead of diminishing. His office on the top floor of a decorous and painstakingly preserved brownstone intimidated her with its Old Masters' prints and leather-bound books; and Faith wasn't easily intimidated. Growing up without a mother, she'd learned early to stand on her own two feet.

Now that she was here, Faith couldn't think what to say. What she'd envisioned on her drive over was simply rushing into Walter's arms and whispering the happy words into his ear the moment she laid eyes on him. But Walter still stood behind his desk, his hands shoved into the pockets of his charcoal slacks, a pinched smile on his lips.

"I didn't think you'd mind," she said, although it was clear now that he did. She couldn't imagine why. Suddenly her soft flyaway hair felt messy; she caught it behind one ear and wished she'd thought to fix herself up. This office called for something more sophisticated than the green-sprigged cotton jumper she'd put on for the shop this morning. But Faith's closet was short on sophisticated.

"Mind?" he said. "No, of course not."

He'd been lost in his work, that was all, Faith told herself as he walked over and closed his office door behind her. Hadn't he told her when they'd first started dating that it was best not to disturb him at work? That he was so single-minded and focused at the office that it took the entire drive home to even remember he had a life outside the law firm?

Then again, I never really had a life before you.
She remembered when he'd said those words, that
night at his secluded lakeside cabin, where she'd noticed no family photographs, no personal touches.
She'd ached for how lonely Walter's life must have
been.

The memory relaxed Faith. So did the way he now
wrapped his arm around her shoulders and kissed her
cheek and smiled his reassuring smile. He ushered
her to a big cozy armchair.

Of course that was it. Walter always lost himself
in his work. Having her drop in like this had simply
taken him by surprise.

"I'm sorry," she murmured. "This probably
wasn't a good idea, after all."

He sat in a matching armchair. "Is something
wrong?"

She shook her head. "I wanted to tell you in person, that's all. And I just couldn't wait for the weekend."

"Tell me what, Faith?"

The sound of his voice told her he was worried.
How like Walter to worry about her. She smiled. In
all her thirty-six years Faith knew she'd never been
happier.

"We're going to have a baby."

Saying the words thrilled her, caused a wobble in
her voice. She pictured Walter at her side as their
baby was born, ever the calm, steadying influence
he'd been throughout their relationship. She could
see the ring on her finger, something simple but sub-
stantial. Walter would be the perfect father, attentive

and patient and wise. Exactly the kind of man she'd spent all these years looking for.

It had been worth the wait.

Faith looked for Walter's reaction and saw the color drain from his sun-burnished cheeks, saw his expression shift from uncertain to stunned. The fear in his eyes came out of the shadows.

"Oh, my God," he whispered.

Something in Faith froze. Once again this did not seem like the Walter she knew, the Walter who had spent two weekends a month with her and at least one night a week for the past year and a half, who had stood by her side when her father died and given her endless legal advice about her business. This was not the Walter who said he loved her small town and all the people in it, and who had in turn captured every heart in Hope Springs with his easy charm. This was not the man she had known would share her joy in the creation of a new life born of their love.

What was wrong? Where was that Walter?

"You're sure?" he said.

"You aren't happy about this," she said, disappointment creeping into her heart.

"You're sure?"

Faith recognized another stirring of her quick temper and did her best to tamp it down. This was no time for one of her infamous tantrums. "Yes, Walter. I'm sure."

"Oh, my God." He sounded beyond stunned; he sounded dismayed.

A tangle of emotions began to choke Faith. She

shot to the edge of her chair, clutching her purse under her arm. "You're repeating yourself, Walter. I'm sure what you mean is, 'Darling, I've never been so happy. How soon can we be married?' Isn't that what you mean, Walter?"

Even her pointed tone of voice didn't seem to pierce his shock. He stared at her as if he couldn't take it all in. Yes, Faith was definitely getting angry. She felt the flutter in her chest and the way hot and cold shivered along her arms all at the same time.

"Faith, I—"

"I think I'd better go," she said. She really didn't want to make a scene here in front of the Old Masters. "We'll talk this weekend."

"This weekend?"

Faith clenched her fists; that way, she thought, she wouldn't be tempted to close her fingers around his neck. They'd been planning this weekend by phone for days. Walter never stood her up. *Never.* She stood and willed herself not to shake. "This weekend, Walter. The contra dance. The hike to the waterfall."

She would not lose it. She counted to thirty; ten was seldom sufficient to contain her temper.

Her counting apparently gave Walter time to collect himself. He rose and put a hand on her arm. She wanted to shake it off, but didn't. "Faith, I know this seems like rotten timing, but I'd planned to call today, anyway. I can't make it this weekend, after all. Prep for the Thoroughgood trial is taking longer than I expected and..." He shrugged apologetically but didn't look her in the eye. "But we'll talk. We'll get this straightened out. I promise."

"Straightened out?"

"It's not going to be a problem, I promise."

"A *problem?"*

Faith felt hot all over, and ice cold deep in the core of her being. She knew that feeling and she knew she couldn't keep it in check for long. Especially if Walter kept on the way he was going. One more wrong word out of him and she might have to commit murder. And the only attorney she knew who could get her off would be the one surrounded by police chalk lines.

She stormed out of his office, not so blindingly angry that she didn't notice Walter failed to call after her.

Murder is always an option, she thought, seething. But first she'd take the time to put together a better plan. Something foolproof. And maybe even painful.

SEAN DAVENPORT didn't like the tone of voice Walter's administrative assistant used when she called. "Walt has a visitor. I think you'd better get down here."

Sean took off his reading glasses and put them on the yellow legal pad where he'd been making notes for a brief. "Dammit, Brick, what now?"

He took the time to roll down his sleeves and pull on his suit coat. Whatever Walt had going, it wouldn't hurt to cruise in wearing armor. He pinched his nose right in front of the spot where the headache had been threatening for the past hour and pondered the foolishness of hanging on to his friendship with Walter Brickerson. The things that had drawn them together as frat brothers seemed less compelling for men who'd just celebrated birthday number thirty-nine for the second year in a row.

Snugging his necktie back into place, Sean left his office.

He turned into the softly lit corridor leading to Walter's office and was instantly plowed into by someone heading out in one heck of a hurry. He put out his hands to steady himself and grasped the arms of a woman with fury in her eyes.

Uh-oh. Not again.

"Take your hands off me," she huffed, the threat of dire consequences in her husky growl.

Sean didn't need further instruction. He dropped his hands. "Sorry. I shouldn't have—"

"And get out of my way."

He stepped back. She continued her whirlwind departure from the law firm of Brickerson, Cowell, Brickerson and Davenport. As best he could tell, she was petite and unadorned, the possessor of flyaway fawn-colored hair and an earth-mother kind of dress swirling around slender calves.

Not exactly Brick's type.

"Son of a bitch," Sean muttered. "What have you gotten yourself into now, pal?"

FAITH WAS RUNNING late in a town where few people ran because nobody worried about a minute here or there. Hope Springs was like that. Laid-back. Calm.

Faith was neither of those things. But Hope Springs was also tolerant and put up with her, anyway.

Her shoes tapped along the cobblestone path that ran along the ledge above Ridge Lane, the town's main street. Before facing work this morning she'd gone into the woods that separated the town from Heritage Manor to spend a few minutes at the tiny chapel. She did that sometimes, looking for more calm than she naturally possessed. Usually it worked.

The path she was on ran from one end of town to the other, from Cookie's Twice-Loved Treasures on the north to the imposing Heritage Manor on the south, with flights of rickety wooden steps every two blocks. Faith descended one of those flights of steps now to get down to Ridge Lane.

She glanced at her watch. Ceramics class had started ten minutes ago, on the button. Kelsy would have seen to that. Kelsy and Donna were used to Faith's tardiness.

And her temper, which had gotten her into trouble again, she thought.

"Say, Faith!"

Faith turned toward the voice. She should've stayed on the path all the way to the shop; she could've avoided this. Clem Weeks waved a tire iron in her direction and walked toward her from the tidy green garage on the corner of Ridge and Loblolly. Clem's faded denim overalls were clean, but her face was streaked with grease. Her chestnut braid was pulled up under a cap touting auto parts.

"You tell Walter I got that rebuilt transmission he asked me to look for, okay? I'll do the job the next weekend he's in town."

Faith nodded at the young woman who'd apparently never outgrown the tomboy stage of adolescence. "I'll tell him," she said, and kept walking.

If he ever speaks to me again, she thought.

The week since she'd gone to Walter's office had been harder than Faith had imagined. Harder even than the week after her father died, and that had been the worst week of her life.

Of course you had Walter at your side then, she told herself as she passed the front window of the *Hope Springs Courier*. She kept her eyes on the sidewalk because she didn't want to have to stop and chat. She sighed, knowing her reluctance to pass the time of day with her neighbors was precisely why she was particularly late for work today. At this very minute Times Square Crafts was overrun with chatty women. Being closemouthed was a social aberration in small Southern towns. This week, however, Faith wasn't up for chitchat.

But Ridge Lane only ran for six blocks before hitting the highway out of town, so it didn't take her long to arrive.

Times Square Crafts had been named by the previous owner when someone quipped that Hope Springs's craft shop was a lot like Times Square— sooner or later the entire world seemed to pass through the doors. It operated in an old house near the north end of Ridge Lane. The gingerbread trim was painted various shades of green, the siding a cheery shade of peach. The porch swing would have been inviting but for the threatening glare of Genghis Khan, the fourteen-pound Siamese cat who served as night watchman and appropriated the well-stuffed cushions on the swing every morning.

Inside, two spacious front parlors were devoted to colorful displays of handcrafts. Antique cabinets and pie safes and baker's racks were filled with the colorful clutter of quilting supplies and framed cross-stitch samplers and ceramic knickknacks. An elegant mahogany rolltop desk held an adding machine and a tidy—thanks to Kelsy—stack of receipt books. The formal dining room, visible from the front between double pocket doors, had been converted to classroom space.

A dozen pairs of eyes looked up from a massive wooden table as Faith slipped in the front door. Conversation didn't slow down, but some of it turned in her direction.

"That watch of yours stop again?" Kelsy asked, a good-natured grin on her face as she looked up from demonstrating glazing techniques to the students.

The woman who had taught Faith geometry in the tenth grade said tartly, "She's never been on time a day in her life."

"I was early once," Faith said, but only because some kind of reply was expected.

"So I heard," Kelsy retorted. "Your pop said you were born a month early. He said that was the only time. Right?"

Faith walked into the classroom, which had been expanded by knocking out the wall between the dining room and the old kitchen.

"You're looking peaked again today." Donna tossed a damp towel into the industrial-size sink.

"She sick?" asked the wife of the postmaster. "I hear there's some kind of spring cold going around."

"I told you yesterday I'm fine."

She wasn't, of course, but she wasn't about to admit to God and everybody that she had managed to muddy the waters with Walter. Like her, most of the other women around the table thought Walter Brickerson was the perfect man. Good-looking, rich and kindhearted. Intelligent, successful and sensitive. A man who brought flowers and called faithfully and elevated your pulse.

Yes, Walter Brickerson was the perfect man, but Faith had made a big mistake, just as Donna had predicted. Bursting into his office like that, while he was in the middle of his work, his mind caught up in life-and-death situations—she should have known he'd be distracted and then in shock from her news.

And in typical fashion she'd made the situation worse by getting angry. Pop always said her temper was going to be her downfall.

Right again, Pop. And it's darned irritating from a man who bailed out on me ten months ago.

Anyway, she'd called back to apologize and Walter had been his old wonderful self. He'd said everything she'd needed to hear—that she was the most important thing in his life, that he loved her more than anyone, that he couldn't believe he'd been such an insensitive dolt. Faith's anger and trepidation had melted away as they always did.

Of course they hadn't really talked about the baby

again, because Faith had the good sense not to make the same mistake twice. They would talk the next time he came, after big mugs of hazelnut decaf and her special blueberry pancakes, maybe even the last batch of Pop's homemade sausage from the freezer.

Except that Walter hadn't been able to make it for the weekend. And so far this week she hadn't heard from him. But she would. Poor guy, this case was wearing him out. He would surely make it this weekend and they could talk about the future. The baby.

Then why did she feel so grumpy? Even Donna and Kelsy could see it.

"If you've got a cold, you can take yourself right home and put your fanny to bed," Kelsy said, shooting Faith a conspiratorial glance that said she was glad to cover for her friend. "I'm in no mood for picking up germs."

"Shoot, Kels," Donna said, "the mood you're in you might as well come down with a cold. You better be looking for a new fiancé—your disposition goes right downhill when you aren't getting a little regular loving."

Everyone laughed. Faith was grateful for the distraction. Kelsy, her curls pulled back in an untidy knot, snapped at Donna, "When I need your advice on my love life, I'll give it up altogether. Why, you've been threatening to work on your own *amour*—or lack of it—ever since the last of your kids took off for college. Well, I hate to tell you this, but it's spring already and I haven't heard any fireworks out at your place."

"Don't rush me," Donna drawled. "I'm working

on it. I've lost ten pounds in aerobics class. And next week the gray hair goes. In a few weeks I'll be a regular coquette.''

Faith smiled. At forty-two, Donna had three nearly grown children and a husband who had settled into middle-aged apathy. She was ready to shake things up.

Kelsy said, "Gonna wash that gray away, huh? You decided on a color?''

Donna shrugged. "Well, I guess I'm the jet-black type?''

Maude, who had worked at the Snippy Scissors before she retired and thus qualified as a professional consultant in matters of beauty, studied Donna carefully. "That's too easy for an African-American woman. You want to shake things up, you ought to go the brazen-blond route. What do you think, Faith?''

Faith wrinkled her nose and made an effort to get caught up in the conversation. "Blond? Don't you think that's a little...bold?''

Donna studied herself in the mirror over the sink. She looked terrific to Faith, but Faith knew what her friend saw in that mirror—an ebony-skinned woman who'd put on twenty-something pounds since she'd walked down the aisle, who wore reading glasses on a chain around her neck, whose salt-and-pepper hair was cropped close for a minimum of fuss and whose husband hadn't been the most amorous partner in the past few years.

Donna sighed. "It's going to take something bold to get Tom's attention.''

Faith reminded herself once again how lucky she was to have found Walter. The life that lay before them was nothing short of heaven. They would live in Hope Springs of course, where their sons and daughters would attend the same schools Faith had attended, make friends with the children of people Faith had grown up with.

They would keep Walter's cabin, too. It would be a wonderful weekend retreat. She remembered going to the rustic little cabin for the first time, how impressed she'd been that a man with Walter's money chose to live so simply. He could afford the grandest house in Richmond, but instead, he'd built his little four-room cabin and pared his life down to the things that were truly important. Why, a man like Walter—

Through the open front door, Genghis Khan screeched a warning. Faith looked up; her first thought was that Walter had come. Her heart took a momentary leap. Then she realized it wasn't Walter at all, but another man who might have been cut from the same mold. Like Walter, he was tall and slender, with shoulders as broad and sharp as blades. His tan wasn't as deep as Walter's, his hair was darker and his expression less relaxed. But he was dressed in the kind of suit Walter wore and he carried a monogrammed leather briefcase. *SPD.*

Faith thought she recognized him, but she couldn't imagine from where.

"Miss O'Dare?"

His voice reminded her of Walter, too. Very cultured, very educated and very commanding. The

shop grew quiet, and Faith knew all attention had
been turned to their unexpected visitor.

He looked right at her when he spoke, as if he
recognized her, too.

"I'm Faith O'Dare."

"I'm Sean Davenport. Walter's partner."

Before his introduction sank in, Faith noticed that
both Donna and Kelsy had moved a little closer to
her. Rallying, it seemed to her. Fear struck her hard
and swift. "Walter. Something's happened to Walter."

"No, no, Walter's fine. He...I..." Sean Davenport's dark gaze shifted slightly, taking in the others
in the room. "Perhaps we could speak in private."

Something was wrong. Faith knew it. She heard
the sharp intake of breath from someone behind her.
Her knees grew a little wobbly and her insides turned
upside down. "No, I..." She felt Donna's hand on
her elbow. She was going to need her friends for this,
she knew it. "No, please, there's no need for privacy."

Walter's partner looked at the other women,
seemed to plead with them for understanding. Donna
inched closer to Faith and announced in her no-
arguments voice, "We've got no secrets, Mr. Davenport."

He nodded, took a deep breath and said, "Well, if
you're sure..."

"We're sure," Kelsy said.

Faith had never fainted in her life, but she wasn't
certain she could hold up for much more hemming

and hawing. "What's wrong? What's happened to Walter?"

"It's about the...the baby, Miss O'Dare."

A collective startled gasp came from the group sitting around the work table. Someone murmured, "The *what?*" Donna's hand tightened on Faith's elbow.

"Miss O'Dare, are you sure we shouldn't—"

"What about the baby?" Faith said, her heart tripping so hard she was certain he must be able to hear it from where he stood.

"Well...there's no easy way to say this, Miss O'Dare. But the truth is, Walter is...married."

CHAPTER TWO

DISBELIEF GAINED an instant chokehold on Faith. Married? Walter? What did this slick so-and-so think he was up to?

"You're crazy," she said, struggling to steady her voice.

Sean Davenport shook his head, teasing loose a brown wave over his right eye. His eyes were the same sable color. And they held sympathy.

Faith shook her head more emphatically than he had. "I've known Walter Brickerson for eighteen months. He's not married and I want to know what you're trying to pull."

"And I've known Walter twenty years," said the man who claimed to be Walter's partner. His voice was soft, but it resonated with authority. He approached and propped his briefcase on the worktable. "I was best man at his wedding."

Faith's response caught in her throat. Her disbelief was beginning to dissipate, losing ground to the ugly doubt sweeping up from her gut.

Donna tightened her hold on Faith's elbow and said in her most challenging voice, "And when was that? How can we be sure you're telling the truth and not just..."

He pulled a legal file out of the briefcase, halting Donna's interrogation. Through the fog of her stunned emotions, Faith sensed everyone at the worktable leaning forward to see what magic Sean Davenport would produce from his expensive leather briefcase.

Inside the file was a photograph. A wedding photograph. A young Walter resplendent in a dove gray tuxedo with a lovely woman decked out like a fairy princess clinging to his arm. A half-dozen bridesmaids and enough flowers to make the payroll at Bitsy's Flower Bower for the next year. Faith's disbelief vanished. Her doubt bloomed into outrage.

The rotten so-and-so had been married!

Faith's breathing grew shallow. She opened her mouth to speak, but the highway from head to mouth seemed shut down by gridlock. Nothing came out but a gasp.

"That's an old picture," Kelsy pointed out. "So he's been married before. That doesn't exactly—"

Another photograph appeared.

"And this was last year," the devil's messenger said. "At their eighteenth anniversary."

The room was silent except for the blood pounding in Faith's ears. She took in the photograph, a glossy eight-by-ten of the perfect family. A well-groomed woman with that moonlit blond hair only the very rich can wear with confidence. Her silver dress was simple and understated, the kind of thing Faith had never worn and probably never would. A thousand-dollar dress.

Walter was looking down at the woman in the

photograph as if he adored her, touching her champagne glass with his. Faith knew that look. Intimately. At least she'd thought she knew it. He was wearing the gold bracelet Faith had given him for his last birthday. She'd saved for it for six months.

Flanking the happy couple were four girls, so touched by wealth and beauty they didn't even have that look of youthful awkwardness about them.

"His daughters," she murmured.

"That's right," Sean Davenport said. "Amanda and—"

"No!" Shaken out of her stupor by the six privileged happy faces in the photograph, Faith ripped the Kodak moment right through the middle of Walter's smile. Then she flung the pieces in Sean Davenport's face. "I don't want to hear any more. Take your photographs and your—"

"But, Miss O'Dare, Walter asked me to—"

"Walter can take a flying leap off Dane's Peak. And you can follow him, Mr. Davenport. Now get out of my shop!"

Faith was angry now, boiling, fighting, raging mad. And it felt good. Better than the pain she'd felt in that searing moment of betrayal when she couldn't deny the truth. She gave herself over to the anger and promised herself a good cry later, in the privacy of her backyard, while she incinerated every single item Walter Brickerson had ever given her as a token of his undying love. The dangling heart earrings. The cashmere sweater. The cherub for her flower garden. Did concrete burn? she wondered.

Never mind. It would certainly smash. She envisioned the pickax in her garden shed and could hardly wait.

"I know you're upset," Walter's partner was saying in that calm, soothing voice that was beginning to drive Faith's rage from a stage-one brushfire to a stage-four inferno.

"Get out," Faith said, her voice lowering menacingly.

"You see, it's important for you to understand that—"

Donna snatched his briefcase off the table and shoved it against his chest. "It's important for you to understand that Miss O'Dare asked you to leave. And if you're smart, you'll get your pin-striped ass out of here."

He drew a deep breath, and Faith found herself staring into his eyes once again. They were deep and dark and held an understanding that didn't comfort Faith one iota at the moment. "Fine. But perhaps later, we could—"

"Out!" Faith took a menacing step in his direction.

The top of her head reached the tip of his chin, but he backed up nevertheless.

"Okay. Okay."

He turned and walked toward the door. Faith realized she was quivering, her knees as weak as Jell-O. Then he stopped.

"In all fairness, Miss O'Dare, you should hear me out. For the sake of the baby."

That did it. Faith started for him, shaking off Kelsy's restraining hand.

"You leave my baby out of this," she said, grabbing a hearth broom decorated with gingham ribbon and dried flowers. She brandished it in his direction.

Sean Davenport held up a hand, fending off her weapon as he walked out the front door. Faith followed him, ready to strike a lethal blow with the broom if necessary.

He paused beside the gunmetal gray BMW angled against the curb along Ridge Lane. "But you shouldn't let your anger over Walter's despicable behavior—"

"Get out of my town!"

"—and it was despicable," he continued as if she weren't screeching at him at the top of her lungs. "But you shouldn't let that obscure the fact that this is Walter's baby, too. His responsibility, too."

Rage burned white-hot at the core of Faith's being. How dare he! "This is not Walter Brickerson's baby! This is *my* baby! And my baby doesn't need anything from a lying cheating scoundrel like your lowlife partner."

He stood there with one hand on the door of his car, the other hefting the briefcase in which he had carried the truth that had shattered Faith's life. He looked at Faith once again, his heart in his eyes. He was as good as Walter, she realized suddenly. Able to look so sincere, so genuine. Oh, God, what a fool she'd been.

"Just go," she said, her anger suddenly spent. "If you really want to do something for me, just go."

He nodded and got into his car, one that was like

Walter's in all but color. He pressed the power button
and lowered the window.

"I'll be back," he said, "to check on you. After
you've...after things calm down."

Faith clutched at the final vestige of anger in her
heart, the only thing keeping her from losing it at the
sympathetic sound of his voice. She shook her broom
and yelled after him as his BMW purred down Ridge
Lane. "Don't you dare come back! And you tell
Walter to stay away, too. This baby doesn't need
Walter. You tell him I said that!"

The BMW rounded one of the many curves in
Ridge Lane and was gone.

Faith stood on the sidewalk, watching the bend in
the street where he'd disappeared and knowing she
would give almost anything to take back the last ten
minutes. To beat back the ugly truth and restore her
fantasy world.

"Oh, Pop, where are you when I need you?" she
murmured.

Numb and wounded, she turned to make her way
back up the front steps to Times Square Crafts. She
could go to the back room for a moment, collect
herself, then stumble home for the day. Donna and
Kelsy would understand.

But as she turned, Faith realized she wasn't alone
on Ridge Lane. Bama and Torrence Preston stood on
the corner of Presidents' Drive outside Preston Re-
alty. Bama whispered behind her hand when T.J.
Chrichton came out of the bakery next door. In the
other direction a handful of people had spilled out of
Sweet Ida's Tea Room, and the part-time librarian

stood on the front stoop of the library two doors down. A low buzz was already coming from that direction.

Faith's secret, it seemed, was out. The Hope Springs grapevine would work its magic, and by afternoon the only person in town who wouldn't know that Faith O'Dare was pregnant by a married man was old Lavinia Holt, who summarily dismissed all gossips from her presence and thus still didn't know that the next in line for the Matherly fortune had come out of the closet last fall.

On the Times Square porch, Faith's two partners and the entire ceramics class stood watching her. She smiled at them wanly, certain she should feel humiliated, instead of hollow.

"Well," she said loudly enough for everyone to hear, "at least you won't have to buy a wedding present, too."

Then she let Donna put an arm around her shoulders and draw her into the comfort of her motherly embrace. Maybe she wouldn't wait for the privacy of her backyard to cry, after all.

TIMES SQUARE CRAFTS was a quiet place that afternoon.

Oh, plenty of people came by in hopes of hearing more. But Donna managed to squelch most of the curiosity with nothing more than a look.

Raising three kids did pay off sometimes.

She stared at Kelsy across the table. Her young partner looked troubled, her freckles standing out starkly against her pale cheeks.

"I think I'm going to be sick," Kelsy said.

Donna nodded. Pregnant. Expecting a baby. She couldn't imagine anything worse. Babies consumed your whole life.

"How can she ever trust another man?" Kelsy said. "How can *I*?"

"Since when do you trust men, anyway?" Donna asked pointedly, even as she felt gratitude wash through her. At least her Tom was as trustworthy as the snow was deep in January.

"What's that supposed to mean?"

Kelsy sounded offended, but Donna knew that a woman didn't break four engagements if she had a lot of faith in men. Donna had always suspected Kelsy bailed out of all her relationships because that was less frightening than waiting for a man to bail out on her. But she'd introduced that topic with Kelsy before and hit a brick wall.

"Faith will be all right," she said to avoid another wrangle with her young partner.

"But she's alone," Kelsy whispered, as if afraid of saying the words too loud. Afraid they might be contagious.

"And expecting," Donna added, thinking she, too, ought to cross herself or otherwise protect herself from a similar curse. But before she could, the front door burst open and another of the town's curiosity seekers rushed in.

It was Tom, looking grim. "Tell me it's not us." He put his hands on his wife's shoulders. "I heard somebody at the bank talking about somebody over here expecting a baby. Donna, it's not us, is it?"

Donna laughed. "Tom, it's been eighteen years since the last one. You can't be serious."

She saw the tension go out of him and he pulled her into a hug. "I have to tell you, babe, it scared the living daylights out of me."

IF THE BLACK-TIE SOIREE had been for anything but Walter Brickerson Senior's seventy-fifth birthday party, Sean would have begged off. Even if it had been planned for sometime other than the evening after Sean's trip to Hope Springs, he would have invented a plausible excuse and called in his regrets.

There weren't many things Sean hated more than trussing himself up in a tux and wishing he'd remembered to get a haircut in time. The dress shoes always pinched, the starched collar always scratched, and his hair was always one week beyond well groomed.

But Walt Senior was one hell of a guy.

Unlike his son, who Sean was having trouble convincing himself wouldn't benefit from a solid right hook to the jaw here in front of the cream of Richmond society.

"You're quiet tonight."

Beverly's voice startled him. He mustered a smile for Brick's wife, hating the feeling that he was now part of the duplicity. *Damn you, Brick.*

"I'm always quiet at these things," he said. "Hate 'em, remember?"

She smiled. "You wouldn't hate them nearly so much if you'd relax and circulate."

"I could circulate or I could relax. I can't do both," he said, aiming for a lightness he didn't feel.

Beverly's silken laughter washed over him, and for a moment it gripped him as potently as it had all those years ago. She was so different now, as they all were, he supposed.

Except maybe Brick. Same old Brick.

Tonight Beverly was the epitome of understated sophistication in a slate blue sheath. The silk skimmed her lean curves; diamonds glittered at her throat. When Sean first met her more than twenty years ago, she'd already had the look of wealth about her. But it had been fresh and unadorned, and her eyes had sparkled with adventure. He'd fallen for her the moment he met her, a kid from the wrong side of the tracks who, thanks to an Ivy League scholarship, had been rubbing elbows with people who had never even set foot on his side of the track.

But Beverly's spell wasn't the only one Sean had fallen under during his first year in Boston. He'd met Brick. Glib, charming Brick, who had more money than good sense. Brick had taken Sean under his wing—and shortly after relieved him of his girlfriend.

Finessing women had always been Brick's specialty. He'd perfected his technique over the years.

At this precise moment he was exercising those skills on the new trophy wife of one of the judges who had come to pay respects to Senior. The trophy wife was burgundy-maned and statuesque, dressed in curve-hugging glitter. Brick's demeanor was all propriety, but Sean knew the look in his old friend's eyes.

How could he? With the most wonderful wife in the world, with four adorable daughters, with one woman already so furious with him he'd be lucky if she didn't sue him for every penny he'd ever made or could ever hope to make. With all that, and here he was lining up the next conquest.

And a dangerous one at that. The last thing the firm needed was for Brick to tick off a judge.

"How are the girls?" he asked, realizing he'd let his gaze linger on Brick too long. He hoped Beverly hadn't noticed.

"Awful," Beverly said, warm affection in her eyes despite her pronouncement. "Bailey is doing her utmost to convert herself into a boy—she discovered last week she's getting breasts. Taylor wants to dye her hair purple, Amanda is hormonal, and Brooke got her driver's license last week."

"Should I start taking the bus?"

"I highly recommend it."

As they chatted about the girls, Sean felt guiltier with each anecdote. Didn't he owe it to Beverly to tell her the truth? After all, Brick had been deceiving her for more years than Sean could count. If she knew, couldn't she then get on with her life?

He remembered his mother's expression every time he'd had this conversation with her. She'd sit there in the kitchen of the neat little house that was the best she would allow him to buy her and narrow her dark eyes at him. *You butt out,* she'd say. *What Beverly Brickerson doesn't know she probably doesn't want to know. When she's ready to deal with it, she'll see the truth herself.*

His mother's words brought to mind Faith O'Dare. In truth, he'd hardly been able to get her out of his thoughts since leaving Hope Springs that morning. He'd seen how quickly her denial had been replaced by shock, then fury. But she had, for a moment, wanted to turn her back on the truth. Maybe his mother was right.

And look how much pain the truth had brought Faith O'Dare. He'd seen it in her eyes. He wasn't sure he could bear to see it in Beverly's eyes, knew he couldn't be the bearer of those tidings himself.

Lucy Davenport was a wise woman. Sean decided, as he often did, to do what she suggested.

But small talk with Beverly while he carried the truth in his heart was too difficult, and he made his escape from her as quickly as possible.

But wherever he turned, it seemed he encountered another reminder of Brick's duplicity. He stumbled into a conversation with a young attorney Brick had seduced four years earlier. She asked about the rumor that Brick's marriage was on the rocks, a rumor Sean denied. He was introduced to the burgundy-haired trophy bride, but her gaze kept straying over his shoulder to Brick.

He had to get out of here. He had to loosen his collar. He had to quit obsessing over what Brick had done. But before he could go, he had to pay his respects to Senior.

Sean sought out the guest of honor and found him holding court in the library, where the haze of cigar smoke hung heavy and redolent. The high-ceilinged library, like the rest of the old Tudor mansion in the historic neighborhood known as the Fan, was opulent, filled with dark leather and soft lighting. It was the kind of room Sean had never learned to feel comfortable in, the kind of room that always threw him back to the three-room apartment where he'd grown up. There had been no high ceilings, no leather, no soft lighting in that building. Only noisy pipes and threadbare upholstery.

But there had also been plenty of love. So Sean could recognize affection when he saw it, and he saw it now. Walt Senior brightened when Sean walked through the door and waved him over. Sometimes it seemed to Sean that his old mentor loved him almost as much as he loved his own son.

Sometimes he even thought Walt respected him more than he respected his own son. Walt was no fool. He knew what Brick was like.

"Keeping yourself too damned scarce tonight, son," the old man said. He gestured to the decanter on the table between them. "Have a brandy."

Sean shook his head. "I've had my limit."

Walt grunted and smiled. At seventy-five he still looked hearty. His color was good, his eyes still bright. "Happy to hear some of us know what our limits are. Tell me, Sean, what's Brick up to?"

Guilt gnawed at Sean again. Could he lie to Walt? Did he dare tell the truth? He hesitated.

Walt gave him one of those granite-hard stares that had shaken plenty of people on the witness stand during his fifty-year career. "Again?"

"Walt, maybe you'd better talk to Brick about it."

"Loyalty's a fine thing, son. But only where it's deserved."

Sean thought about the college buddy who had insisted on introducing his friend to his father. *Just meet him. He'll set you up with an internship with the firm. Let me swing this for you, Sean.* How could you repay such a debt? he wondered.

"Walt, you know what Brick is like. I'm not going to change him and neither are you."

Walt frowned. Sean knew the old man never liked hearing that his power had limitations. He savored a sip of his brandy and finally nodded his head. "I know. And I wouldn't mind a bit if whatever he's gotten himself into this time blows up in *his* face. I just don't want it blowing up in Beverly's. Or in the firm's."

Sean nodded.

"See if you can contain things, son."

Sean almost smiled. He remembered Faith O'Dare's fury and wondered if there was any way to contain it should she decide to point that fury in Brick's direction.

No, Brick deserved the full effects of that wrath. And if Faith O'Dare didn't dish it up, Sean made up his mind to see that some kind of justice was finally served on his old buddy.

CHAPTER THREE

THE DOORBELL on Faith's front door was broken, a fact most folks in Hope Springs already knew. So when she heard the squeak of the screen door, she cursed herself for not thinking to lock it.

When she heard footsteps ascending the stairs, she knew it must be Ida Monroe. Even in Hope Springs, only the proprietor of Sweet Ida's Tea Room would dare barge right upstairs without first giving an inquiring holler.

Faith tossed a stack of letters into the box sitting at the foot of the bed and turned back to her topsy-turvy closet.

"I'd keep those if I were you."

Faith didn't bother to turn at the sound of Ida's whispery voice. She dropped to her knees and dragged forward the small chest at the back of the closet. "Why?"

"Evidence."

Faith turned, settling the chest between her knees. Ida was nosing through the box, picking up things to examine them more closely. She lifted her long blond hair, which should have turned gray at least a decade earlier, away from one eye so she could slip on her reading glasses. A drugstore item, they hung from a rhinestone chain and rested on her generous bosom. She opened one of the letters.

"You don't want to get rid of anything you might need as evidence, dolly."

"I don't want any evidence," Faith said. "I'm burning it all."

Ida peered at her over the glasses sitting on the end of her pug nose. "That's my girl. Mature. Rational. Always using her head."

"Don't start, Ida." She reached for the letter, folded it and placed it with the rest beyond Ida's reach.

She opened the chest, a small carved ebony box Pop said her mother had found at a flea market in Washington, D.C., years before Faith was born. Roberta Sanders O'Dare had used it for her treasures—Faith's baby bracelet from the hospital, her wedding pictures, things like that. When Faith found the chest in the attic in her fifteenth year, the chest was only half-full, symbolic of a life cut short. Roberta O'Dare had died of leukemia at thirty-one, when Faith was only seven. The chest had become her link to her mother, a sacred place she visited when the sorrow of being motherless grew too strong.

When she'd reached thirty-one, it had somehow seemed right to begin using the chest herself.

Right now her only thought was to obliterate all evidence of her own stupidity so that her own son or daughter wouldn't someday rummage through her life and lose all respect.

"What a dummy," she muttered.

"For throwing all this stuff away? I'll say." Ida was still going through the box.

"You know what I mean."

"I'm taking this cashmere sweater." Ida held the peach-colored confection over her bosom and stepped up to the mirror.

Faith knew there was no prayer of a fit, but she also knew there was no arguing with Ida. Her next-door neighbor, who'd seemed ancient to Faith when she was a child and now seemed to grow closer to Faith's age with each year that passed, had become a sort of surrogate mother. She'd dispensed offbeat advice that contrasted wildly with the prudence and wisdom Pop had specialized in. She'd demonstrated that women don't always need a man to be happy or successful. And she'd proved that age is only a state of mind.

Ida sat in the rocker beside the window overlooking Timber Gap Lane. From Faith's room this time of year, before the trees leafed in, you could see the Holy Comforter Episcopal Church directly across the street and anything in Hope Springs that was higher than two stories. Which was pretty much limited to Heritage Manor, up on the hill, and the municipal building three blocks away. The municipal building, at four stories, towered above everything else on Ridge Lane.

"You gonna beat yourself up over this?" Ida asked. The rocker began its familiar creak. "Act like you're the only woman who ever got snookered by a married man?"

"I'm thirty-six," Faith said, fingering a lace handkerchief that had been her mother's. "College educated. How could I have been so dumb?"

Ida smiled, revealing a network of fine lines. "Dolly, you've never been dumb a day in your life. You know, don't you, that—"

The front door squeaked and a breezy voice called up the stairs. "Yoo-hoo! Faith? You up there?"

Ida swore, her voice that of a seductress and her language that of a sailor. "It's that old bat Mrs. Levenger."

Mrs. Levenger was probably younger than Ida, a point Faith was just irritable enough to consider mentioning. "You left the door open."

"You left it that way first," Ida whispered. "If we're very still, she'll go away. With that walking cane of hers, she'll never make it up the stairs."

"People all over town tonight will be saying I'm a naive sap," Faith said, shoving aside the chest and getting up off the floor. "No need to have them saying I'm rude, too."

Ida followed her. "That's your father's influence, you know. Patrick was too nice for his own good."

Loretta Levenger, who had retired as headmistress of the Blue Ridge Academy for Girls three years ago, stood at the bottom of the steps, a covered casserole dish in one hand, her silver-headed cane in the other. When she saw Faith, her beaming smile immediately shifted into the sympathetic look usually reserved for funeral parlors and hospital waiting rooms.

"You dear child," Mrs. Levenger said. "I brought macaroni and cheese. My mother's recipe. Birdie and I thought you might not feel like cooking tonight."

Birdie was Mrs. Levenger's spinster sister-in-law.

Faith swallowed a sigh and smiled as graciously as she could manage. She wondered if her eyes were still red from the hour she'd spent crying after Donna drove her home.

She was sniffing the casserole dish and mouthing appropriately appreciative remarks when a rustling at the front door caught their attention. Ginny Bryant and her six-year-old son stood on the porch, peering through the open door.

"We got pie," Dustin said, thrusting a foil-wrapped pie plate in Faith's direction. "We gonna eat it now?"

Faith wanted to close her eyes and groan. For one thing, she hated Ginny Bryant's sweet-potato pie. For another, she knew this would not be the end of it. She glanced at Ida, hoping for help, and got only a faint smile and a whispered comment as they all paraded toward the kitchen. "Guess we know what happens next."

"We make tea?"

"Nah. Vera Templeton always brings tea."

And so she did. In fact, by suppertime the little 1920s bungalow where Faith had grown up was as full as it had been the day of Patrick O'Dare's funeral. People from all over town had responded to Faith's crisis the way they always responded to crises. They brought covered dishes, heavy on the desserts. They stayed to eat and to sympathize. They clucked over Faith, hugged her and told her exactly what she should do. And they bad-mouthed Walter Brickerson.

"He's too low for words, Faith." That was Bitsy from the florist's.

"He's a man," said Birdie Levenger, who had been jilted herself a lifetime and a half ago. "What can you expect?"

"Now wait a doggone minute..." came a male voice.

"This one's worse than most. He certainly had me fooled."

"I could see it written all over his face," Birdie said.

"Why, Birdie, I saw you flirting with him at the church supper not one month ago."

"Why, I never..."

Hoping to fade into the background, Faith wandered from room to room, grateful she lived in a place where people cared so much. A cynic, she knew, might have said they were only here out of nosiness. But even after all that had happened this day, Faith couldn't find it in her to feel that way. She believed in people, in their innate goodness. Another legacy from her father. And one she didn't intend to let Walter Brickerson rob her of.

"You've hardly eaten a bite, dear," Reverend Haigler said, his own plate piled high with Virginia ham and green bean casserole and Ida's famous yeast rolls.

"I've had plenty," she said, although he was right. "I'm really not that hungry."

"You're eating for two now," Mrs. Haigler said gently, then turned a frightening shade of pink at her husband's frown. "Oh, dear. I hope I haven't said the wrong thing. It's just that, well, since that awful man came to town this morning, well, it seems everyone has heard.''

"And you don't have a damn thing to be ashamed of," interjected Tood Grunkemeier, who had loaded up the front seat of his pickup truck with dried apples and jugs of homemade cider. "Begging your pardon, Reverend. But it's that scoundrel Brickerson who ought to be ashamed."

"Exactly," said Cindy Martin, who was passing with an empty plate on her way to the kitchen. "Imagine sending somebody else to do his dirty work for him like that."

"Man ought to be tied up by his..." Tood paused, seemed to remember that he wasn't surrounded by his barbershop cronies and finished, "Toes. And his friend next to him."

For the moment, it seemed, Faith was immune to the mention of Walter. She felt as if she'd buried her feelings for him somewhere deep and dark so they couldn't hurt her. She could dig them out and deal with them later.

But the mention of Sean Davenport brought all her emotions rushing to the surface again. Her pain over his unwelcome revelation filled her once again with roaring anger, and she realized she hadn't made great strides in becoming like her gentle-spirited father. Her heart began to race with the residue of the morning's anger just thinking about Sean Davenport. He'd come marching into her life with his fancy suit and his pricy briefcase and his luxury car and shattered every dream she had. He might as well have been serving papers; her dreams were no more important to him than that. He was just doing his partner's dirty work.

What really made her angry was that she didn't entirely believe that. She'd seen sympathy in his eyes. Understanding and compassion.

Then Sean Davenport's face shifted and transformed into Walter Brickerson's equally sincere face. The one he'd worn each time he said he loved her. The one he'd worn on a night just like this one, with the whole house full of people paying their respects to Patrick O'Dare. Walter had been the perfect partner that night, compassionate and warm and understanding exactly what she was going through.

And he'd been wearing a pin-striped suit just like the one Sean Davenport had been wearing earlier today when he'd looked oh, so compassionate.

Maybe a little bit of cynicism wasn't an entirely bad idea.

Faith slipped away, leaving Tood Grunkemeier to defend his opinion of justice in the matter of Walter Brickerson and Sean Davenport.

She encountered Kelsy, who sat on the bottom step in the foyer, a plate of German chocolate cake on her knees, talking to Ida.

"She should sue his butt," Kelsy said. "He ought to pay through the nose for this. Right, Ida?"

Mandy Powell stuck her head around from the living room and said, "You take his money and you'll have to put up with his interference forever. He'll be wanting weekends and Christmas and trying to tell you what school to send the kid to."

The thought sent a chill through Faith.

"Not if his wife's got anything to say about it," Kelsy pointed out.

A heated discussion followed and Faith kept walking. As she passed through the dining room, she overheard her high-school English teacher saying to the librarian, "Nothing says she has to keep this baby of course."

And Faith shivered again.

She wanted them gone, out of her house. And at the same time she dreaded being alone with reality.

When the evening eventually wound down and people began to trickle out the front door, each of them with a little pep talk and the offer of a shoulder to cry on or a friendly ear to listen, Faith was glad when Ida once more sank into a rocker, this time on the front porch. Faith joined her, pulling one of the rockers that had belonged to her grandparents close to the railing so she could put her feet up. Her feet never had reached the porch when she'd sat in these old rockers.

"Now, where were we?" Ida said. "Oh, yes, you were saying what a dumb cluck you are and I was saying you're smart as a whip and there's nothing dumb about trusting a man who gives you every reason to trust him."

Faith closed her eyes. The smells of spring were all around her, dominated by the wisteria vine from Ida's yard, which had somehow insinuated itself onto the trellis at the end of Faith's porch. It was just as well, for she'd never had the patience to coax much out of the climbing roses that were supposed to be

there. The bells at the Baptist church were beginning
their nine-o'clock chiming.

"At least I'm apparently not going to be ostra-
cized," she said.

Ida laughed. "They mean well."

"I know." And as heavy as her heart was this
evening, as unlikely as the possibility would have
seemed three hours earlier, Faith had drawn some
comfort from the houseful of people who had rallied
to her support.

Hope Springs was that kind of place. Nestled in
the Blue Ridge Mountains of Virginia, the eight
thousand people who lived here year-round were
mostly folks whose families had been in the town for
generations. Although the town was often inhabited
by more visitors than residents, the locals never lost
sight of the fact that Hope Springs was their home.
The well-to-do and sometimes the well-known came
for hiking and horseback riding and golf at Heritage
Manor, but the residents paid them little mind. Oh,
they fed them in more restaurants than you might
expect in a town this size, entertained them and
opened shops for them. But as far as the people of
Hope Springs were concerned, life here was about
schools and churches and drugstores and whether the
municipal pool could afford to hire a lifeguard each
summer so the town's children could swim safely.

Hope Springs was simply home, despite its history
as a spa resort with a grand hotel.

Tonight Faith had been reminded of that at a time
she needed it most.

"I guess I should have seen the signs," Faith said.

"He never introduced me to his friends. We never went out in Richmond."

"But he took you to his house," Ida reminded her gently.

Faith thought about the rustic lakeside cabin Walter said he lived in. "He probably rents it by the hour."

For a few minutes the creaking of the rockers was the only sound in the night.

"What are you going to do?" Ida asked at last.

"I don't know. I was thinking about getting to know Mrs. Walter Brickerson."

"That would serve him right."

Faith imagined Walter sitting on his suitcase in front of a big antebellum-style mansion.

"Or I could take out an ad in the Richmond paper," she fantasized. "Full-page. So all his high-placed friends will know exactly what kind of man Walter Brickerson is."

Saying his name aloud left a bitter taste in her mouth.

"Or you could try to let it go and not let the anger consume you," Ida said. "You know, harboring resentment is like drinking poison in hopes of killing somebody else."

"Now who sounds like Pop?"

"Oops. Sorry. I hate it when I step out of character like that."

"I do know one thing," Faith said, remembering the comment she'd overheard about giving up her baby.

"What's that, dolly?"

"I'm going to raise the happiest baby this town's ever seen. It's going to be loved and treasured and proud to be the next generation of O'Dares."

Ida stood and paused beside Faith on her way off the porch. "Being a single parent isn't easy."

"I had a good role model."

Ida ran a hand lightly over Faith's hair. "That you did."

"Besides," Faith said as Ida started down the front stairs, "she'll have the best substitute granny anybody's ever had."

"Granny?" Ida's soft voice rose with alarm. "You teach this child to call me Granny and I'll tell him about the time you climbed the spire at the church."

Faith grinned in the dark. "You wouldn't."

"Try me."

Then Faith was left alone at last with her heartbreak and the one dream no one could rob her of. *She was going to be a mother.* She hugged her knees to her chest and closed her eyes and consoled herself with thoughts of holding her own baby girl seven short months from now.

"We won't need a thing from men in pin-striped suits," she said, knowing she would believe it soon.

THE COURTROOM was still empty. Sean liked it that way. It gave him time to focus his energies, to gear up for whatever battle would be played out once court was in session. He stood, took his reading glasses from his inside breast pocket and a file from his briefcase. He would run through the information about his client's financial dealings one last time.

Concentrating wasn't easy this morning. He couldn't get Faith O'Dare out of his mind.

She'd stayed with him all night after he left the party for Senior. The contrast between her forthrightness, her freshness, and the stilted, jaded atmosphere at the Brickerson home played across his mind time and again. There was no pretense in Faith O'Dare.

No, none at all. She despised him for his friendship with Brick and didn't mind letting him know it. He couldn't blame her for that. But it weighed on his mind.

Loyalty's a fine thing, son. But only where it's deserved.

That was what Walt Senior had said, and Sean couldn't get that out of his mind, either. His loyalty to Brick was long-standing, going back all those years to Harvard, when Sean was odd man out, the illegitimate son of a hardworking telephone operator. Sean had been working as a waiter the night he and Brick had met. They'd seen each other in classes before that, but Brick was clearly out of Sean's league and they'd never even exchanged nods.

But on this night Brick was treating his frat brothers at a pub near campus, running a tab and playing big shot. Sean kept their pitcher of beer full and cold. When it came time to settle up and Brick's credit card came back over the limit, Sean had made what turned out to be one of the most important decisions of his life. He'd unobtrusively called Brick aside to explain what was happening. Brick sobered instantly.

Sean could see in the rich young man's eyes his fear
of losing face with his friends.

Using his tips, Sean covered for Brick.

Brick had paid him back many times over.

"You're early."

Brick's voice didn't surprise Sean. He turned. His
friend stood in the aisle, his megawatt smile bright-
ening his face.

"I'm always early," he said, also not surprised
that Brick didn't know that about him. Brick, he had
realized long ago, didn't pay attention to much but
himself.

"Rollins v. Rollins?"

Sean nodded.

"Tough case. Knock 'em dead, buddy." Brick
raised his briefcase in salute.

"Brick, what are you going to do?"

Almost imperceptibly Brick's smile faded. "About
what?"

Sean frowned. Brick raised a conciliatory hand and
glanced around to make sure the courtroom was still
empty.

"Okay, okay. About her."

Sean clenched his jaw. "About *Faith*. And your
baby."

"Look, I... What *can* I do?"

A good question. Sean had racked his brain for the
answer and there was no good solution, nothing that
wouldn't cause upheaval in plenty of lives.

"I mean, leaving Bev to marry her would hardly
be fair to my family."

Sean felt himself bristle. As if Faith would marry

him at this point. As if any woman in her right mind would marry him. "Faith deserves better, anyway."

Brick had the good grace to look sheepish. "Maybe. Sure. Listen, about Beverly. You're not going to do anything noble, are you?"

"I don't know what I'm going to do, Brick."

"Think about Amanda, buddy. Think about Brooke and Taylor and Bailey."

"*You* think about them next time you're feeling randy."

"Getting a little self-righteous, aren't you?" Brick's voice was tight.

Sean worked his jaw some more and kept silent.

"Listen, we all need a wake-up call from time to time. Think of this as mine. I'm no kid anymore. I know I've got a great family. And I'll stay on the straight and narrow from now on." He grinned. "On my honor as an attorney."

In a field where honor was sometimes viewed as a relative matter, the vow evoked little confidence. "And your baby?"

Brick hesitated. "Should I go talk to her? See what she needs? I could set up a trust fund. Or if she wants, the firm could find a good family."

Sean took a moment of pleasure in the image of Brick getting a taste of Faith's wrath. "Yeah. That's a good idea. But, Brick, don't mention adoption. Let her bring it up if that's what she wants."

Somehow he didn't think so.

"Leave it to me," Brick said, already beginning to back down the aisle to the door.

"When? When will you go?"

Brick shrugged. "Soon. As soon as I can get away. I'll have Brenda check the appointment calendar. It may have to be after Thoroughgood goes to the jury, but...soon."

"She needs to hear from you now, Brick."

"I'll do the best I can. I can't just pick up and go on a whim, you know."

"You did before."

Brick gave him one more irritable glare and was gone. Sean swore softly. Faith O'Dare would get no help from that corner, that was clear. It could be weeks—months, even—before Brick's present case went to the jury. Then of course there would be another excuse. And another. Sean had seen these things end before and knew his old friend believed in making a clean break.

Sean sighed. He wondered if Faith O'Dare had some vestige of hope that the father of her baby would show up, contrite and loving. Offering moral support or financial support or even a quick divorce and a wedding ring.

"Brick, you're a real jerk," he murmured as the court recorder came in and started to set up.

Maybe he'd better go himself. Just to make sure she was okay. After all, she was pregnant and alone.

Pregnant. Intense uneasiness stirred in him.

It's not your responsibility, he told himself. But that sounded like a cop-out. He would see that the mother of Brick's baby had what she needed even if Brick couldn't be bothered to do the right thing.

The pulse of a headache started behind his eyes.

What possible help could he be to a pregnant woman?

"Isn't the smell of that paint making you sick?"

Donna's question made Faith pause. She gingerly sniffed the paint jars she was capping after the morning acrylics class.

"Nope."

"And here I am having sympathy morning sickness. Listen, girl, thank your lucky stars. Nothing—I repeat for emphasis, *nothing*—is worse than morning sickness."

From the corner of her eye, Faith saw Kelsy nudge Donna. Donna looked up, frowned and said, "Oh. Sorry."

Faith propped paint-smeared fists on her hips and squared off to face her partners. "Why?"

Donna squirmed. "Well, you know."

"Because being pregnant and unmarried might be worse than morning sickness? Is that what you mean?"

Kelsy rinsed a sponge in the sink and said, "Now, Faith, don't get riled up. It's probably not good for the baby."

"And jilted by a married man," Faith said. "Let's not forget that part."

"Faith!"

"Well, it's true. And there's no reason in the world why anybody—much less the two of you—should dance around it. My situation isn't exactly a state secret."

"Still," Kelsy said, "we should be sensitive to your feelings."

"My feelings are fine and they don't need pampering," Faith said, turning back to her cleanup chores.

None of that was true of course. But she refused to play the victim. She was pregnant and she had committed the unspeakable crime of having an affair with a married man. In both cases she should have been smarter. But it was too late for regrets. Too late to do anything but make the best of where she was. Whining wouldn't help.

Crying herself to sleep wouldn't help, either, although she'd given it a shot that first night.

Since that night almost a week ago she'd focused entirely on the baby she carried. Walter was a dead issue for her. Her love for him had apparently died on impact with the truth, even though the pain of betrayal lingered as sharp as a fresh wound.

"Okay, then," Kelsy said. "Have you talked to Walter?"

"No, I haven't talked to Walter." There. It didn't even hurt to say his name.

"When are you going to?"

"I'm not sure I am."

"What?"

"What's the point? He knows where I am. He knows I'm pregnant. He's obviously not interested."

"He should be made to pay."

Sometimes Faith felt that way, too. Sometimes she wanted revenge. She wanted to wreck his life. Except that the more she thought about it, the more she could see the great gift even in Walter's despicable behavior. She was pregnant. A new life grew inside her. Was that really something for which she wanted to exact revenge?

"Kelsy's right. You can't just let him off the hook."

"If I try to punish Walter, he won't be the only one to get hurt," Faith said. The picture of Walter's wife, his four daughters, still haunted her.

"That's not your fault. It's his. Maybe they deserve to know."

"Maybe they do," Faith said. "But I'm not going to be the one to tell them."

"Leave her alone," Kelsy said. "She's probably been talking to her old man again."

Faith smiled. It was true. Over the past week, she'd thought a lot about what her father would have done. *Take the high road,* was what Pop always said. After she'd made the decision, she'd felt instantly calmer. In her heart she'd known that she and her baby would be all right.

She wiped her hands on a towel. "I'm going to take some books out on the porch and figure out a project for next week's knitting class."

Kelsy rushed to the rack up front and thrust a booklet into her hands. "A baby blanket would be nice. There's a dear one in that booklet. It has a duck embroidered in the middle."

Faith promised to give the duck blanket fair consideration, then escaped to the front porch. She nudged a grumbling Khan to one side on the swing.

"Won't be long before I'm as big as you," she

said to the big Siamese, who tolerated a rub behind his ears. He purred, but his look reminded Faith that he did so only to appease her. "Don't worry. You'll still be king of the porch."

The knitting booklets were full of lush sweaters and cozy afghans, even a sweater-and-scarf project that would be fun for a class that liked to see fast results. Besides, Birdie Levenger had signed up, and the big needles would be easier for her to handle with her arthritic fingers. But Faith kept coming back to the baby blanket. Kelsy was right. It was dear. She imagined cuddling it around a soft warm little girl with sleepy eyes and a dimpled smile.

She was smiling, happy with her daydream, when she heard the deep rumble of a car pulling up to the curb. The engine sounded like Walter's BMW, and her heart leaped. What would she do? Say? Feel?

There was no need to wonder. The BMW wasn't Walter's. Sean Davenport walked up the sidewalk and onto the porch. His necktie was loosened, but he was still a pin-striped kind of guy. A carbon copy of Walter.

"How are you feeling?"

His question was the last thing she expected.

"Why do you care?"

"Because you're a nice lady who's gotten a raw deal."

"Nice ladies don't get mixed up with married men," she said, knowing she sounded testy and not even caring. Sean Davenport had no business showing up here pretending to be sensitive and considerate. That was one routine she wouldn't fall for again.

"Brick has a real gift for that kind of thing."

Faith felt her cheeks go pink, but she refused to lower her eyes. "Does he?"

"I'm afraid so."

She wondered if that meant her baby had a lot of half brothers and sisters out there, but she didn't want to hear that yet. "Tell him not to worry, I don't intend to make his life miserable over this."

The surprised reaction on Sean Davenport's face caught her eye, and Faith found herself studying him for the first time. His face was not nearly as perfect as Walter's, but there was something friendly, almost comforting, in its slight imperfections. His chin was square and as prominent as his nose. Disturbing the symmetry was his mouth, small with lips that looked firm and determined. His hair was dark, shot through with silver.

His eyes were tender, compassionate.

Faith narrowed her own eyes, unwilling to be taken in. Walter's eyes, too, had been convincing.

"He wants to help. Financially."

His gaze flickered away and she knew he was lying.

"I don't want Walter's money."

"You're better off without him." He glanced at the color photo of the baby blanket in her lap. "Both of you."

Faith slapped the magazine closed and stood. "I've already figured that out."

"But if there's any way *I* can help..."

"Why on earth would I want your help?" She advanced on him, not knowing why he was pretending to be nice and not caring to find out what scheme he had up his sleeve.

"Well, because I know that having a baby alone isn't easy," he said. His brown eyes were expressive.

"I'm not alone," she said, feeling her anger rise as she sensed his unwelcome sympathy. "I have friends. A lot of them. The kind of friends you don't have to make excuses for. And all I want from you is for you to get in your car and go away and never come back to Hope Springs again."

He studied her. "You're sure about that?"

"I certainly am."

And as she watched him do exactly as she'd suggested, Faith told herself she should be relieved. Told herself she *was* relieved.

Then she sank back onto the porch swing, wondering why relief felt so much like one more disappointment.

CHAPTER FOUR

LEVELHEADED. ANALYTICAL. Those were a couple of the words Sean's friends always used to describe him, and he noted there wasn't a single mention of being rash or obstinate.

So why was he standing on the front porch of a woman who had made it painfully obvious she wanted him to stay the hell out of her life?

Sean couldn't answer that question. So he did the only thing he could. He knocked on the screen door, fighting to keep himself from peering inside the story-and-a-half house with its wide front porch and cedar-shake shingles. If Faith caught him doing anything that looked remotely like spying through her open front door, that would clinch it for sure.

"Come on in!" called a cheery voice from somewhere inside the house. "It's open."

Sean hesitated. Her lively tone startled him. It didn't fit the mental picture he'd been carrying of her, in which she'd been sorrowful, crushed, needy. He also felt certain she wouldn't have extended the invitation—and certainly not that cheerfully—if she'd had any clue who was doing the knocking. Still, that was hardly his fault. He opened the door and walked in.

The house was old-fashioned, and that warmed him. Hardwood floors gleamed around the edges of well-worn rugs. Wreaths of yellow roses decorated the wallpaper, conjuring up images of old wartime movies. A dark walnut library table held a Tiffany-style lamp and a careless pile of mail on a crocheted runner. On one side of the foyer was a formal living room with a high-backed sofa flanking a fireplace hidden behind an iron screen. On the other side was a cozy room with bookcases and a TV. The books crooked a beckoning finger at him, but he ignored the temptation.

"I'm up here!"

Shrugging, he climbed the stairs toward her voice. Rows of family photographs lined the wall leading up the stairs. Prominently featured in the photographs was an imp-faced little girl with flyaway blond hair and a smile that promised trouble.

Sean realized he'd never seen her smile. He paused a moment to enjoy the sight and made up his mind that he would see that smile in person before he left today.

He found her in the first room on the right at the top of the stairs. She sat spraddle-legged on the floor, which was covered in a sheet of plastic. A boom box sat beside her, purring jazz. She wore jeans and a frayed golf shirt the size of which announced that it had originally belonged to someone larger than this 105-pound woman on the floor. Her hair had been pulled back with one of those stretchy poofy things Brick's preteen daughter used, but strands straggled out to graze her cheek. She was bent over a book, chewing the end of her thumb. Stacked to one side were rolls of wallpaper, a tray, bottles of solvent and a tidy pile of tools for wallpapering.

"You're just in time," she said vaguely, not looking up from the book that held her frowning attention.

"Good," he said, taking off his leather jacket and hanging it on the glass doorknob. "Believe it or not, I'm pretty handy around the house."

Her back straightened in a shot, and the thumb she'd been chewing flew to hook a loose strand of hair behind her ear. Her ears were tiny, he noticed. A good fit for the rest of her.

"Who let you in?"

"You did."

"I most certainly did not!" She stood up and Sean wondered how far along her pregnancy was. She wasn't showing. Far from it. Faded canvas pants hung loosely from her narrow hips.

The narrow hips troubled him. Would she have complications? he wondered. He decided to ignore the uneasiness that crept into his head. Not his problem.

"Sure, you did," he said, trying a smile. "I knocked on the front door and you said, 'Come on in. It's open.' And then when I came in, you said—"

"But it wasn't supposed to be *you!*"

"Do you interrupt everybody like that or is it just me you don't like to hear talk?"

"Just you," she said. "Specifically, exclusively *you.*"

"Okay. I can be pretty quiet." He took a step into

the room and began examining the boldly striped wallpaper, a contrast to the rolls of paper with the yellow ducks stacked on the floor. "Just tell me what to do and I'll try to keep my mouth shut."

She took his jacket off the doorknob—she held it as if it might impart a deadly virus, he noticed—and thrust it at him. "I don't need your help."

"Sure you do." He leaned over to pick up a can of wallpaper stripper. "Shouldn't you stay away from these fumes? It says right here to use a dust mask."

"Only if you're spraying it. I'm sponging."

He continued studying the cautions on the back of the can. "Provide adequate ventilation. It says that, too."

Her reply was as stuffy as the room. "The windows are open."

He looked over his shoulder at the three windows in the room, all of them tightly closed. He looked back at her, saw her disgruntled expression as her gaze followed his. She marched to the closest window and began tugging on it.

"Well, they will be open," she said.

Except that it didn't budge when she threw her weight into it and shoved. He decided to let her struggle with it while he opened the other two. They'd been painted shut more than once and it was no easy task. By the time he finished the other two, she was breathing heavily with her determination to prove herself.

She stepped back from the window, her chest rising and falling with exertion and, he speculated, anger. She glared at him.

"I'm getting used to your scowl," he said, reaching out to press the tip of his finger to the crease between her pale eyebrows. "It's going to lose its power to intimidate me soon."

She almost laughed, he could tell. He saw her lips quirk and the corners of her soft gray eyes crinkle, but she turned before she gave herself away completely. He wouldn't have told her for the world, but her flashes of temper appealed to him after the silent withdrawal he'd experienced during the final years of his marriage.

"Open the window, then."

"My pleasure."

When he was finished, she was once again holding his leather jacket out to him. "Thank you. And goodbye."

"You know, I worked as a paper hanger once. In college."

"You made that up."

"No, I didn't." He rolled up the sleeves of his gray turtleneck when he noticed that she'd let the arm holding his jacket drop to her side. "Actually I'm a rotten liar."

"I know."

"You do?"

She studied him so intently he grew uncomfortable. The expression in her eyes remained tense, her shoulders never relaxed. But she did at last hand over a can of stripping compound and a sponge.

"You start over there." She pointed to the back wall. "I'll start over here."

They retired to separate corners.

The jazz was soft, the sounds of springtime seeping through the open windows softer yet. Birds. A chattering squirrel. Children down the street, their shrill cries muffled by distance. All sounds Sean wasn't accustomed to hearing in Richmond. In fact, he might never have identified the squirrel if he hadn't looked out the window to see the offended creature apparently reprimanding him for the intrusion.

"It'll make a nice nursery," he said, noting the rambling backyard that would also one day make a wonderful playground for a little boy or girl.

A touch of anguish twisted at his heart, an old familiar feeling that he set aside as he always did.

"It's my favorite room," she said.

He wondered why. The striped wallpaper they were laying waste to had a masculine feel to it. Someone before Brick, he speculated. An ex-husband?

"I'm surprised you don't use it yourself, then," he said. A direct cross-examination at this point probably wouldn't turn up much helpful information.

She nudged up the volume on the boom box.

He made a face at the squirrel, who also turned away. He noted the open door on the tidy shed out back and the plot of ground near the back of the yard that was separated from the rest by railroad ties. It looked a little overgrown, although a pile of weeds had been chopped up to reveal a tiny patch of rich brown earth in one corner. Bright green gloves and a mud-caked hoe lay to one side.

He'd never hoed weeds before, but he supposed he could always learn.

He caught himself before he said so out loud. *One thing at a time, Davenport.*

"It's a big room for a nursery," he said. "But it'll be nice later for bunk beds and toy boxes."

She murmured noncommittally.

"Lived here long?"

About as long as it took her to decide to answer, he bet.

"Thirty-six years."

Thirty-six. A good age. "No, I meant in the house."

"So did I."

He stopped his work and turned to look at her. She had climbed part way up a stepladder, allowing the stripper to work. Her slender arms reached for the top of the wall. She didn't have many curves. Even her shoulder blades were visible beneath that shirt, probably left over by whoever had vacated this room. Sean was surprised Brick had had the good sense to find her attractive.

He frankly couldn't believe either man had had the poor judgment to leave her behind.

Another bad line of thought, he admonished himself.

"Wow," he said, grabbing hold of her last comment. "Your whole life in this house? No fooling?"

"That's right."

"What's that like?"

"Well, you get pretty good at stripping wallpaper," she said, turning to look at his wall, then hers. She lowered her gaze pointedly at him.

"I'm slow, huh?"

"Deliberate," she said. "Attorneys aren't slow, they're deliberate. That's what—"

She stopped abruptly, then turned back to the wall. She didn't have to finish. He'd heard Brick say it every time he needed an excuse for procrastinating.

"All attorneys aren't the same," he said. And he turned back to his own wall.

He worked in silence for a while, his thoughts on images of growing up in a house like this, with a yard to play in. Like Sean, Brick's child might have a single mother, but that child's life would be significantly different from his own childhood.

He had a hunch the one thing that wouldn't be different was a dedicated mom. He'd had one; he bet Faith O'Dare would be one, too.

"Why does he do it?"

The unexpected question from the other side of the room was so softly posed he almost missed it. He crossed to the boom box and turned it down.

"Heck if I understand," he said.

"But you're his partner. His friend."

Sean had been exploring the meaning of friendship this past week and hadn't yet come to a conclusion. "Brick is complicated. He's got everything—money, power, prestige."

"A beautiful wife and daughters." She raised her chin and tossed a defiant look over her shoulder as she said it.

"Yes. A beautiful wife and daughters." He wanted to tug her down off the ladder, pull her against his chest and comfort her, mostly because he could tell she was striving valiantly to show she didn't need anyone's comfort. Was that to be his fate, always wanting to comfort women who didn't want his help? "But it's never been enough. It's like there's a hole in his gut. And no matter how much stuff he pours into it, it just gets bigger, emptier."

It disturbed Sean that he might as well have been describing himself, as well.

She turned on the ladder and looked at him, once again looping a stray strand of ash brown hair behind one of those tiny ears. "Well, of course it gets emptier. You can't fill that hole up with *stuff.*"

She looked so certain and so surprised that he needed to be told.

"You can't?"

That was when she smiled. It wasn't the impish smile of the little girl in the pictures along the wall; it was softer, tempered by things that little girl hadn't yet learned, Sean supposed. "Not according to Pop."

"Your father?"

She nodded and hoisted herself onto the seat at the top of the ladder. Her feet were bare, he noticed, her toenails tipped in bright orange. "Pop always said we had to fill ourselves up with things you couldn't touch. Or see. Things like love and compassion and giving."

Sean had to admit there hadn't been much of that in his life these past few years. And it was a cinch that his expensive condo and his expensive car and the people with expensive hobbies he'd surrounded himself with hadn't helped him with his empty feeling. "What does your father do?"

"He was the postmaster. He died. Ten months ago."

He thought about the striped wallpaper and the oversize golf shirt. "I'm sorry. And your mother?"

She pursed her lips and stared at her rubber-gloved fingers. "I was seven. When she died, I mean."

"Oh. I am sorry."

So she was all alone. He told himself that didn't necessarily mean she needed him.

"Well, you get used to it. Only having one parent, I mean."

He averted his eyes and nodded. He thought of his own fatherlessness. He could have used that to connect with her, maybe, but that was the kind of thing Brick would do. He kept his mouth shut.

"So," she said, "I'm living proof that children can turn out perfectly fine with only one parent."

"I guess so."

"Good." She nodded and jumped off the ladder, landing with barely a sound. "But you do have to have a nursery. Right?"

"Right?"

"Then we'd better get busy."

She turned up the music again.

They'd made good headway by lunchtime, when she stopped to make them peanut-butter-and-banana sandwiches, iced tea and apple slices. He sniffed at the sandwich, took a bite under her challenging gaze and discovered it was tolerable. He wondered if she'd ever bullied Brick into peanut butter and banana and couldn't imagine it.

How could you continue deceiving a woman who was guileless enough to serve you peanut-butter-and-banana sandwiches?

By the end of the day the walls were stripped and prepped. Sean offered to come back the following Sunday, but she told him Times Square Crafts was closed on Mondays and she could finish papering the next day. He thought he might check in the next weekend, anyway, to see what else he could do for her. But he didn't mention it. Easier to get forgiveness than permission.

He stood at the curb admiring the way she hid a yawn behind her hand. As delicate as she looked, she didn't have delicate-looking hands, he'd noticed earlier in the day. They were small, certainly, fine-boned. But the nails were utilitarian, short, and the skin looked tougher than the rest of her. A worker's hands.

"Thanks for your help," she said. "I'd still have a lot left to do if you hadn't stuck around."

"My pleasure."

She smiled again, but not the smile he hoped to see. "You're still a lousy liar."

"You said that earlier."

Her smile faded. She gave the barest of nods.

"Why?"

"You said Walter wanted to help. Financially. That was a lie."

In that one case he wished he'd been a better liar. He nodded. "I'll work on it."

"Not on my account."

"Right." He opened his car door, reluctant to leave, no matter how good a hot shower and a cold beer sounded.

"Sean?"

It was the first time she'd said his name.

"Yes?"

"Are you married?"

He shook his head. "Not anymore."

She nodded. "Not that it matters. I guess...I guess I just wanted to be sure I could tell. Whether or not you really are a bad liar."

"Sure. I understand."

And he did. She'd let him into her house and fed him lunch and accepted his help. A month ago she would have trusted him without question, because that was the kind of person she was, the way she'd always lived, he supposed. But today, thanks to Brick, she had to ask.

And would probably still find it hard to be sure.

He waved as he drove away, watching her in his rearview mirror. She rolled her shoulders as she walked back up the steps to her front porch. She needed a hot shower for the kinks, too.

He shouldn't have let her work so hard, he told himself when he hit the winding highway back down the mountain toward Richmond. She might not look it yet, but she *was* pregnant. Pregnant women shouldn't be knocking themselves out the way she had today.

Maybe he would call her when he got home, make sure she was okay.

Back off, Davenport.

But he had trouble not worrying. Anything could happen. He knew that, deep in his gut where his fears hid.

And you can't do a damned thing if it does.

He pinched the bridge of his nose, hoping to fend off one of his tension headaches. He turned up the radio to drown out his thoughts, but it was hopeless. He'd done all he could today. He'd helped out. He would find a way to help again. Because trying to get Faith to accept his help had begun to fill that empty spot in him.

That empty spot had been around a long time— since Rachel had walked out four years ago. Maybe before. But this time, he told himself, things would be different.

Except that Faith didn't want his help any more than Rachel had.

FAITH COULDN'T BRING herself to tell Donna that Sean Davenport had helped her strip the old wallpaper in Pop's room. And that omission told her more than she wanted to admit about what had happened at her house that day.

She had capitulated. Let down her guard. Admitted the Trojan horse into her house. Into her baby's nursery, for heaven's sake!

Picking through the glassware on a table near the front window of Cookie's Twice-Loved Treasures, Faith pondered what it could be that Sean wanted from her. Was he reporting back to Walter? They must have some devious plan in mind, of that she was certain.

Then why had she let him stay? And why couldn't she tell Donna?

"Are these romantic?" Donna asked, and Faith looked up to examine the onyx candlesticks her partner held aloft from across the sea of knickknacks and antiques that filled the old barn.

"Oh, yes," Faith said, wondering why anyone would give her opinion about romance credence any longer. "Definitely romantic."

"Good. I'll take 'em."

Cookie Langtry looked up from the Victoriana magazine he was studying and said, "What you needin' with romantic, anyway? You kickin' Tom out?"

"Right," Donna said. "I've got Cary Grant coming for dinner tonight and I want to make sure the mood is right."

"Cary Grant's dead," Cookie said, resting his magazine across his rotund belly and his hands behind his head. The lacy nosegay on the cover of the magazine made a colorful accessory to his faded overalls. "'Course some folks say Tom's been dead for years, and you've been feedin' him supper right along."

"Mind your own business, Cookie," Donna snapped.

"Don't mind me," Cookie said. "I'm just an observer of human nature. And I observe that you've lost weight and colorized your hair. So maybe Cary

Grant *is* droppin' by tonight. Stranger things have happened.''

Faith found a milk pitcher decorated with a bright yellow flower that would look cheery on her kitchen windowsill. She found a wicker chaise longue that would be perfect on her front porch, shaded by Ida's wisteria climbing up her trellis. She could see herself stretched out on the chaise next spring with her new baby. She could make a pretty floral cushion for it, and a pillow to place at her back. She and little Alyson could doze off together every afternoon.

"Alyson O'Dare has a nice ring, don't you think?" she said to Donna as she wistfully turned away from the wicker chaise.

"The other boys are gonna tease him something awful," Donna said. She nodded toward the chaise. "You ought to get it. Treat yourself."

Faith shook her head. "Not today. I'm going to need so many things, and that's just an extravagance. Besides, it's going to be a girl. I know it. Sarah said we'd find out next week."

"Good. I don't want you getting too attached to Alyson before you find out you're carrying an Allen."

Faith knew why she was so convinced this baby was a girl. She had convinced herself it would be easier to raise a girl alone than it would be to raise a boy. She remembered all the times she'd longed for a mother, and how, as wise and wonderful as Pop was, sometimes a girl just needed a mother. It would be the same for a boy, she supposed. Sometimes a boy just needed a father, and she hated the thought of coming up short in her child's life.

So it would be a girl. She was certain.

Either way, sometimes kids had both parents and still turned out lousy. Look at Walter. Even Sean Davenport.

Just thinking about Sean made her irritable, because she couldn't believe how easily he'd charmed her into letting him stay. She remembered studying him and reaching the conclusion that, despite their connection, Sean was probably nothing like Walter. Standing there in his jeans and his worn leather jacket, his hair falling over one eye, he'd convinced her that the only similarities between him and Walter were the cars they drove and the suits they wore to court.

Sean looked looser, more like someone you'd go on a picnic with. Or strip wallpaper with. He'd even liked her peanut-butter-and-banana sandwiches, and Walter had always brought sprouts and avocados and sun-dried tomato bagels for their weekend lunches.

You're a fool, she told herself. *They're cut from the same cloth, and here you are trying to convince yourself they're different. You don't need Sean Davenport to fool you. You're doing a fine number on yourself.*

She frowned and held up a baby quilt draped on the corner of a chair. It was antique, but she could make one of her own for less money.

"Oh, Faith, look! A cradle!"

Grateful for a distraction from her troubling self-examination, Faith made her way to the back of the crowded barn. Tucked between a white enamel pie safe and an old wringer washing machine was a dusty, often-painted cradle. Faith fell in love with it instantly, because she didn't see the broken rocker or the chipped paint in layers of yellow and red and blue. No, Faith saw the hand-carved spindles that would be revealed when the paint was stripped, and the gentle rhythm to which the cradle would move when the broken rocker was repaired. She could see a baby's downy head nestled on a pillow, a hand-made quilt tucked beneath its fat little chin.

And wasn't that just like her, always believing she could see a treasure beneath a surface that any reasonable person would label junk?

"Let's take it home," she said.

She wasn't ready to give up salvaging lost treasures. But at least she could learn to limit herself to salvaging inanimate objects and pick her people a little more carefully.

CHAPTER FIVE

SEAN PUTTERED awkwardly around the kitchen, taking orders from his mother. He'd been doing it all his life, and he apparently still didn't know his way around a kitchen. It was written all over him that here was a man who didn't know a paring knife from a pickle fork.

"What *is* a pickle fork, anyway?" he asked as he gingerly plucked piping hot biscuits out of the dented pan his mother refused to give up.

Lucy Davenport looked at her son quizzically, then continued serving up plates of pot roast, new potatoes and carrots. "A *pickle* fork. Those rich people you hang out with may need a fork just for pickles, but if you ask me, one fork is sufficient for pickles and pot roast."

Sean grinned. "How am I ever going to earn my place in society with a mother like you?"

"Sit down at the kitchen table, Mr. Big Shot," she said, her pride evident, despite her teasing tone.

After a lifetime of working as a telephone operator, starting in the old days when they wore heavy headsets and plugged cords into lighted boards, Lucy Davenport had been grateful for the early retirement her son's success had made possible. She was grateful for the little two-bedroom brick house he'd bought for her, although she'd refused the more spacious house he'd had in mind.

And have nine rooms to dust and vacuum when five is gracious plenty? she'd protested. His assurance that he would hire help for her had been met with one of those looks that told him it was pointless to argue further. She wasn't yet sixty, she'd pointed out briskly, and hardly in need of servants. *I'd be old and fat in three months,* she'd said, *sitting around letting people do for me.*

Sean's mother hadn't been willing to become the lady of the manor. Which Sean supposed meant she was wiser than he. Because, hard as he'd tried all these years to fit into Richmond's upper-crust society, Sean was still more at home in his mother's small house, wearing a pair of jeans and eating pot roast, than he'd ever been in a dinner jacket sipping brandy and nibbling sushi.

He might have crossed the tracks when he got to know Walter Brickerson, but he was still only comfortable on the side where he'd grown up. Over there, he was an impostor, waiting to be found out.

Over here, he would always be Lucy Davenport's boy. And that was something he'd gotten pretty darned good at over the years.

He savored the pot roast while his mother told him what had gone on since their last dinner date. She'd started a yoga class with one of her neighbors, but only because Scotti Yount assured her it would keep her limber. Helen Grammar's daughter was getting married again. And Lucy was thinking about getting a puppy to replace old Marvin, who'd died a year ago. The Newsomes had a litter, all of them black-and-white spotted.

"And you know I've always been a pushover for a spotted puppy," Lucy said.

"Want me to fence the backyard?"

Her brown eyes lit up. Lucy Davenport had been barely nineteen when Sean was born. Her skin was still fair and smooth, her eyes bright, and her dark hair had less gray than her son's. "Would you?"

"I'd love to."

"You do too much, you know."

"Don't start, Mom."

She frowned and went to check on the blueberry pie in the oven. "Well, you do. You think you're supposed to save the world."

"No, I don't. I just like seeing my young pretty mother with a happy face."

She turned off the oven and took the pie out to cool. "Then how about showing me my young hand-some son with a happy face."

"I'm happy."

"Maybe." She poured two cups of coffee into chipped mugs she had also refused to give up for a new set of china. "You look troubled." She sat. "You always look troubled."

He didn't like the feeling he was gossiping, but there wasn't much he kept from his mother. He pushed his plate away. "It's Brick."

Her disapproval flickered and vanished in an instant. Lucy Davenport had never been one to judge others, but she had stopped admiring Walter Brickerson Junior a long time ago. "Oh?"

He registered her expression, as he had many times, and heard himself saying something even he hadn't expected. "What would you think if I quit the firm?"

Her eyes grew wide. She sipped her coffee and Sean knew she was considering her words carefully. "I'd think you must have a darn good reason and I'd be behind you all the way."

The Loyal Mother Response, and he knew every word of it was true. "What else?"

"I'd think you'd be breaking Mr. Brickerson Senior's heart."

Sean thought of Walt Senior and knew that would be the hard part about severing ties with Brick.

"What's happened, son?"

Now Sean considered his words carefully. This was what he'd come here for of course—to lay this out before his mother and try to gain her clarity, her wisdom. But now that the moment was here, he felt awkward about it.

Sean had known for a long time, since before he understood the full implication really, that his mother and father had never married. The first time he asked why he didn't have a father, she'd told him his father hadn't been able to stay with them; he had other things he had to do that meant he couldn't be in their family. The older Sean got, the more he admired the grace with which his mother had excused a man she must have loved. She hadn't wanted to taint her son's feelings for the father he'd never seen, and in the process she'd given him even more to admire in her.

But he knew that her circumstances probably colored how he felt about Faith's situation. And he knew she would suspect that, too.

"It's another woman. Again." He forced himself to press forward. "Only this one's different, Mom. She's a good person. She's not sophisticated and cagey like some of the others. He cooked up this elaborate scheme—she lives out of town and he visited her regularly, took her to the lake house on weekends, the whole nine yards—and she never even guessed he was married. And...now she's pregnant."

As he had expected, his mother's empathy showed in her brown eyes. "Oh, dear."

"Mom, he's got no remorse. It's like nobody matters but him. Not Beverly or the girls, not Faith—"

"Faith?"

"That's her name. Faith O'Dare." A rush of emotion flooded him as his lips formed her name, feelings too complicated to analyze at the moment. Feelings so strong they frightened him. He made himself think about his partner, instead. Those were emotions he knew how to handle. "Brick doesn't even seem to understand that he has some responsibility to her, to the baby."

He let the silence hang between them, knowing his mother would begin to talk when she had digested all this. He trusted her judgment. She would tell him if he was overreacting. Maybe she would tell him to butt out, to stay away from Faith O'Dare.

He almost hoped that was exactly what she'd say.

He didn't need an entanglement. Especially an entanglement with a pregnant woman. But he was having trouble convincing himself.

"A man like Walter... I hate to say this, Sean, but she'll be better off without him."

"I know that, Mom. I think she does, too." He remembered the cold fury in her gray eyes that day on the porch at Times Square Crafts. Faith's love for Walter Brickerson had died a swift death, if he was any judge. "I guess what I'm wondering is whether I'll be better off without him, too."

"You don't have to be his friend just because you work in the same firm," she said.

"But if I sever the friendship, what about Beverly? How do I explain things to her?"

Lucy sighed. "You always forget that it isn't your job to make the whole world happy, Sean. Nobody hired you to protect everyone."

Sean had heard that from his mother so many times he knew the words by heart. But he couldn't really feel that truth in his heart. He'd felt responsible all his life, even as a child. Although she'd never expected it of him, Sean had stepped into the role of man of the house as soon as he'd realized his family didn't have one. No matter how often his mother had urged him to have fun, to be a kid, Sean had always helped out, behaved himself, tried to shift some of the burden off his mother's shoulders onto his own. Forty, he supposed, was too late to do much changing.

"But—"

The arch of his mother's left eyebrow stopped him. He smiled. "I know. You're right."

For the rest of the evening he told her about the cases he was working on and the latest office gossip and about the young boys he was teaching to play basketball.

The blueberry pie was heaven, the cup of coffee bottomless and the conversation easy. The evening drew to an end too soon.

And although Sean knew his mother hadn't given him any direct advice on how to handle the situation with Brick, he knew that sometime over the next few days something she'd said tonight would trigger his resolution. That was the way it always seemed to work. Lucy Davenport never told him what to do; instead, she'd taught him thirty years earlier how to listen for the solution himself.

But as he slipped into his leather jacket and kissed his mother on her cheek, she took both his hands in hers and said, "This woman, Faith, she may be better off without any help from Walter Brickerson's best friend, too."

He started to protest, but she shook her head. "Just think about it."

"I will." A promise that wouldn't be hard to keep. He could think of little else.

KELSY FELT GUILTY even listening to her latest ex-fiancé with Faith in the room. She turned her back to Faith and whispered into the receiver.

"I'm not changing my mind," she said.

"But, Kels, I love you."

His voice was so pleading, so tender. She couldn't remember when one of her jilted fiancés had reacted with so much despair. Maybe Steve really did love her enough to make it work. Maybe Steve wouldn't walk away from her someday down the road. Maybe…

Wishful thinking, she told herself, glancing again at Faith.

"You'll get over it," she said, wondering if her words sounded as callous to Steve as they did to her.

"You'll change your mind," he insisted.

"No, I won't," she said. She remembered all the times her mother had changed her mind, allowing her father back into the house time and again after he'd vanished for months, returning with no explanations and a boatload of insincere remorse. Granted, Steve had never done any of those things. But Kelsy knew she had to hang tough. She couldn't waffle and weave once she'd made a decision.

"Aw, baby, don't do this. I know what you're thinking, and I'm not like—"

"It isn't that," Kelsy said, regretting that moment of weakness when she'd told Steve everything. He'd been the only man she'd been able to share the whole story with. He'd seemed different from the rest, tenderhearted and understanding. He hadn't minded talking about things like that. She'd honestly believed that Steve was different.

That hadn't stopped her from being ruled by her fear.

She glanced once again at Faith. They'd all believed Walter was different, too. Even Kelsy hadn't

been able to detect his deceit, and she'd always believed she could sniff that stuff out after a lifetime
of being exposed to it.

But she hadn't. And that frightened her. Even she
could be fooled.

"Steve, it's over. Nothing is going to change my
mind."

FAITH WAS IMPATIENT to wear maternity clothes, but
her body wasn't cooperating. Now that she was
barely four months pregnant, the baggy pants she
sometimes wore actually fit for the first time. So she
had to content herself with other ways of making this
pregnancy real.

She'd gone for the ultrasound, a procedure that
had revealed a healthy baby boy growing inside her.
Tears had welled up in her eyes as she watched the
tiny being, and she'd looked up to see that Sarah was
also wiping away tears with the sleeve of her white
lab coat. The ultrasound photograph was taped to the
mantel at Times Square Crafts. About ten people a
day came by for a glimpse at the town's newest res-
ident-to-be.

Clem, from down at the garage, had squinted at
the grainy snapshot and said, "You're sure that's a
baby?"

Kelsy, who had taken a very proprietary air with
the photograph, said, "See, there's his little feet and
there's his little eyes."

A whole troop from Fudgie Ruppenthal's barbershop came by one morning. "Want to see the little
feller," Tood Grunkemeier said, sounding for all the

world as if he expected to determine whether "the little feller" looked more like Faith or Walter.

And, in fact, when the four old men left, Fudgie grumbled, "See. Told you we wouldn't be able to tell."

"Aw, hell, Fudgie, you'd know if you weren't blind as a bat. It's a wonder you ain't cut somebody's throat giving a haircut."

"I'm not blind. *You're* seeing things."

Using the garden hose to rinse the paint remover from the cradle she'd dragged into the front yard after work, Faith smiled at the memories of all the caring people who had traipsed through the shop the last few days. She heard a pickup truck slow to a halt in front of the house and looked up. The side door of the bright red truck boasted that it was from Hurd's Hardware. She watched as Chuck Hurd got out, waved a hand and reached into the truck bed for the buckets of stain and varnish she'd ordered the week before.

"You didn't have to bring my stuff," she said, turning off the hose and walking out to meet him on the front walk. "I'd have stopped by after work tomorrow."

Chuck shook his head and set the buckets on the steps. "Nope. Free delivery's just part of this month's Maternity Special."

"Well, thanks." Faith smiled. "Glass of tea for your trouble?"

"Don't mind if I do."

He was waiting in one of the rockers when she returned a few minutes later with two tall glasses of iced tea. Barrel-chested and thick-armed, Chuck dwarfed her grandmother's rocker.

"Fixin' up a cradle, I see."

Faith sat in the other rocker. "Got it from Cookie's. He said it used to belong to the Tarkingtons."

Chuck's gaze wandered to the section of red-tile roof that showed through the trees. Heritage Manor, built by the Tarkington brothers almost 175 years earlier, was visible on the hill that rose on the other side of Ridge Lane.

"Cookie'll say anything to make a sale."

"I know," Faith said. "But if I want to believe it, I will."

Chuck leveled a pair of stern brown eyes on her, and she read the reproach in them. He thought she'd been too eager to accept Walter's lies, too. She put her bare feet up on the railing and ignored his judgmental gaze. Chuck was a nice man, but just because they'd dated most of their senior year in high school didn't give him the inside track on figuring her out. Chuck Hurd was not an expert on Faith O'Dare; if he had been, she might have gone to the senior prom with him, after all, and they might be fighting about whether or not to allow their daughter to wear a backless dress to her own prom.

But he wasn't and she hadn't and they weren't.

"You're a dreamer, Faith," he said.

"No, I'm not," she said, although she suspected there was a fair measure of truth in what he said.

"Just like Pat."

She didn't even bother to dispute that. Pop had

been a dreamer; it was one of the things she loved about Patrick O'Dare.

"What are you going to do?" he asked.

"There's only one thing to do," she said. "I'm going to get ready for my baby and then do the best job I can when he gets here."

He glanced at her again, but she kept her eyes averted. "Won't be easy."

"Life never is," she said. "Smooth seas don't make good sailors."

He chuckled. "You gonna do that to this young'un? Dredge up all Pat's malarkey and raise up another generation on it?"

Faith smiled again. "Why not? It worked pretty well for me."

"That's a fact." He set his half-empty glass on the wicker table between them and shifted in his chair to face her. "Faith, I've been thinking."

She nudged the railing with her bare toes to set her chair to rocking gently. "Yeah?"

"You shouldn't have to do this alone."

"I told you, I'll be fine, Chuck. I have the whole town to fall back on. You know that."

"But that's not the same as having a...partner."

She kept silent.

"So what I was thinking was that we used to get along pretty well. Don't you think? Back in high school?"

"Chuck—"

"Now let me finish, Faith. You know we always did have fun." He reached over and took her hand.

"Sometimes things were downright special between us."

Faith didn't look up, because she didn't want to be reminded of the memories he was obviously trying to evoke. Kissing Chuck Hurd had not exactly been the peak sexual experience of her life, and she certainly didn't want to dwell on memories of his clumsy attempts to seduce her.

"We go back a long time, Faith, and I've always had this warm spot in my heart for you. You were the first girl I ever really wanted to—"

"Chuck, don't."

"Okay, okay. But I loved you all those years ago. That's what's really important. Together we can make a real family for this baby. He'll have a name, a good future in this town. Why, Hurds have run the hardware store in Hope Springs since 1909, Faith."

She didn't tell him that anybody who could read the sign over the door knew that. She also didn't tell him that her baby would have a name and didn't need his noble offer. But if she didn't put a stop to this soon, she might lose her temper and forget that the man meant well.

"Chuck, that's real sweet of you," she said, slipping her hand out of his damp grip. "It really is. But I don't need a marriage of convenience."

"Don't look at it like that," Chuck said. "We were in love once. We can fall in love again."

"We were kids then. That's not love, that's..." She faltered in the face of his eager expression.

"I want you to think about this, Faith. In all seriousness. It's the best answer. If you'll think about it, I know you'll agree.''

She shook her head and stood.

''Just think about it. You'll see. You can depend on me, Faith.''

She didn't want to depend on Chuck. She didn't want him kissing her on the cheek, either, but he did it before she realized what was happening. Then he was waving from the truck, that big smile on his ruddy face. ''You need anything, you let me know, you hear?''

He didn't wait for an answer. Through sheer force of will, Chuck expected to make her do exactly what he wanted. Faith remembered now why she'd broken up with him six days before the senior prom. He'd bought her an engagement ring without any prior discussion. An ugly gold engagement ring that he'd expected her to accept. He'd had the timetable all figured out. He was willing to grant her one year of college—to get that out of her system—then they could be married the following June. The only way she'd been able to get his attention, to convince him she meant no, was to break up with him. To refuse his phone calls. To go to the prom alone.

Francie Hartsell had liked the ugly gold ring, and the styleless wedding band that matched it. Chuck and Francie had been married ten years before she ran off with the tennis pro from Heritage Manor.

That had been six years ago, and Chuck hadn't tried to push any wedding rings on anyone else since.

''He'll get over it,'' Faith murmured to herself, determined to forget what had just happened. The last thing she needed in her life at the moment was one more complication.

She had forgotten, however, the way minor events in Hope Springs could take on a life of their own. When she passed the post office the next morning, Ivalene stuck her head out the door to ask if it was true that Chuck had proposed. By lunchtime Ida said her first three customers of the morning had informed her that Faith and Chuck were finally going to tie the knot. And the kid who filled the *Courier* box at the corner of Ridge and Loblolly said she'd heard that Chuck Hurd was really the father of Faith's baby.

By the time she got over her fit of temper, Faith had decided that the best thing to do was ignore it all.

That was why, when Kelsy came by on her way home that afternoon, Faith was at least able to hear her partner out without losing her temper.

"Are you sure you did the right thing? Saying no to Chuck?"

Kelsy sat on the front porch railing, looking down as Faith began sanding the newly stripped cradle.

"Positive," Faith said.

"How can you be so sure? Shouldn't you at least—"

"I don't love him. He only *thinks* he loves me."

"But for the baby's sake—"

"For the baby's sake I wouldn't dream of marrying a man I don't love. I would've expected you, of all people, to understand that marriage isn't to be taken lightly."

Kelsy looked down at the left hand that had worn

four different engagement rings. She grinned sheepishly when she looked up and, not for the first time, Faith wondered what made Kelsy so shy of commitment.

"I understand that," Kelsy said. "But Chuck is different. Everybody knows what Chuck is like."

"Dull?"

"Steady. Besides, even in my case things would be different if I were pregnant. Which I'm not."

Faith glanced up at Kelsy's hasty pronouncement.

"But if I were pregnant, I would make every effort to fall in love. Fast."

"Kelsy, you can't force love. You know that."

"But you could give it a shot at least. Unless you're still in love with Walter."

Faith stopped sanding and her stiff shoulders slumped. "No, I'm not still in love with Walter. But I'm too bruised to think of loving again for a very long time."

She didn't say, "Maybe ever," but she thought it.

"Oh, Faith." Kelsy jumped off the railing, clearing the hedge of waxy yellow acuba. She dropped to the ground beside Faith and touched her shoulder. "I'm sorry. I'm such a big mouth sometimes."

Faith smiled. "It's okay. It's just that I can't love Chuck and I don't have to settle. The baby and I will be fine. We'll have each other."

"And he'll have his aunt Kelsy." A bright smile replaced the contrition on Kelsy's face. "What are you going to name him?"

Faith took a lackadaisical swipe at a rough knot in

the wood on the side of the cradle. "I don't know. I haven't thought about it yet."

"How about Dexter? I dated a boy named Dexter once and he had such presence. You know, I probably should have married Dexter."

The rumble of a familiar engine halted Faith's reply. She knew a BMW engine when she heard one. And she had finally stopped expecting the engine to belong to Walter's car. "Oh, no."

Kelsy bristled, instantly protective. "What's *he* doing here?"

"Interfering."

Kelsy stood. "Want me to run him off?"

Faith stood, too, and turned toward the street. Sean was walking to the front gate, two white bags from Luisita's Tex-a-Tavern in his hands and a bundle under one arm. He wore a tentative smile on his lips.

"Thanks, but I can handle him."

"I don't like him coming around here upsetting you."

Faith smiled and told herself she was responding to Kelsy's mother-hen attitude, and not to Sean's smile. The man was a pest. Just like Chuck, he couldn't take no for an answer.

"Hi." He stayed on the other side of the gate, and Faith knew he was waiting for an invitation to enter.

She struggled with herself. Shouldn't she tell him to leave? She remembered how hard he'd worked stripping wallpaper.

Kelsy took a step toward the gate. "What are you doing here?"

He waved a bag. "Dinner. Luisita said her frijoles

offer one hundred percent of the nutrients needed by mothers-to-be. She seemed to know her business.''

Faith thought about the three little Mendozas he had probably seen running around at Luisita's.

''Mexican food?'' Kelsy asked skeptically.

''Tex-Mex,'' Sean corrected her. ''That makes all the difference. Luisita said so.''

Kelsy glanced at Faith.

''I'll be fine,'' Faith said.

''*He'd* give me heartburn even without Tex-Mex,'' Kelsy said, opening the gate wide. ''I'll be at Donna's. In case you need anything.''

She stared pointedly at Sean's back.

''I'll remember that,'' Faith said.

Kelsy started down the sidewalk, stopping long enough to say, ''Dexter. Give it some thought. Dexter O'Dare. What a great name!''

Faith nodded. ''I'll think about it.''

She turned to Sean, who stood there with his bags and his bundle. ''Dexter?''

''She wants me to name the baby after one of her old boyfriends.'' Faith wiped her dusty hands on her denim skirt, took one of his bags and started toward the house.

''It's a boy?''

''Yes.''

''You had an ultrasound?''

She nodded and began placing containers of food on the wicker table between the rockers. ''We'll eat out here if that's okay.''

''And everything was all right?''

She didn't look up because his concern came

through so loud and clear she didn't want to see it in his eyes. "Of course. You didn't have to bring dinner, you know. I'm capable of feeding myself."

"Will they be doing any other tests?"

She handed him a paper napkin wrapped around plastic utensils and gestured to one of the rockers. He sat, but he didn't take his eyes off her. When she looked at him, she realized he didn't seem concerned at all, just downright worried.

"Everything's fine," she said, irritated by his worry. She didn't want anyone fretting over her, especially not Sean Davenport. "You came here to eat, so eat."

"My mother says I worry too much," he said as they began their meals.

She didn't like him talking about his mother, either. She didn't even want to think he had a mother. She wanted him to be Walter's friend and nothing more. Not human, not likable, certainly not someone whose mother doted on him. Of course, he didn't look like any mother's dream tonight. He was wearing the leather bomber jacket again over a faded T-shirt and another pair of snug jeans. His hair still needed cutting and his five-o'clock shadow made him look like trouble.

Which is what he is.

"You should listen to your mother," she said tersely, enjoying the food in spite of herself. Luisita must've told him her favorites.

He frowned. "I know."

Faith coached herself not to eat so quickly, although if she did, Sean would be gone sooner.

"You're refinishing an old cradle."

She nodded, giving him no encouragement.

"I suppose you stripped it yourself."

She heard the disapproval in his voice and looked up, irritated once again. "Your point?"

He looked exasperated. "The fumes, Faith. You have to remember the baby."

She clenched the fist that held her napkin. "Don't you dare lecture me about taking care of my baby."

He set aside his empty carryout box. "I'm not lecturing."

"It's none of your business."

"I happen to care. I'm sorry if that makes you angry."

How dare he be so rational with her? How dare he look at her with those soulful eyes of his and address her in that kind, concerned voice? How dare he sit here on her porch looking absolutely at home?

"I'm not angry," she said through clenched teeth.

The cough he hid behind his hand had started out as a chuckle, she knew it. She wanted to throw her box at him, but it still had frijoles in it and she wanted every bite. Darn him.

"I brought you something," he said, thrusting a package in her direction.

She stared at the package, then at him. He was smiling, a charming smile that clutched at her.

Then she remembered it had been a roguish smile that had first attracted her to Walter.

"I don't want a present," she said, appalled that she sounded so childish.

"Well, it's not really for you. It's for Dexter." He

started tearing the paper off the gift. "And *he'll* want it."

"His name isn't Dexter and..."

She faltered as the paper fell away, revealing a huge stuffed duck exactly like the ones on the wallpaper he'd helped her with a week ago. It was adorable. Irresistible.

Like his smile? she chided herself.

"Sean, I can't... You know this isn't..."

"Just take it," he said softly.

Something caught in her chest and she realized even his voice was irresistible.

"No," she said, refusing to touch the downy soft toy. Refusing even to put her hand close enough to his to take it from him. "I can't. And you have to stop offering."

"Why? Why can't you just let me be a friend?"

Because she might have been naive once, but it wasn't going to happen again.

CHAPTER SIX

SEAN WAS SURPRISED to realize how familiar the main drag of Hope Springs was becoming to him.

He'd parked in the municipal lot behind the bank and the bookstore and headed for Hurd's Hardware. Towering shade trees anchored the corners of the parking lot, their new spring growth fluttering in a late April breeze. Hurd's, enormous display windows flanking its double wooden doors, covered about one-third of the block of Ridge Lane between Tarkington Drive and Old Dominion Drive. On the Tarkington Drive corner stood a video store with movie posters screaming from its narrow window; on the north side of Hurd's was Ferguson's IGA Supermarket, Curls and Swirls Salon, then the Ole Virginny Diner, its sign and menu posted in the window both in the shape of the state.

Sean had been back to Hope Springs about once a week since his first trip five weeks earlier. He couldn't say that Faith was any friendlier, but the town was getting downright inviting.

Actually, he speculated as he waved at the startled ladies he could see through the plate-glass window of Curls and Swirls, Faith seemed to build the wall that separated them a little higher each time she saw him.

"I'm not letting you in my house anymore," she'd said the week after he'd brought frijoles and tamales.

And the time after that, with an edge in her voice, "I'm just going to pretend you aren't here. What do you think about that?"

But none of it deterred him. He felt good about what he was doing. Released, in a way, from whatever emotional prison had held him since Rachel left.

He had cleaned gutters that were still clogged with last fall's leaves, listening to her shouted protests the entire time. He had washed and waxed her father's car after discovering that Brick had promised to do the job, even though she showed no signs of wanting either to sell it or use it herself. He'd met her next-door neighbor and self-appointed protector, Ida, last week and learned why the garden plot behind her house was lying fallow. Faith had run out of energy to till it herself and refused to ask for help, according to the blond proprietor of Sweet Ida's.

And that was why today he was walking down the broad sidewalk on Ridge Lane headed for Hurd's Hardware.

A musty earthy scent assaulted him when he entered the open front door of Hurd's. Bags of peat moss were stacked by the door; bins of nails lined the opposite wall. Iron skillets and lightbulbs and drill bits cluttered row after row. A burly man with thinning blond hair and a blue plaid shirt stood behind the counter, booted foot on a three-legged stool.

He studied Sean, barely nodding when Sean greeted him.

"Do something for you?" he asked, putting his foot on the floor and straightening when Sean approached the counter.

"I'd like to rent a tiller."

"A tiller?"

The man made it sound like an object only found in vessels from uncharted planets.

"That's right. I understood you have equipment to rent."

"You're a flatlander." The sandy-haired man leveled the words like an accusation. "Mind if I ask what you'd be needing with a tiller?"

Sean kept his expression placid, despite his irritation. Small towns were different, he reminded himself. Maybe the man was just showing interest.

"I'm helping a friend with her garden."

The man behind the counter sized Sean up some more. Sean hoped his twitching jaw wasn't noticeable. He slipped his fingers into the back pocket of his jeans and pulled out a credit card. He put it on the counter between them. The clerk didn't even acknowledge it.

"Reckon that friend'd be Faith O'Dare."

"Reckon you'd be right," Sean said, giving in to the urge to echo this man's challenging tone.

"Reckon you'd be Sean Davenport, then."

"And you are...?"

"Chuck Hurd."

He said his name as if that would explain an attitude that bordered on belligerent.

"Mind if I pass on a little advice this morning, Mr. Davenport?"

"I'd rather have a tiller."

Anger became a dark cloud in Chuck Hurd's eyes. "Folks in Hope Springs have noticed you hanging around. And some of 'em feel it's their neighborly duty to remind Faith that big-city fellows aren't very trustworthy."

Of course. Everyone was protective of Faith. Sean should have expected that. And he should have realized that his attentions wouldn't have gone unnoticed.

Still, he didn't feel inclined to defend himself to this sour-faced guardian at the gate. "I'm sure Faith appreciates their concern."

Actually he was sure of anything but. He could pretty easily imagine Faith's bristling reaction to any buttinskies who dared tell her how to run her life. She might agree with them wholeheartedly, but she wouldn't appreciate unsolicited advice any more than she appreciated his unsolicited help.

"Nope," Chuck said. "And that's why I'm talking to you, instead of her. Faith gets riled."

"Maybe I get riled, too."

"You I can handle," Chuck said, rolling his shoulders and placing his broad hands on the countertop.

Sean suspected that was so. Sean hadn't lifted a fist to anyone since Rodney Prescott accused him of being a dirty bastard in the fourth grade. Rodney Prescott had bloodied Sean's nose, and Sean had realized not everyone was cut out to be a brawler.

"Does this mean you aren't going to rent me a tiller?"

"It means Faith has all the help she needs right here in Hope Springs."

And for a moment Sean saw glimmering in Chuck Hurd's eyes the genuine devotion that prompted this macho display. How could he be angry with that? It did, however, give him a moment of uneasiness he couldn't quite label.

"I'm going to till Faith's garden today," Sean said, looking Chuck squarely in the eyes. "I can do it with one of your tillers or I can head back down the highway until I find another town and another hardware store. What'll it be, Chuck?"

"Why are you so damned interested in Faith?"

"Because she's been treated shabbily by someone I know."

"So you're going to play white knight?"

That was when Sean recognized the flicker of emotion in Chuck's face. Jealousy. He felt a moment of uncertainty. What was he doing here mucking around in Faith O'Dare's life? There must be plenty of men, even in a small town like Hope Springs, who'd be glad to have a woman like Faith. She didn't need help from someone like him, someone motivated by old baggage and fresh guilt.

Then he caught sight once again of Chuck's big clumsy hands and thought of them on Faith's fair skin, in her soft hair. It was a mismatch so flagrant it made his blood boil.

Chuck Hurd might have his sights set on Faith,

but Sean didn't have to roll over and make it easy for him.

That was when Sean recognized his own jealousy.

"Is my money good here or not?" he snapped.

Twenty minutes later he was unloading the tiller from the trailer Chuck Hurd also let him use for the day. The storeowner's final words echoed in his head even as he heard Faith's back door open and close.

Be careful. You do any damage and your credit card won't come close to paying what you'll owe.

Sean knew the less-than-friendly warning had nothing to do with the tiller or the trailer. And he wondered for a moment if Chuck Hurd and all the others in town who thought he ought to stay away from Faith were right. What could he possibly do to help her that someone else in this town couldn't do better, more safely? After all, he knew that each time she saw him it reminded her of Walter Brickerson.

He should leave and never come back.

But as he watched her walk down the stone path toward him, he knew he wouldn't do that. He also knew there was nothing noble in his motives.

Faith touched something in him, something that hadn't been touched in years. In some perverse way her emotional strength in this crisis helped him look at his own vulnerability without feeling he came up short. And the fragility of her appearance—which he knew had nothing to do with what was inside her—gave him hope he had something to offer her, even if it was only cleaning gutters and tilling gardens.

She carried a steaming mug, and her hair still

looked disheveled from sleep. Even her eyes wore that muzzy look that said the coffee hadn't yet kicked in. She wore a dress this morning, one of those soft cotton dresses in pale yellow, flowing around her knees and calves as she walked, molding itself intimately to her rounding belly. The reality of her pregnancy hit him like a thunderbolt, squarely in the gut, almost taking his breath away.

Oh, God, he thought. *What am I doing? I've lost my mind.*

He swallowed hard and hoisted the tiller over the railroad ties that edged the garden.

"You just don't listen, do you?" she said, ending on a yawn that made her narrow face look like the face of the little girl in the photographs on the stairwell wall.

"I could use a cup of coffee," he said, beginning to bargain with himself. If he got through this one day, he'd never come back. He would leave her alone, which was what she and everyone else in this town wanted. He would disentangle himself.

"It's decaf," she warned him, gesturing apologetically in the direction of her tummy.

"Then maybe I'd better just get to work," he said. "Get this done and take the tiller back to Hurd's before Chuck sends out a posse."

She sat on a stump and curled her feet under her. They were bare again, he noticed, slender feet with toes this time painted bright pink. "What did you do, steal it?"

"You'd have thought so."

She chuckled, giving him another glimpse of the

child she had been. He imagined the baby she carried would look the same way, devilish but innocent. He'd like a little boy like that.

Dangerous territory, Davenport.

"He wasn't giving you a hard time, was he?"

"Well, he didn't mention tar and feathering."

She laughed. "Folks around here aren't crazy about the company you keep."

"So I hear. They think I ought to stay away from you."

"They're busybodies." She frowned. "But that's not the company they object to."

"I know. They think I'm like Brick."

"Aren't you?"

He dug the front blade of the tiller into the winter-toughened soil and paused. "No."

Then he flipped the switch and took out his frustration on Faith's garden.

FAITH WATCHED until her mug was empty and the stump grew uncomfortable. The way he went after the soil reminded her of her father. Any time Pop had been angry or irritable, he'd always taken it out in physical work, and she'd have sworn that was what Sean was doing. His chin jutted forward, his brow creased in a ferocious frown, and whenever he hit a clump of roots he gave the tiller a mighty jerk.

The ground gave way beneath his determination, softening.

Back in the kitchen, she washed up after breakfast and started a pot of soup for their lunch. He was out there streaked with dirt and sweat so she could grow tomatoes and corn this summer. What else could she do but feed him?

While she peeled potatoes and diced carrots, he drew her attention time and again. As the sun rose higher and the morning chill burned off, he slipped off his T-shirt and tossed it onto the stump where she'd sat. He was slender, but his back and chest were chorded with taut, convincing muscles. Dark hair threaded down his flat belly and disappeared. His skin was bronze. Like her father's.

The second comparison of the day to her father irritated her and she turned away from the window. Sean Davenport couldn't hold a candle to the kind of man Patrick O'Dare had been. And she needed to keep that in mind.

When she had the soup simmering on the stove, she took a tall glass of iced tea out to him. He saw her coming and killed the motor on the tiller, pausing to wipe his face and hands on his cast-aside T-shirt. Perspiration beaded on his skin.

His nipples were dark and taut, ringed with springy curls.

Faith looked away. Then looked back as he drank, swallowing half the glass in one long gulp. She'd never before thought about the loveliness of a man at work and wished she hadn't thought of it now.

"I'm almost done," he said. "I'm going to work in some manure. Chuck said that was the thing to do. Then we can plant this afternoon."

She shook her head. "I'll plant next week. After work. It helps me wind down."

She didn't want to tell him that she liked getting

her hands in the dirt, doing her part in the eternal process of bringing food out of the ground. It made her feel connected to something bigger than herself, and she didn't want that spoiled by having a stranger looking over her shoulder.

He was hardly a stranger any longer, but never mind that.

"If you're sure."

She nodded. "I have soup ready for lunch."

"Thanks."

She hesitated but couldn't stop herself. "Maybe I'll go with you when you go back to Hurd's. I need to pick up seeds and tomato plants."

He smiled, and she realized there was nothing roguish about his smile. It wasn't like Walter's at all. Instead it teased her gently and made her relax.

"Your friend Chuck might not like that, us showing up together."

"My friend Chuck can mind his own business."

"He might call out the militia."

"The whole town can mind its own business. I don't need them to run my life, you know."

"I know. But they don't."

"They will."

AND THAT WAS HOW Sean found himself later that afternoon getting the grand tour of Hope Springs from Faith O'Dare. All he'd had to do was appeal to her stubborn streak.

He should've felt guilty. After all, she'd let him clean up in her bathroom and lent him a plaid shirt that must have belonged to her father. Then she'd fed him three bowls of homemade soup, thick with her own canned tomatoes, corn and lima beans. She'd even taken an iron skillet off the wall and made corn bread, one of those Southern mysteries that even the best blue-plate diners couldn't get right.

Faith's was perfect, moist inside, crunchy outside, the way Sean's mother made it.

Hope Springs was becoming the land of day-dreams. Weekends in the yard, homemade food, a pretty woman who lifted his heart and made his spirits come alive for the first time in years.

A pretty, *pregnant* woman.

That part was hard to forget. He grew nervous thinking about it. More than nervous. Downright afraid.

Nothing to worry about, he'd reminded himself as they settled up with Chuck Hurd. She was young and healthy and there was nothing to fear.

Still, he felt the fight-or-flight response whenever his gaze wandered to the barely rounding belly beneath her soft, swishy dress. His pulse buzzed in his ears. His chest felt like a convention of hummingbird wings. Perspiration gathered on his upper lip.

This is not the same, Davenport. Can the theatrics.

So he'd concentrated on putting her tomato plants and green-bean plants and all her little packets of seeds in his car—she couldn't believe he didn't mind a little dirt in the trunk of his BMW—and then he'd said, "Show me around?"

She'd surprised him by agreeing.

They walked from one end of Ridge Lane to the other. On the north end she showed him the stone welcome sign he'd never seen because he'd always come from the south. The imposing structure read, "Welcome to Hope Springs. Population 8,497. Established 1833. You'll Need No Other Medicine but Hope."

"They say that's out of Shakespeare," she said, "but I don't know. Hope Springs used to be one of the most popular spa destinations on the entire East Coast early in the last century. They said the hot springs could work miracles."

"And can they?"

She shrugged. "Well, I've never exactly seen a miracle."

"Maybe it depends on your definition of a miracle."

"Maybe."

They passed a junk-and-antique store, then a stone gas station that had been built in the early days of automobiles. The stone fire station next door was from the same era. On the corner across the street, an old train station showed signs of renovation. A neat stack of roofing sat in the front. Cans of paint were piled by the ticket window. Scraps of lumber were scattered around.

"That's the old depot," Faith said. "The train hasn't come through here in more than twenty years, and some people thought we ought to tear it down. Build a big new grocery store."

Sean winced. "That would be a shame."

"It's going to be a Southern-folklore museum. They're having the grand opening later this summer."

A block later she led him up a rickety flight of wooden stairs to a cobblestone path that ran parallel to Ridge Lane, overlooking the rooftops of the little shops on the street below. The path wandered through the woods, but here and there you could see through the newly budding trees to the bustling street below. And every two blocks or so another flight of stairs led down to Ridge Lane.

The path was filled with the sights, sounds and smells of the woods. Birds and squirrels chattered at them. Other smaller critters buzzed near Sean's ears from time to time. At one point he heard the babble of water. The flowers of wisteria vines, hanging like sweet-smelling bunches of pale purple grapes, overpowered him with their fragrance. Once they broke out of the woods long enough to take the narrow footbridge that crossed above Manor Parkway. Then they were back in the woods.

"It feels as if we're the only people for miles," he said. "Is this your own private path?"

She laughed softly, and he looked up quickly to catch her fleeting smile. "Hardly. The path gets overrun sometimes in the summer when the town is full of tourists. Fortunately most folks still prefer the bridle paths or the cart paths."

She gestured away from Ridge Lane, and he could see a pristine putting green in the distance. Ringed in mountain laurel and dotted with wildflowers, the golf course ranged toward the mountains in the distance.

"The view must be magnificent," he said.

"They say people who've never hit a golf ball

leave here hooked on the game, seduced by the view.''

They strayed off the path then, and Sean wondered where she was leading him. But it didn't seem to matter, and he wasn't sure whether to blame that on the seduction of the scenery or his guide. She was surefooted even off the cobblestone path, stepping over roots and fallen trunks that marked the handiwork of beavers. She led him around a trickle of water over moss-slick stones into a shaded clearing. The remains of a small stone building stood in its center. Inside the ruined doorway was a bench and an altar.

''What was it?'' he asked.

She walked through the nonexistent doorway and sat on the stone bench. He followed. It was dark, damp and cool here, and he felt the warmth of her bare arm through his sleeve. The hairs on his arm stood at attention; he had to make an effort not to shiver.

''A chapel,'' she said, almost whispering. Her hands were clasped in her lap and her eyes were trained straight ahead. ''They say one of the Tarkington girls had it built when her lover went off to fight for the Confederacy so she could pray for him every day.''

He followed her steady gaze and saw that he was, indeed, looking at the remains of an altar. Most of the cross remained.

''And did he come home?''

She smiled. ''He was a Matherly.''

He knew, from the other stories she'd told him on

their walk, that the Matherlys now owned Heritage Manor. "Good. I like stories with happy endings."

She lowered her gaze and he wondered if she was thinking of her own less-than-happy ending.

"Me, too," she said, standing.

He followed her out of the clearing and on to the final stairway back to Ridge Lane. They wandered through neighborhoods this time, passing a day-care center tucked between Dogwood Avenue and Birch Street. He saw the two-story brick high school and the stadium where the Hope Springs Wildcats had been the 1989 state champions, according to a fading sign.

And he met people. The librarian looked him over critically, smiling with vacant politeness. Walker Shearin, editor of the local paper, a silver-haired man a few years older than Sean, studied him as carefully as the librarian had, but with more warmth in his smile. A pretty young nurse grew uncomfortable as soon as she learned he was an attorney; then she scurried away.

"I don't seem to be inspiring much trust in the people of Hope Springs," he said wryly.

Faith shook her head, setting a few strands of soft hair at her forehead adrift on the spring breeze. "That's just the way Libby Jeffries is. It's not you, it's lawyers."

Her voice filled with sympathy. Sean wanted to smooth her whisper-soft hair. He wanted to touch the hollow at her temple, trace it to the hollow beneath her cheekbones. He shoved his hands in his pockets.

"Oh?" he said, although he didn't really care. The

only thing he cared about at that moment was Faith, tender-spirited Faith.

The woman who was pregnant with his best friend's baby. *Get a grip, Davenport. This is reality, not fantasy.*

"She was a witness once in an attempted murder trial. She was just a kid. I don't think she's ever gotten over it."

She hugged her bare arms to her chest, then looked up and gave him a wan smile. "Not every story has a happy ending."

He wanted to say more, to assure her that hers would. But he couldn't of course. He wondered, not for the first time, what the heck he was doing here.

The last person they ran into on their trek back to his car was a courtly looking gentleman wearing a wide-brimmed straw hat and bright pink suspenders, and leading a pair of Corgis on leashes the color of his suspenders. Faith and the old man embraced warmly before she introduced them. Melvin Guthry, it turned out, was not only the town's sole attorney, but Faith's godfather, as well.

Sean felt uneasy.

"Enjoying your visit to Hope Springs, I trust," the old man said, tugging sharply on the pink leashes and bringing the two tiny dogs to heel. They sat patiently, wagging their tails, their pink tongues lolling, their eyes raised expectantly to their walking companion.

"Yes," Sean said. "It's a lovely town."

He knew he couldn't look a longtime attorney squarely in the eyes without revealing too much. He also knew he couldn't evade a longtime attorney's gaze without also revealing too much. He was sunk.

He tried believing in his heart he hadn't been having entirely inappropriate feelings for Faith O'Dare all day. Everyone knew you could fool the lie detector if you really believed the lie.

He doubted he'd passed.

"Will we be seeing a lot of you, Mr. Davenport?"

The old man must have been a master at cross-examination. He asked the question so casually, as if Sean's reply hardly mattered in the grand scheme of all the evidence to be presented. Sean knew better. And he didn't know which answer would prove to be more incriminating.

He thought about pleading the Fifth, but he knew the message that conveyed. Guilt.

Sean wasn't even sure what the charges were at this point, but he knew he was guilty.

"That's...up to Faith," he said, thinking that might be clever enough to get him off the hook with her godfather.

Then Faith grunted. "Since when?"

Melvin chuckled. "Well, if you make it back to our fair town, I hope you'll feel free to stop in for some brandy and a cigar. We could talk state politics. No one here likes talking state politics with me."

"That's because you switch sides just for the sake of argument, Melvin," Faith chided, giving him a peck on the cheek.

"Nonsense," he said. "It's because I always win my argument. And no one can take a true challenge any longer." He jiggled the leashes, and the two Corgis jumped to their feet. "Can you take a true challenge, Mr. Davenport?"

Another trick question from the prosecution. "I like to think I can."

"Good. Good. Come by sometime. We'll find out for certain."

On the short drive back to her house with her tomato plants and her seed packets, Faith chatted about Melvin Guthry and her father. Both widowers, they'd been best friends for as long as Faith could remember. Patrick O'Dare was the optimist, Melvin Guthry the cynic. At least, those were the roles they played. It was only after her father died, Faith said, that she realized crusty old Melvin was as softhearted and idealistic as her father had been.

"He misses Pop terribly," she said, placing her tray of bedding plants on the sidewalk. Her voice was wistful.

"And so do you."

She nodded. "And so do I."

Once again he longed to touch her. When she looked up at him, he almost believed she wanted the same thing. Just a touch. A connection. Something to keep the ache at bay, even if only for the moment.

Could he take a true challenge? Not this one.

All the way home he told himself that keeping his distance was the best thing for Faith. But all the way home he couldn't ignore the mocking voice that said it was the best thing for the coward in him.

By the time he reached his sterile condo, with its expensive leather couch and trendy artwork and its French doors overlooking a tiny enclosed patio he hadn't bothered to dress up with a single plant, Sean was restless. He was irritable. He was discontented. He kept thinking of Melvin Guthry's words about challenge. He kept thinking of the loneliness in Faith's eyes. He kept thinking of her warm flesh, so close he could almost feel it as he had in the damp shade at the chapel in the woods.

And he kept thinking of the feminine way her dress molded so demurely to her swelling body.

It grew late, but he couldn't go to bed. He couldn't read the suspense novel whose story had been so compelling the day before, or listen to CDs. The longing in him was too intense. He thought he'd buried that longing years ago. And here it was, back again. Unearthed by Faith O'Dare and the life growing inside her.

He started getting ready for bed, although he knew he wouldn't be able to lie there in the dark. He turned back the sheets. He brushed his teeth. He set his clock. He sat on the edge of his bed, then decided to take out the suit he would wear the next day.

But when he opened his closet door, he knew the suit wasn't what he was after.

Hand trembling, he reached for the box on the back of the top shelf. His fingertips felt the film of dust on the box. He brought it down, anxiety a living force in his chest. He gripped the box in both hands, set it on the bed, mindless of the dust.

He lifted the lid.

The first thing he saw was a portion of the blue-and-white banner: It's a Boy! He'd bought the banner himself, in anticipation. Sean's heart pumped fast and hard, making it difficult to breathe, difficult to swallow. Next he saw the ultrasound photo. Even if he'd been wearing his reading glasses, the grainy image wouldn't look like much, he realized, but he had always read so much into it. His chin. Rachel's fine, expressive fingers.

Something broke loose in his chest. A sob. He laid the photo down.

Rachel had thrown it all away after the miscarriage. Sean had salvaged it from the trash, certain in his heart they would have another chance.

He'd been right, too. There had been three more chances. And three more miscarriages.

After each one it seemed that the more he needed to get close to Rachel, the more he tried to help her, the more she shut him out. She'd grown bitter and distant. After the fourth miscarriage, she'd left the hospital with her mother and never come home again.

Sean felt the dampness on his face and wiped at it with the back of his hand. He hadn't cried in years. Maybe not since the second miscarriage.

Then, at the bottom of the box, he saw the tissue and took out the final tiny bundle. He held it for a moment, unsure he could look at it, knowing he couldn't stop himself. He folded back the tissue, revealing the small baseball jersey he'd bought for the son who had never been born. He touched the letters in the team name on the front. It smelled a little musty now, and he thought of the waste.

Then he thought of Faith and the son she now carried. He thought of a little blond-haired baby wearing this jersey and knew, somehow, that would make him happy.

The image lightened his heart. And as he turned out the light and crawled between the sheets, the tiny jersey still visible in the glow from his alarm clock, Sean knew some of his wounds were healing.

But the healing, he realized, had little to do with the hot springs in the town of Hope Springs and everything to do with a miracle called Faith O'Dare.

CHAPTER SEVEN

FAITH WALKED around the worktable at Times Square Crafts feeling like a fraud of the worst kind. The only one who seemed to notice was Ghengis Khan, who had ambled through the open front door and bedded down atop the storage cabinet in the workroom. The lofty perch was the Siamese cat's favorite spot for keeping a disdainful eye on whatever class was going on at the moment.

At this moment Khan was leveling his reproachful look at Faith. *You fraud,* his blue eyes seemed to say. *Consorting with the enemy behind our backs.*

He lowered his eyes to slits and rested his chin on outstretched paws.

"You're such a lucky young woman," Norma Featherstone said as Faith helped her master a dropped stitch in knitting. "Not even a hint of morning sickness. Gracious sakes, but that's a blessing."

"She's got a few blessings coming to her," said Hezzie Stuart, and all the heads around the table nodded.

Faith knew her smile was unconvincing, but it hardly mattered since all eyes were trained on the balls of soft yarn and the sheets of instructions around the table. A mohair shawl, a beret-style cap and the duckling baby blanket were the choices she'd offered the class. Needles clicked slowly and mounds of yellow, mauve and red were being slowly converted to things useful and beautiful.

Well, Norma Featherstone's shawl might be less than art, Faith had to admit. But beauty was in the eye of the beholder, as Donna had reminded her last week when Norma had selected her red-and-green yarns. A Christmas gift for someone very special, Norma had said, and they'd all prayed they wouldn't make Norma's list come December.

Faith had also prayed that some topic of conversation would come along to take the place of her pregnancy, but so far that particular prayer hadn't been answered.

"Those sweet little dresses you always wear make wonderful maternity clothes," Hezzie said approvingly. "Very feminine."

Donna grinned as she came through with a box of supplies that had just been delivered by UPS. "I'm just glad she's finally starting to show. I was beginning to think she was going to go through the entire pregnancy weighing 105. Shoot, *she's* the one who's pregnant and here I am gaining all my weight back."

Faith laughed with them, although the extra weight was becoming disconcerting to her. She'd always been very petite, and it crossed her mind that she was grateful not to have seen Sean Davenport for two weeks. What would he think of her now?

Guilt gave her a sharp jab. There she was again, thinking about Sean Davenport. More and more, it seemed, she had to be vigilant about reminding herself who Sean was and what he represented. He was Walter's friend. Walter's partner. The mirror image of the man who had lied to her and turned his back on her.

Her reminders rarely worked, however, and she felt guilty every time she thought about him. What would these sweet uncomplicated women think of her if they knew about the crazy thoughts she'd been having about Sean Davenport? She kept thinking of his bare chest, streaked with grime and sweat from laboring on her behalf. She kept thinking of the tender understanding in his eyes every time he looked at her. She remembered his soft laugh and the way her skin had tingled with his nearness as they'd walked along the wooded path two weeks earlier.

Some of her thoughts were friendly, trusting thoughts, and that was scary enough. But other thoughts were almost...well, they were downright...

She shook her head. She couldn't even allow herself to give word to the feelings.

Thank goodness he'd gone away and hadn't come back.

"She won't get off scot-free," Donna was saying, and the words startled Faith back to attention. "She may have an easy pregnancy, but wait till there are diapers to change."

Faith adjusted the size-eight knitting needles in Abbie Lynne's hands and said, "Donna, I thought you were going to change all the diapers for me, you're such an expert."

"Not me," Donna said. "My mothering days are over. Don't get me wrong—I love babies. But I've served my time with diapers and formula. These days I'm a vixen.''

At last all the conversation turned to Donna's new image. Amid talk about Donna's new size-ten wardrobe and her flirty new hair color and the contact lenses that had replaced her bifocals, Faith was able to forget—almost—that she was feeling things she shouldn't for Sean Davenport.

As DONNA PUT the finishing touches on her romantic dinner for two, something kept bothering her. Something she couldn't put her finger on.

She had the wine, the candles, the lovey-dovey ballads on the CD player. She looked smashing in her new red bodysuit, even if it was a little snugger than it had been when she'd bought it a month ago. Back to salads for lunch this week.

But not tonight. Tonight was date night and she felt as giddy as she had all those years ago when Tom used to pick her up in his father's sedan and take her to the ice-cream parlor for a double-dipped cone.

Only tonight she wouldn't have to slap his hands away and fight so hard to hold on to her control.

Date night had become Donna's favorite night of the week these past few months. Now that she could be a wife again and not just a mother.

Still, something was bugging her, the way she felt those Sunday mornings when she rushed out without making sure she'd unplugged the iron. She had the nagging feeling she would see something she'd missed if she just stopped and looked around.

As soon as she finished uncorking the wine, she would take a few minutes to figure out what it was.

But before she could return the wine bottle to the cooler, the back door opened and Tom slipped his hands around her waist from behind. His lips were on the nape of her neck and his chest was solid against her back.

"Mmm," he murmured. "The woman of my dreams right here in my own kitchen."

Donna's heart began to race. She turned to him with a lazy smile. "Come here, lover, and I'll make you forget the mother of your children."

In the process she entirely forgot that some unsolved riddle had been nagging at her.

SEAN WAS SHOPPING for a new handbag for his mother, who tagged along at his side. Women's accessories were on level three, so there was no reason for him to take the escalator up to the fourth floor. The only thing on level four was baby furnishings.

"The lining is barely ripped," Lucy protested. "This purse will do me another five years. I can't see the extravagance of another— What are we doing up *here?*"

Sean looked around at baby clothes and stuffed toys. A good reply escaped him. "Ah...I'm not sure."

Lucy stared up at her son. "You've been seeing that woman, haven't you?"

That woman. The phrase rankled him. "Her name is Faith, Mom. Faith O'Dare."

She sighed. "Oh, heavenly days, Sean Patrick

Davenport. What are you thinking, getting involved with...with Walter Brickerson's..."

"She's not Brick's anything, Mom," he said quietly, walking toward the department-store displays of cribs and musical mobiles and tiny clothes. "I told you she didn't know anything about Beverly. She's not a bad woman."

"I'm sorry," Lucy said. "I didn't mean to imply she is. Of all people I know better than that."

Sean looked down at his mother's contrite, troubled face.

"It's just such a sticky situation, Sean. She needs to sever those ties. And you certainly don't need to get caught in the middle."

"I know."

He did know. But he hadn't been able to get Faith's secondhand cradle out of his mind. He hadn't been able to banish the image of a tiny little body wearing the baseball jersey that still lay on his bedside table. He'd even added another image, this one more dangerous than all the rest—Faith nursing a child. Her breasts would be small, perfect. And he would touch the plump cheek of the baby at her breast, then look into Faith's eyes, and they would share a moment of supreme joy.

The baby in his daydream had Sean's dark hair, Sean's stubborn chin. And the woman in his daydream carried the gleam of Sean's reflection in her impish gray eyes.

"I don't see how it can hurt to give her a helping hand," he said, even as his daydream reminded him precisely how this could hurt.

He'd had such dreams before. He didn't want to watch them die again. Couldn't bear it, in fact.

"This isn't even about her, is it?" Lucy asked. "It's about the baby. About *your* babies."

"Don't, Mom."

He wished it was that simple. That was part of it, maybe. But it had been about Faith long before the reality of her pregnancy had set in for him. In fact, if she'd been visibly pregnant when he'd first met her, he probably would have turned tail and run. True challenge, indeed.

But he hadn't run and it was too late now.

"You're going to buy her a crib?"

Lucy's astonished question made Sean realize he was examining the cribs, fingering their price tags and checking out their construction. He let a price tag drop and stepped back. They were in Richmond's best department store, surrounded by the best nursery items in town. But as he looked around, Sean remembered the stubborn look in Faith's eyes when she'd refused to accept the stuffed toy he'd taken her before. She wouldn't appreciate his generosity.

"Of course not," he said.

He looked at his mother and knew from her expression that his protest hadn't convinced her.

"I suppose you're thinking of this for your condo, then?"

"She wouldn't take it," he admitted.

"Good for her."

"Besides, none of it looks like Faith," he said, studying the fancy designer cribs.

"And what does Faith look like?" Lucy asked.

He thought of her bare feet on the dew-damp ground and her all-business hands brushing back vines and limbs in their trek through the woods. "Down-to-earth. Faith is real people."

Lucy sighed again, more deeply than the last. "Oh, dear."

"What?"

"You're not just trying to take care of her because Walter's abandoned her, are you? You're in love with your Faith O'Dare, and there's no point in denying it."

He took his mother by the elbow and pointed her toward the escalator. "I hate it when you're such a know-it-all."

"You hate it when I'm right."

She was right about that, too.

KELSY'S HANDS trembled.

She shoved the evidence back into the box from the drugstore and buried it at the bottom of the wastebasket in her bathroom.

"Not possible," she whispered, reaching behind her for the edge of the tub and lowering herself onto it before her knees gave out. "It's got to be a mistake."

She closed her eyes to keep the room from spinning around. For days she'd told herself her suspicions were silly, the result of all the attention Faith's pregnancy was getting. Kelsy had always been careful, determined she would never get caught. But little things kept adding up, and she'd driven thirty miles to Browerton for one of those home pregnancy tests.

Just to prove to herself how silly she was being.

She'd been back twice, hoping for different results.

The truth could not be denied any longer. And Kelsy knew she didn't have the courage to face it.

AT TIMES SQUARE CRAFTS the first of June was always the week for the annual sidewalk pottery sale. Kelsy was a superb potter, and the students in her ongoing class—more than a dozen people came every Thursday night from places in a hundred-mile radius—exhibited flair and distinction. Some tourists, most of whom were city dwellers from up and down the East Coast, planned their entire vacation around the event.

But the first morning of the sale Kelsy was late.

"I don't like this," Faith said, leaning one of the folding tables against her tummy so she could unfold the legs. She looked down the block in the direction Kelsy always came from. The only people she saw were a few early-bird tourists drifting in and out of Sweet Ida's Tea Room. "It's not like Kelsy to be late, especially on the first day of the pottery sale."

Donna looked glum, too, but Faith was getting the notion her partner's expression had nothing to do with concern over Kelsy's whereabouts. "Hmm?"

Faith grasped the tabletop and with a grunt set it upright on the sidewalk. Donna had dropped to the ground beside a box of pottery, but she hadn't yet opened the box. She simply stared at it.

"Donna, get a move on!" Faith glanced at her watch. "We've got two hours."

Donna looked up at Faith, her forehead wrinkling, her eyes growing blurry. Then, with no further warning and no further provocation, she burst into tears. Stunned, Faith ran to her friend and dropped to her knees beside her. She put an arm around Donna's shoulders and said, "Donna, what is it? I'm sorry. I didn't mean anything. Please don't cry."

Donna sniffled. "No. I won't. It's not... You didn't..." Then she began to sob in earnest. Faith patted Donna's frosted hair, feeling helpless.

Eben Monk, no doubt on his way to the barbershop, paused on the front sidewalk and stared at them. "Got problems?"

Faith shook her head. "We're fine, Eb."

Eb looked doubtful. He dug in the front pocket of his old seersucker slacks. "Got a kerchief here somewhere."

He finally found it and brought it over. It smelled of tobacco and fried bacon. Donna glanced up through her flooded eyes, spied the handkerchief Eb was waving under her nose and said, "Oh, God."

Then she jumped up and vanished into the house.

Faith shrugged. "Thanks, Eb."

Wondering how they would ever get the sale under way on time, Faith nevertheless knew what came first. Friends never took second place to business or money. She followed Donna into the house, prompting a disgruntled meow from Khan, who was never happy with disrupted routine or excessive traffic on his porch.

"Get over it," Faith said, giving him a rub behind the ears in passing.

She found Donna in the rest room pressing a damp paper towel to her forehead. Her complexion was faintly tinged with green.

"You're sick," Faith said.

Donna gave her a baleful look.

"You should go home."

"I should shoot myself."

"Now, Donna, you know we can manage."

"I may shoot *you*, too."

"Me? What did I do?"

"I think I caught it from you."

"What are you talking about?"

Donna's chin puckered and trembled again. "Oh, Faith, I'm so mad at myself I think I'm going to kill Tom."

"You know you're not making one lick of sense."

Donna took a long deep breath. She turned and splashed water on her face one more time. "I'm pregnant."

Faith felt a smile creeping up on her and realized from her friend's expression that rejoicing was not in order. To hide her smile, she put her arms around Donna and gave her a big hug. "Oh, Donna. I'm—"

"If you do anything but commiserate with me, I'll kill you, too." She shrugged out of Faith's embrace, squared her shoulders and started back outside. "Come on, we've got work to do."

"But if you don't feel well..."

"I'm not likely to feel well for the next twenty years," Donna snapped. "About the time I get this one off to college, I'd say. Just in time for arthritis and Alzheimer's. And if I hear one single congratulations, if one single person insists I ought to be grateful, I might just take a hostage.''

Faith was glad Donna had stormed ahead of her. She could smile without danger of being discovered. Of course, she understood her friend's dismay. For two years all Donna could talk about was getting the last of her three children out of the house. Finally having a chance to be a woman first, a mother second. Faith knew this was a shock. But she also had to believe that once the shock wore off, Donna would be thrilled.

She put a hand on her own belly, where she had recently felt the first flicker of movement—of life. What woman wouldn't be thrilled?

When they reached the front porch, they almost passed right by without realizing that Kelsy was sitting in the porch swing, tightly holding a grumbling Ghengis Khan on her lap. She was staring straight ahead and didn't seem to notice the cat's impatience or her partners as they came out of the shop.

What now? Faith thought, looking in dismay at the boxes and tables that needed to be set up in attractive displays within the hour.

"Kelsy?"

Kelsy looked up, loosening her hold on Khan, who rumbled a protest over the strange behavior his people were exhibiting. He jumped out of her lap and disappeared into the azalea bushes.

"Oh, Faith, what am I going to do? I'm not like you. I'm not strong and brave like you."

"What are you talking about?" Why wasn't anybody making sense this morning? She looked at Donna, who shrugged.

"I broke my engagement too soon."

"What do you mean?"

"I'm going to have a baby!"

Then Kelsy, too, was crying.

Faith wasn't sure her legs were going to hold up. She walked over and sat next to Kelsy. She held the younger woman's hand while she cried. Donna walked back onto the porch and stared at them.

"Omigosh," Donna said. "It's an epidemic."

"Well," Faith said, "at least you two have given the people of this town something to talk about besides me."

Neither of them seemed happy for her good fortune.

CHAPTER EIGHT

SEAN SAT in the courthouse cafeteria, pushing squash casserole around his plate and wishing his mother was wrong.

How could he have let himself fall in love with Faith O'Dare?

A hand clasped his shoulder. "I can't believe a partner of mine is eating courthouse cafeteria food."

Brick sat down beside him, a cup of coffee in his hand. Sean wasn't glad to see him. He didn't want to tell Brick that he'd been eating in the cafeteria because he wanted to avoid running into Brick at all their familiar lunchtime haunts.

Sean pushed his plate away. "I don't have much stomach for ten-dollar lunches, Brick."

Brick peered at Sean's nearly full plate. "It appears you don't have much stomach for the cafeteria food, either. What's wrong, Sean? You haven't been yourself lately."

Sean felt the throb of the headache that had become a nearly permanent fixture in his life in recent weeks. "It's a boy, Brick."

"What's a boy?" Brick waved and flashed a smile at one of the assistants from the district attorney's office. He looked back at Sean, still smiling and unconcerned. Then it sank in and his smile vanished. "Oh. That. A boy?"

Oh. That. Sean felt like shaking his partner until his teeth rattled. He would have given anything for a son; Brick himself had often said he wanted a son. How could he speak of it now as if it mattered no more than another hamster for Amanda? "Are you really going to pretend nothing has happened? Can you really do that?"

"She hasn't asked me for anything." Brick reached for another packet of artificial sweetener and stirred it into his coffee. "I'm not unreasonable, you know. If she wants anything, she knows where I am. But I'm not going to go looking for trouble. I doubt if she's very happy with me these days."

"You got that right."

"What's that supposed to mean? She hasn't been harassing you, has she? If I'd thought for one minute that she'd try to drag you into this, I never would have asked you to go up there." Brick looked and sounded like the injured party.

"Brick, you really are a horse's rear end. Do you know that?"

"What?"

Sean stood. "You're the father of this baby. Does that mean anything to you?"

Brick looked around. "Can you keep it down, Davenport?"

"I hope she sues the pants off you. I hope she takes you for money you haven't even earned yet."

He took satisfaction in the way Brick's carefully tended tan paled. He knew damn well Faith didn't want a penny from Walter Brickerson. But it wouldn't hurt a bit for Brick to stew over it awhile. Sean turned and walked away, anger still heating his blood.

After court adjourned—he lost his temper and the judge almost ruled him in contempt of court when Sean knew it wasn't the court he held in contempt at all—Sean got into his car and drove toward the outskirts of town. He threw his tie and his suit coat into the back seat. He rolled up his sleeves. He would drive through the countryside surrounding Richmond until his irritation subsided.

He shouldn't have been surprised seventy minutes later to find himself looking at the Hope Springs town-limits sign.

He parked in the municipal lot, a good five blocks from Faith's neat little house. Just because he was in Hope Springs didn't mean he had to see her. He could walk around town, duck into the bookstore, maybe take the cobblestone path and visit the chapel again.

Or maybe he'd just take a quick peek in her backyard. See how the garden was coming. See if it needed weeding.

It was all lame rationalization, he knew. The truth was, he couldn't stay away from Faith. He was falling in love with her, and there was no way to stop it from happening.

She was watering the garden when he got there. She wore a pair of baggy shorts that almost covered her knees and a T-shirt that might have been her father's. Her hair was pulled back in a haphazard ponytail. Her feet were bare and she was squishing her toes in the mud being formed by the water leaking from the nozzle of her hose. But it was all Sean could do to take his attention off her tummy. The baby was growing. That was a good sign, wasn't it?

"How does your garden grow?" he asked.

She jumped, startled. When she saw him, she turned the stream of water in his direction and caught him with the spray. It was his turn to jump.

"Better when I'm not contrary," she said, turning the nozzle to stop the flow of water. She dropped the hose.

He grinned and wiped the mist off his face. "And are you contrary?"

"Only when strange men sneak up on me."

"I'm not so strange."

"That's not what my neighbors think," she retorted. "They think any man who hangs around when a woman he doesn't even know is pregnant must be strange."

"I know you. Better all the time."

"But you have to admit, it is strange." She gestured toward the house. "Come on. I'll pour us some tea."

He followed her into the house, which was cool and dim despite the June heat that had warmed even the mountain regions that day. She poured tall glasses of tea and led him to the rockers on the front porch.

"Is this what everybody does this time of day?" he asked, thinking of all the people he'd seen in rockers and porch swings as he'd walked down Dogwood Avenue to her house on Timber Gap Lane.

"Of course. It's a Southern thing."

"Maybe. But it's not a Richmond thing."

"Then I'm glad I don't live in Richmond."

Sean mulled that over. Sometimes these days he wished he didn't, either. "But you've got no symphony. No art museums."

"No traffic," she continued. "No exhaust fumes. But we do have a community band that puts on a concert twice a year—Fourth of July and Christmas."

"And a folklore museum," he added.

"Soon. The grand opening's in a month."

"So what else do you need?"

She frowned. "You're switching sides. How am I supposed to trust a man who switches sides?"

Sean set his glass on the wicker table between them. "I've never been on Brick's side. Not in this."

"Haven't you?"

"No."

She didn't say anything. He kept waiting for her to say she believed him, that she understood, something. But she didn't.

"Brick is wrong," he said at last, unable to stand the silence any longer. "He's always been wrong about this. He takes good people and screws around with their lives."

"I don't want to talk about Walter."

"I just wanted you to know I don't excuse him. Or make excuses for him."

"But you're best friends."

He took some satisfaction in saying, "Not any-more."

"Then why are you here if you're not keeping an eye on me for him?"

"Is that what you think? Dammit, Faith. You can't think that."

"What am I supposed to think?"

Sean sighed, his emotions a tangle of impatience and understanding. "I care. About you, about the baby. That's all." He wanted to tell her the whole truth, but he couldn't. He hadn't talked about the miscarriages to anyone, and he couldn't start now with a pregnant woman. "You know, I always prom-ised Brick that if he had a son I'd be the godfather. I said I'd be there no matter what. I'd still like to live up to that promise."

Faith stood abruptly. "This isn't Walter's son. He's *my* son. *I'll* decide if he needs a godfather."

Sean saw the anger flash in her eyes before she turned and faced the street, arms crossed tightly be-neath her breasts. He stood, turned her toward him. He left his hands on her shoulders, hoping to feel her relent.

What he felt, instead, was a deep raw longing.

"Don't shut me out," he said, frightened by the hoarse anguish in his voice.

"I have to shut you out," she said, her own voice strangled by emotion. "Can't you see?"

"No, I can't. All I can see is..." He leafed through his Harvard vocabulary for new words, something she hadn't yet heard that might make a dent in her doubt. But he knew words were inadequate. Words would never get through the wall she'd built.

So he put one finger under her chin and raised her lips to his. He touched them gently, a mere breath of pressure. Her lips were soft and tasted of the spring air. Something tight and painful inside him burst free and soared.

He pulled back, looked into her eyes. They were dark and confused.

"Never do that again," she said, her voice low, the implied threat unconvincing.

Sean dropped his hand, backed away. He'd made another mistake. But he wasn't sorry. "I can't promise you that."

Then the confusion in her eyes dropped away, the anger returning.

"Whose idea is all this?"

"What?"

"Walter's?" She took a challenging step in his direction. He caught her fragrance again and felt once more that surge of need. "You come in and seduce me, cast some doubt on my character, and Walter's off the hook. Is that the game plan, Counselor?"

The emotion that had blossomed in his chest began to wither again. The hurt was sharp. "Maybe I'd better go."

"That's a darn good idea. You tell Walter his little scheme won't work."

"We'll talk about this later, Faith. When you're calm."

"No, we won't," she said. "You know, Sean, we

have a sheriff's department in Hope Springs, and I might just call it the next time you show up on my doorstep.''

He wanted to talk some sense into her, to make her see that this was nothing but a wild idea her mistrust had given birth to. But he'd seen her temper often enough to know that trying to talk to her now would only make things worse. He walked off the porch and into the lowering dusk. He looked back before he rounded the curve in Timber Gap Lane, but she was no longer on the porch. She hadn't yet turned on any lights in the house, either. He wondered what she was doing.

And he longed to do it with her, even if all he could offer was a pair of safe arms to hold her close in the dark while she muddled through a tangle of difficult emotions.

DONNA'S ATTENTION was riveted on her husband. What would he say? How would he react to the news that was going to turn their lives upside down?

Tom sat in his old recliner, phone to his ear, listening to their son try to wheedle more spending money this month. Tom's side of the conversation was warm and humorous; he loved his kids. He'd always been a terrific father; in fact, like Donna, sometimes he'd focused more on his kids than on his partner. It was something Donna had longed to change before they lost any more time. Tom's springy curls were mostly gray these days, and his spreading middle was hard to hide, even in the double-breasted suits he wore to the bank each morning.

Donna's husband was middle-aged and making no attempts to hide it or run from it.

He was a special man. Comfortable in his own skin. In love with Donna just as she was with him, whether she, too, was sliding into middle age or fighting it tooth and nail, as she had been these past few months. Tom was one of the good ones.

He replaced the phone in its cradle, chuckling. "Thank goodness they're grown and gone."

Donna's heart lurched. "What?"

"They wear me out," he said, directing his easy-going smile at her. "I wouldn't trade 'em for a million dollars, but I wouldn't give you a nickel for another one."

"Oh."

"Now, what was it you wanted to talk about?"

Donna froze. She had to tell him. There was no getting around it. Kelsy and Faith knew. Everybody in Doc Sarah's office knew. If she didn't tell him herself, it would only be a matter of time before somebody walked into the bank and congratulated him, and then the feathers would really hit the fan.

She spoke his name, but her voice cracked. Tom frowned. "What's wrong, babe?"

She couldn't seem to say the words. Every dream they'd had for this part of their lives was about to go down the tube. How could she tell him that?

"Donna, you're scaring me."

On weak legs she got up and walked into the kitchen, to the glass bowl on the counter where they tossed their change. She rooted through it until she found what she wanted. A nickel. She turned and discovered that Tom had followed her. He looked worried. She handed him the nickel.

He shook his head, confused. "What?"

"A nickel," she said. "For another one."

He stared at the nickel, then back at her. "What do you mean? Is one of the girls... We're not going to be grandparents, are we?"

"Worse than that," she said.

Understanding finally seemed to dawn. And Donna saw in his eyes precisely what she'd feared seeing. Disbelief, followed by dismay, then anger.

"Oh, no."

Donna sighed. "Oh, yes."

FAITH SAT CROSS-LEGGED on the floor of the nursery. Moonlight wavered through the open windows, filtered by the flutter of new leaves on the elms and sugar maples. The cradle, with its bright new finish, was a dark shape in the room, the only thing of substance.

Faith put her hands on her belly and closed her eyes. "No," she whispered, "this is the only thing that's real."

A voice in her heart wanted to believe that Sean's kiss had been real. The voice whispered softly, telling her the irrational words she'd hurled at him were lies told by her fears. Lies told to keep her alone, to shut her off from anyone who might hurt her.

Never give your fears power over you. That was what Pop used to say.

But what would he say tonight? What would he

say now that he understood how Walter had betrayed her?

That was Walter, whispered the voice in her heart. *This is Sean. Silly fool, Sean is the one who keeps coming around, who keeps doing things to make your life easier, who asks nothing in return.*

"No," Faith whispered, rocking back and forth, cradling the unborn life in her arms. "No, no, no."

Wasn't the voice in her heart the same one she'd listened to before when Walter came around? She couldn't put herself—or her baby—through that kind of betrayal again.

"I'll be strong," she promised. "I'll keep us both safe."

She had learned her lesson the first time. She didn't need a refresher course. No matter how gently the brush of Sean's lips on hers haunted her.

Silly fool.

KELSY ONLY HAD one person with whom to share her news, and she figured she might as well get it over with.

She drove up the mountain highway to Locklear, the tiny town where she'd grown up. She felt herself grow tighter, smaller with each familiar sight as Locklear came into view. The school, then the church, where she'd always felt too ashamed to hold her head up. The main street she'd drifted up and down like someone lost. Then the house. In those days the whitewashed siding had been peeling, a few of the windows cracked, the yard a brown weed patch.

Now, if anything, it was worse.

She stopped her car and got out, shivering. From her cozy little home in Hope Springs, she sometimes thought about this place and felt as if it had all happened to someone else. Miracles really had happened for her in that little town. In Hope Springs she felt respected and cared for and capable.

But when she came back to Locklear, she still felt like that little girl whose mother everyone had pitied and scorned.

She didn't knock. The front room looked much the way it had looked most of her childhood—a sagging couch, rump-sprung chairs, walls so dingy it would have required sheer luck to guess their color. The lamp in the corner was on, and the smell of frying pork chops came from the kitchen. Kelsy followed the smell.

Anna Beattie Moser looked up, her face bright until she realized it was only her daughter. The look of disappointment was familiar to Kelsy; she tried not to let it matter, as she had always tried when she was a child. Anna was still thin, still pale, her hair faded to the dull color of a very old and much-used copper penny.

"I thought you were Paul," she said in greeting, and turned the pork chops.

"He's back?"

Anna nodded. She was smiling.

Paul always came back, just as he always left again. That had been the way of it throughout Kelsy's childhood, first with her father, then with her stepfather, Paul Moser. And Anna was always either in the throes of trying to charm and please her man so that he wouldn't go elsewhere again or barely hanging on to her emotions by a thread until he came back through the door.

Whichever state she was in, her daughter always felt like an afterthought, a minor irritation whose presence stole time Anna would have preferred to spend on the man she had placed at the center of her universe.

"When are you going to stop letting him treat you this way?"

Anna pursed her lips. "You don't understand."

That much was true. All Kelsy understood was that men would abandon you if you let them. She'd never been willing to let them.

"I'm pregnant, Ma."

Anna took the pork chops out of the pan and turned off the burner. "Pregnant. I guess that means you'll finally tie the knot, then."

"I doubt it."

Anna looked indignant. "What are you talking about? Of course you'll get married. You don't have to let a man treat you that way, girl."

Kelsy wished she hadn't come.

HOPE SPRINGS at dusk had a magical quality. Children chased lightning bugs and cried out shrilly at whatever games kids played these days. Porch swings creaked and neighbors talked over picket fences and hedges of azaleas. People even called out greetings to Sean, as if they knew him or might like to. He knew better than that of course, but the idea had a nice ring to it.

It almost made it possible to forget Faith's accusations. But none of it was enough to wipe out the ache that had begun when he kissed her.

Maybe he *should* go home and never come back.

One of the townspeople he ran across in the growing darkness was Melvin Guthry, filling a collection of bird feeders gathered in the trees of a corner lot. Sean remembered the white-haired old man from his walk with Faith. A friend of her father's, she'd said. The town attorney. The house on the corner where he worked was a tall Victorian, the gingerbread trim painted a contrasting color that Sean couldn't quite distinguish in the fading light. A wooden post and sign perched on the corner: Melvin Guthry, Attorney at Law. Est. 1953.

"It's kind of late for working in the yard," he said, pausing.

Melvin bent over his bag of birdseed, captured another scoopful and poured it into the top of his feeder. "But the air is cooler. The older I get, the harder it is to take the heat."

"Taking the heat can be tough at any age," Sean said.

Melvin laughed and straightened, brushing seed from his fingers. "I take it you have been visiting Faith."

Kissing Faith, Sean corrected silently. "She threatened to call the law on me if I come back."

Another laugh. "Faith has her mother's temper. Roberta could light into you so swiftly you had no time to prepare for the lash. An hour later she was all smiles. Patrick—he was Faith's father—learned to walk away and come back later. It vanishes as quickly as it appears.''

Sean nodded. ''It might've been more prudent of me not to kiss her right after she accused me of keeping an eye on her for Brick.''

''Brick? Ah, Brickerson. Of course.'' Melvin nodded, the sage nod of a judge. ''Yes, I see your problem. Timing is everything.''

''It isn't true, you know. I only want to help. Brick doesn't even know I've been seeing her.'' Sean leaned over and picked up the heavy bag of birdseed as Melvin reached for it. ''But she doesn't trust me.''

Melvin snapped a rubber band around the top of the bag Sean held. ''Well, she probably feels the need to blame someone. You're convenient.''

''Brick should have his butt kicked. That's for sure.''

''A light sentence in my humble opinion. You know, he fooled the whole town, not just Faith.''

Sean followed Melvin back to the house, wondering if that gave Faith any consolation. He doubted it. She was hard on herself. He mounted the steep steps behind Melvin and stashed the bag of seed in the parson's bench Melvin opened beneath the bay window.

''If you're struggling with the aftermath of an ill-timed kiss,'' Melvin said, ''you may need a good stiff scotch. Straight up. What do you say?''

Sean smiled. ''I don't think a citation for driving under the influence would improve my situation.''

Melvin nodded. "Well, then, a cigar at least. You can listen to an old man meander on about his retirement. Surely that could get you in no further trouble."

Sean thought of all the meandering conversations he'd had with Walter Senior over the years. A night like that had its appeal at the moment. "A cigar and conversation sounds like the perfect way to turn the evening around, sir."

"Excellent. Follow me, young man. I'll show you what the law library of a small-town practitioner looks like." Melvin paused under the porch light and studied him. "You know, Walter never did have the time for a cigar with an old man."

FOR THE NEXT MONTH Times Square Crafts might just as well have sported a gigantic banner: Home of the Baby Boom.

Traffic picked up considerably in the small shop. The high-school senior who worked part-time for the *Courier* came by for a photograph for the front page, wrinkling her pimpled brow and asking, "Can't you do something to look a little more pregnant?"

Donna almost took after her with a piece of pottery Kelsy had started the day before.

Ida brought treats she'd concocted specifically with the mother-to-be in mind. "Plenty of milk, not much sugar. Come on, dolly, give it a try."

Clementine Weeks, the town tomboy who owned the shade-tree garage, started hanging out, asking questions and offering to help. But nobody could figure out how an oil change was going to further the cause of motherhood.

"Well, how about if I try my hand at a baby quilt?" Clem said, her big blue eyes eager.

But Donna, Kelsy and Faith had taken one look at Clem's grease-stained hands and expressed doubt that making baby quilts would turn out to be Clem's strong suit. Clem tried, anyway, but at the end of three weeks even she had to agree the result was a disaster.

"That doesn't look much like a teddy bear, does it?" she said, studying the gingham patches she'd appliquéd to muslin.

"Never mind," Faith said. "If we could all make teddy bears, who'd be left to adjust our brakes?"

Even tourists were prone to stop in, browse through the store, study the three proprietors closely and say, "Are you the three sisters who all got pregnant at the same time?"

Faith would glance at Donna's dark complexion and Kelsy's carrot-colored curls and say, "Yes, we are."

The unexpectedly expectant mothers at Times Square Crafts were the hit of the season in Hope Springs. Everyone fussed over them, catered to them and beamed over their expanding midsections. Everyone in Hope Springs was happy about what Tood Grunkemeier had dubbed the Times Square Triplets.

Everyone, that is, except Donna and Kelsy.

"The only thing worse than morning sickness is

morning sickness at forty-two,'' Donna moaned each day after her visit to the ladies' room.

"At least you have a husband,'' Kelsy grumbled. "Look at these ankles. Who's going to want a woman with ankles the size of a loblolly pine?''

"Oh, sure, I have a husband,'' Donna retorted. "He blames me for this. Me! He reminds me every day that we'll be sending this one to college on our Social Security checks. Yeah, a husband is a big help.''

But the furor over the mini baby boom helped take Faith's mind off the fact that Sean Davenport hadn't been back since the night she'd threatened to call the law on him if he returned.

Since the night he'd kissed her.

Most of the time Faith tried hard not to remember that kiss. Other times, the memory would almost fade and she would find herself frantically reaching for the feel of it, the soft emotion of it. She would cling desperately to the scent of him, the taste of him, the firm but gentle pressure of his lips.

She couldn't remember Walter's kisses at all. But Sean's kiss she could remember in enough detail to occupy her thoughts for hours.

She could also remember the wounded look in his eyes when she'd hurled her ugly accusations at him. Accusations she'd made because she desperately needed to do something to shove him to arm's length once again.

Silly fool.

CHAPTER NINE

FAITH KEPT a close eye on her feet as she descended the steps from the cobblestone path. She was grateful she could still see her feet and wondered how much longer that would last.

"You stay off that path, Faith O'Dare!"

The admonition came from across Ridge Lane, where Luisita Mendoza swept the sidewalk in front of the Tex-a-Tavern. "You'll trip over a root or fall down those stairs. That's no place for an expectant lady. You hear me?"

Faith waved and smiled. "I hear you."

Once upon a time the intrusion would have irritated her. She would have resented the implication that she couldn't think for herself. But pregnancy was mellowing her. Each day that passed brought her more serenity and more confidence in her body. She felt strong and happy. Even her heart seemed to have mended nicely.

Life stirred inside her on a regular basis, as it did at this moment. She paused, hand on the post-office door handle, and absorbed the pure joy of her baby's movements. He was a kicker, a fighter, an emotional little creature. Like his mother. She smiled. He responded to barking dogs and the wail of the fire engine. He liked country music better than classical, her touch better than Ida's.

Faith wondered for a moment if that was where her feisty temperament was going, siphoning off to become part of her son.

If so, she liked the idea immensely. She liked her new mellow nature and thought fondly of the day when she would be the voice of reason for this little scrapper inside her. Like her and Pop all over again.

How could she still be brokenhearted, how could she harbor any resentment for Walter, when such a wondrous gift had come from his deceit? She hadn't lost. He had.

More often than she liked to admit, however, she thought of Sean, and a feeling of loss did come over her. He hadn't returned. And she missed him. Not only for the things he'd done for her, but for his interest in the baby. For his smile and the way his eyes lit up when he looked at her.

Thank goodness she'd put her foot down when she had. Sometimes it almost felt as if she'd fallen in love with him. What a disaster that would have been, she thought as she opened her post-office box and retrieved the letters.

Bills, mostly. And a catalog filled with baby toys, which she began to thumb through eagerly.

She didn't notice the envelope from Brickerson, Cowell, Brickerson and Davenport until she was in the shadow of the church spire across the street from her house. She faltered, slowing to a halt. Little Patrick picked up on her alarm and gave a shove to get her attention. She spread her hand to calm him, but her own heartbeat didn't respond to the reassurance.

She waited until she reached the house to open the letter. Her fingers trembled slightly as she closed the front door behind her and dropped the rest of the mail onto the library table. She forced herself to open the envelope slowly, calmly.

"No reason to get into a tizzy," she said. "You don't even know what it is."

When she saw the signature, Faith realized she had expected the letter to be from Sean. But it wasn't, and she hardly had time to be disappointed before the first paragraph of the letter leaped off the page of smoke-colored linen stationery.

Before you fly off the handle, I hope you will agree that the baby's well-being is your first concern and take the time to read my entire offer.

She almost tore the letter in two right then, but she couldn't stand to prove him right. So she kept reading.

I am sure you are aware that my standing in the Richmond community would afford many advantages for the baby. And, as I am sure you must acknowledge, a boy needs his father.

She began to see red. She knew her reaction was also disturbing the baby, but she couldn't slow the surge of rage taking her over as she skimmed the rest

of Walter's letter. He was willing to pay all medical
expenses, plus a lump sum that was more than she
lived on in five years, to see her through recovery
from the birth.

And the only thing he asked in return was that he
be allowed to adopt the baby. That she relinquish all
ties to the baby. Faith's lungs emptied and she
couldn't seem to catch her breath.

The baby. How dare he refer so callously to *her*
baby. He wanted to *buy* her baby.

She gulped for air. Her hands began to tremble so
violently the offending letter shook itself free of her
fingers.

She should have killed him, after all. As soon as
she'd found out what a scoundrel he was, she should
have pushed him out the window of his fancy office
in Richmond. Rage became a ball of white heat in
the center of her chest, spreading through her. She
was too angry to move, too filled with hate to think
of anything but the fact that the man she'd once
loved believed she would sell her own flesh and
blood.

The idea rang in her head, pounded against her
temples.

Then, like a strike of lightning, came a second idea
that ripped a cry of impotent anger from her chest.

He knew her baby was a boy. And there was only
one place he could have gotten that information—
Sean Davenport. Faith covered her face, felt herself
doubly betrayed. She'd been right about Sean all
along. He was spying on her, reporting to Walter.

Faith fell into the black chasm of her rage.

She was on her knees in the living room, pounding the couch cushions with her fists, when a pair of hands grabbed her wrists and stilled them. She turned her tearstained face on the intruder. Ida. Faith realized her breathing was heavy. As heavy as her heart. Her arms went limp in Ida's grasp.

"Dolly, what on earth is wrong?"

Faith melted into her old friend's arms. "Oh, Ida. He wants my baby. Walter thinks he can *buy* my baby."

Ida sank beside her on the floor and Faith curled against her like a child. The fragrance of the tea room—chamomile and honey, cinnamon and lemon—clung to Ida's bright patchwork vest. Faith breathed in the familiar scents like a calming elixir.

"Now, dolly, we all know that man is a son of a you-know-what," Ida said in the softest sweetest voice Faith had ever heard her use. "And what he thinks isn't worth a dime."

Faith felt the slow rhythm of Ida's heartbeat and breathed in time with it. Her pulse began to slow. Ida was right. Walter Brickerson lived in his own sick fantasy world and she didn't have to go there with him. She was grounded in Hope Springs, surrounded and supported by friends. He couldn't touch her here.

Not even if he had Sean Davenport on his side, she told herself, feeling the tender new bruise around her heart.

But that bruise, too, would heal.

DONNA WAS SITTING in Tom's recliner when he came in from the bank, lugging a big cardboard box. She barely looked up, didn't bother to ask what was in the box. She hadn't started dinner and didn't even feel like apologizing for it.

What was she going to do? How could she turn back the clock and undo this thing that was going to consume the next twenty years of her life? The years that were supposed to have belonged to her and Tom.

She loved children. Her children and anybody else's. But dammit, she was forty-two. And she'd wanted something for herself besides raising kids her whole life.

Tom set the box on the floor beside her and leaned over to drop a kiss on her cheek.

Donna flinched. His shows of affection—and there had been plenty, for once he'd gotten over his initial shock he'd been like a gentle suitor again—only served to remind her she wasn't destined, after all, to be a hot babe ever again.

Tom sighed and sat facing her on the couch. "Why don't I whip up something for dinner, hon?"

She hated it when he was patient and understanding. Why wasn't he raging against this as she was? Why did he have to pretend everything was going to work out just fine? "You really think it's that simple? That you can just whip something up?"

She heard herself and knew she was being unreasonable but didn't know how to stop herself. She was so angry, so disappointed. And the only way she seemed able to show it was in the way she treated Tom.

"I could order a pizza."

His patient tone didn't change. That frazzled Donna's nerve endings, too.

"Whatever," she said, knowing that spicy food wouldn't agree with her and knowing already that she would do her best afterward to make sure Tom felt responsible for her discomfort. Why was she doing this? Why couldn't she simply accept things, the way Faith did?

Darn Faith O'Dare for setting such an impossible standard.

Tom called out for pizza, then came back and opened the big box he'd brought in. "I've got something for you."

He sounded hopeful. Donna made up her mind that, for the rest of this evening, she would be pleasant and reasonable and loving.

"Ivalene brought some stuff in this morning," he said.

Donna had a hard time imagining what the elderly postmistress might have that she would be interested in. Tom started pulling things out of the box. Baby clothes. A blanket. Tiny little shoes.

"She said her daughter didn't need these things anymore, that they weren't planning any more—"

Donna felt the tears of rage and disappointment welling up. "I wasn't planning any more, either."

"Donna, listen—"

But she didn't. She jumped up and ran into the bedroom, where she locked herself in with her tears.

TWO WEEKS LATER Faith still remembered every word in Walter's letter.

She remembered Sean Davenport's part in it, too, and her bruised heart still ached.

But Faith didn't tell Donna and Kelsy about the letter from Walter or the way Sean had betrayed her. For one thing she just wanted to forget about it, pretend it had never happened. For another both her partners were too caught up in their own worries. They didn't need to shoulder hers, as well.

"Jimmy's summer job didn't pan out," Donna said. "So he's coming home next week."

Donna's morose tone told Faith exactly how her partner felt about having her son back at the house. Her older daughter, Althea, was also back for the summer, acting, Donna said, as if she'd never run the washing machine or cooked a meal in her life.

"So I'm back to being everybody's mother," she said, sagging into the only comfortable chair in the work area at Times Square. "Even Tom's."

"Only if you accept the role." Marcia Moondancer, who ran Nature's Best Remedies, an herbal shop that was giving the pharmacy a run for its money, had stopped by with another package of her herbal tea. She'd brought some last week, promising it would ease Kelsy's swollen ankles. No one had the heart to tell Marcia—who had been Marcia Greenberg until she visited that ashram out West and came back with a new name and a new vocation—that Kelsy had taken one swallow of the tea and thrown the rest of it out with the trash.

Donna turned her mouth into a little prune, signaling Faith that she was on the verge of saying something she would regret.

"Marcia, did I show you the new tea cozies we got in last week?" Faith pointed Marcia toward the showroom in the front. "When the shipment came in, I said that I thought they'd look just perfect on that display shelf where you keep your teas. Didn't I, Donna?"

The wrinkles of Donna's prune deepened.

Marcia didn't buy any tea cozies, but at least a battle was averted.

They weren't so lucky later that day, when Donna and Kelsy got into it over which of them was having the hardest pregnancy.

"You don't know anything," Donna said, listlessly dusting the shelves in the front of the store. "You're a kid. Your body is up for this. Mine is worn-out."

Kelsy sat at the desk, her feet up on the needlepoint footstool Donna had made the month before. She was near tears. "Call me when your ankles swell up to the size of Tennessee."

"You're a wimp."

"And you're just hateful. You know that, Donna? Just plain hateful."

Faith worked on the computer, designing a flyer for their late-summer classes, wondering if any of them would still be speaking by then. She tried not to get in the middle when her two miserable partners bickered. She tried not to let them see how good she felt about her pregnancy, although it occurred to her that it might give them a united front. They could both turn on her. And she could ignore them.

She was grinning over the prospect when the bell

over the front door jingled. The bickering subsided when Ivalene Harkness marched in, making her daily rounds to deliver mail to the town's businesses. Wiry and fit, the fifty-year-old hefted a sack of mail over her shoulder and held a lone letter in the other.

"Got one here for Faith," Ivalene said, dropping the rest of their mail on the table by the door as she always did. "Certified. Needs your John Hancock."

Faith's fingers stilled over the keyboard. She thought of asking who the letter was from. Thought about refusing to sign for it. But she didn't want to call attention to the letter.

More attention, she amended as she reached for the letter and signed the little green card on the back of the envelope. Donna and Kelsy were already looking her way, more curious than Khan the cat had ever dreamed of being. Faith didn't open the letter. She caught sight of the name of the Richmond law firm on the envelope, and her stomach did a nervous flip-flop. Quickly she shoved it into the big pocket of her skirt. Donna and Kelsy were silent only long enough to see Ivalene out the door.

"What is it?" Donna asked as if she had every right in the world to know.

"You can't just stick it in your pocket like that and pretend it's nothing," Kelsy said. "It could be an inheritance. Can you imagine what we could do to this place with an inheritance?"

"If it's an inheritance, she's going to put it away for her boy's college," Donna said. "That way his lazy butt won't end up back home summers mooching off his poor hardworking mom."

Faith ignored them, tried to get her mind back on the flyer she was creating. But her partners wouldn't be sidetracked. Donna sidled closer, and even Kelsy took her feet off the footstool long enough to march over to Faith.

"So what is it?" Kelsy demanded.

They weren't going to give up.

"Look, it's just something from Walter. Whatever he's got to say, I don't need to hear it. I'll just..."

She took the envelope out and started to tear the envelope in two, but Donna snatched it out of her hands. "Don't you dare! Girl, there might be a check in that envelope."

Faith didn't tell her she would tear up a check just as quickly. "I don't care what's in it."

"Open it, Donna."

Donna opened it and passed the letter to Faith. The two women peered over Faith's shoulders as she read.

Furthermore, and pursuant to this matter, I will therefore institute sole-custody proceedings in the matter of the unborn child should you refuse to engage in reasonable negotiations concerning the well-being of said unborn child.

Faith told herself she couldn't get as angry as she had the first time. It wasn't good for her. It wasn't good for her baby. But she couldn't beat back the cold hard fear growing in her chest.

"What the heck does that mean?" Kelsy said.

"It means that arrogant SOB wants to take Faith's baby away," Donna said.

"What!" Kelsy grabbed the letter from Faith's hands.

Anger, Faith realized, wasn't an option for once. What she felt at the moment was numbing fear. Walter was threatening to take her to court over custody of her baby. A baby he had done nothing to acknowledge in almost five months.

Kelsy continued to rant as she reread the offending letter. "'A more promising future, given the many advantages the Brickerson name and fortune can afford him'! How can he say that?"

It was true, Faith knew, that Walter had more money. More prestige. But she also knew she had grown up without all those things. And she had turned out fine. Better than Walter in her humble opinion.

"Oh, Faith, you've got to see Melvin. He'll tell you what to do."

Faith thought of Melvin, with his gentle spirit and tender heart. And he loved her like a second father. Yes, he would help her any way he could. But he would be powerless against the force of Brickerson, Cowell, Brickerson and Davenport. The top firm in Richmond, Melvin himself had told her many times.

She thought, too, of the stories Walter delighted in telling—the dinner parties and golf outings with all the judges and legal powerbrokers in Richmond. He knew them all, intimately.

Fear became stronger than Faith.

But she knew she couldn't let her fear paralyze

her. Because it wasn't her own happiness that was at stake; it was her baby's. The thought of him being raised by a man like Walter, learning to think and behave the way Walter did, was like a knife through her heart.

She would stop Walter single-handedly if she had to.

GRIM DETERMINATION accompanied Faith all the way to Richmond, all the way up the elevator in the elegant building Walter's firm occupied, all the way past his cucumber-cool administrative assistant.

It saw her through the door to Walter's office, then abandoned her.

She saw Sean first and her resolve almost melted. She was so darned glad to see him that for a moment she forgot everything but the sight of him. He was sitting back on the couch, a picture of professional ease. His suit coat was draped over the back of the couch, his necktie loose, a pair of unfamiliar glasses perched on his nose. He'd finally remembered to get a haircut apparently, because his hair no longer fell over his forehead. He looked trim, tidy and self-contained as he peered over the top of his glasses. Faith had grown so accustomed to seeing him in jeans and a T-shirt that seeing him dressed this way gave her a start of anxiety. But at least it reminded her of why she was here and why Sean was not her ally.

He's just like Walter, she reminded herself. *You can't forget that.*

He stood when he saw her. A moment of welcome danced in his eyes before he caught himself.

"Faith."

That was Walter. He sounded displeased, but only in a minor way. Her presence was no more than an irritation, she supposed. Some of her fear gave way to anger, pumping through her veins like a triple dose of mainlined caffeine. Faith welcomed it. Fear she couldn't handle, but anger she wore like a favorite winter coat. She would make sure Walter Brickerson knew he had underestimated Faith O'Dare. She would let him have it, and with great pleasure.

"If you ever threaten me or my baby again, I'll have you disbarred!" She had no idea if she could do any such thing, but it sounded good, so she let the words fly.

"Threatened! Brick, have you—"

"Disbarred! You don't have a leg to stand on. I have every right—"

"You have no rights to my son." Faith took his letter out of her pocket and tore it into tiny pieces, tossing them onto his desk. "But I have rights against harassment. Don't call, don't write and don't you dare show your face in Hope Springs."

"Harassment? Brick, what the hell is she talking about?"

"She's out of control," Walter said. "Can't you see that? Why, a woman like that has no business raising—"

Faith shook her fist in his face. "Don't even say it!"

She felt hands on her shoulders and knew they

belonged to Sean. She shook them off. "And you're no better than he is."

"What happened, Faith?" His voice soothed her, the way it always did. "Tell me what's going on. What was in the letter?"

"As if you don't know." She made her voice as scathing as she could.

"See what I mean?" Walter said. "She's delusional."

"Shut up, Brick. Faith, how did he threaten you?"

"He said he's going to..." She couldn't get the words out. She took a deep breath. "Sue me for custody."

"What?"

At the unmistakable outrage in Sean's voice, Faith felt the starch go out of her legs. She sank into a chair.

"Now, Sean, don't go off half-cocked. That's only part of the story."

"And what's the other part, Brick? Maybe you'd like to have her locked up somewhere just for good measure."

"Given her behavior today—"

"Oh, for... Just shut up, Brick, before you really tick me off."

"He offered me money," Faith said. "Offered to *buy* my son. And when that didn't work, he threatened me."

"You offered her *money* for her baby?"

"For medical expenses, for heaven's sake," Walter said. "You seem to have forgotten, Sean, that this baby is mine, too."

"No, it's not!" Faith jumped to her feet. "You gave up any right to this baby when you lied to me about who you are. You gave up any right to this baby when you didn't even acknowledge its existence for months. You don't exist in this baby's life. And I'll do whatever I have to do to keep it that way."

"You don't have that much power, Faith O'Dare," Walter snarled. "What do you think you'll do—get that old man in that one-horse town of yours to go against me in court?"

Faith knew he was right, but she didn't intend to allow him to see that for a single moment.

"Don't push me, Walter. Don't mess with my baby. You'll find out how much power I have."

Then she turned and left, storming out as she had stormed in, hoping she could make it out of the building before fear once again overtook her.

CHAPTER TEN

SEAN WATCHED FAITH stride out of the office, knowing he'd never been so glad to see anyone in his life.

For weeks now barely a waking hour passed that he didn't think of Faith. Her soft hair she couldn't quite figure out how to control, which suited her perfectly as far as he was concerned. The way her gray eyes grew stormy with anger. The clothes she wore that always looked as if they'd been bought for someone slightly larger, even after her pregnancy had begun to show.

He couldn't get her out of his mind, and he didn't intend to let her get away without talking to her again, without trying to smooth things over between them.

But first he had to deal with Brick.

"I'm glad I had a witness to that," Brick said, wiping his hands as if to dust off Faith's unpleasant presence in his life.

"So am I," Sean said.

"You can see she isn't stable enough to care for a child."

Sean's fingers itched, made a fist against his will. He tried to imagine the shock on Brick's face if his partner punched him right now, right here.

"Does Senior know about this?"

Brick looked almost uncomfortable. "He knows enough."

Which meant Senior knew Brick's version of the story.

"And how about Beverly? How much does she know?"

Brick squirmed. "I told her I had a line on a baby boy. You know she'd be willing to adopt."

"But you haven't told her it's your baby boy, have you, Brick?"

"Look, what's the point in stirring up that kind of hornets' nest?"

"You really think you can manipulate this thing any way you please, don't you?"

"Come on, Sean. Faith'll cave in. She knows she can't fight me. And I'll see to it she's compensated. You know that. I'm a fair man."

At the wounded look on his partner's face, Sean lost it. Almost as if it had a will of its own, his fist tightened and took its best shot at breaking Walter Brickerson Junior's patrician nose.

The effort seemed to have been successful, so Sean walked out and went in search of Faith.

FROM THE FRONT STEPS of the brownstone he saw her on a bench in the park across the street. Her shoulders shook as if she was cold, but it was almost July and he knew better.

She was crying.

He darted through traffic, becoming aware of the

ache in his knuckles and hoping Walter was experiencing a damn sight more than an ache.

He could hear her sobs as he approached, racking painful sobs. Emotion welled up in his own chest, and he fought it back. He knelt in front of her, feeling helpless. He didn't have answers, couldn't make promises. He didn't even have a tissue.

"Faith," he said softly, "don't worry. Please don't worry."

"Go away."

"He's not going to take your baby away."

"And who's going to stop him?"

"I will."

She glared at him through eyes the color of the Atlantic on a dreary winter day. "Likely story. You're the one who told him it's a boy."

"Faith, it wasn't like that. I just—"

"What else did you tell him?"

He got up off his knees and sat beside her. He desperately wanted to take her hands in his, to pull her head to his shoulder and touch her hair. He wanted to make it better, dammit. But his hands were tied.

"I know you don't believe me, but I am not on Walter's side."

Something seemed to catch her eye. "What's that?"

He looked where she was pointing, at the specks on the starched right cuff of his shirt. "Oh. I expect that's Brick's."

"It looks like—" she swallowed hard "—blood."

"Don't worry. I didn't kill him. I only broke his nose."

"You broke his nose?" Her voice quivered.

He rubbed his knuckles. "I hope to hell I broke something."

"You *hit* him?"

"Well, it didn't look as if you were going to do it."

She stared at him for a moment, looking stunned. Then she broke into delighted laughter, brushing tears away as she flashed that impish little-girl smile he'd hoped for all these months.

"If I'd known that's what it would take, I'd have punched him a long time ago."

She sniffed. "What?"

"To get you to smile. I've tried everything. I just didn't know it was going to take violence."

She laughed again. "I have to admit I've thought of doing it myself plenty of times."

"Good. Then that's taken care of and we can forget about Walter Brickerson."

Her expression grew sober. "I can't afford to forget. He's a powerful man. He...he could do it, couldn't he?"

"He's counting on you to cave in. He won't make this public. His father won't stand for it, and he isn't willing to risk his wife's wrath."

"She doesn't know?"

"He's got pulling a fast one on women down to a science," Sean said. "He's desperate for a son. Beverly's had four daughters and she says that's all the babies she's planning to have."

"You mean he would take my baby and not even tell her the truth?"

He nodded. She shuddered.

"How could I have been so blind about him?" she said, another tear trickling from the corner of her eye.

"All of us have been blind," Sean said. "But he's not going to lay a finger on your baby."

She looked at him, a longing for reassurance in her eyes. He took her hands then and leaned forward to place a light kiss on her forehead. His lips lingered and he felt her relax against him. He put his arms around her and felt her rigid body give way to his embrace. Then he heard himself say something he knew in his heart he had no business saying.

"Nothing's going to happen to your baby, Faith O'Dare. I promise."

KELSY SPENT an hour after work in the little chapel in the woods. So by the time she arrived home, she was feeling some measure of peace. Maybe she could handle this unexpected bump in the road of her life. Maybe she did have what it took to make a commitment, to raise a kid who wouldn't grow up feeling she never quite measured up.

Maybe she even had it in her to call this baby's father and try to put together a life for the three of them.

Then she walked onto her porch and saw the truth sitting there—in the form of her mother.

Anna's face was bright. Her clothes and hair

looked perfect. She was trying. But Kelsy saw the strain in the lines of her face, the dullness in her eyes.

"How's my girl?"

Kelsy stifled a sigh and sat on the top step. "Fine." She didn't return the question. What was the point? Anna wouldn't have told the truth even if Kelsy was genuinely interested in listening. Which she wasn't. She knew it all without asking.

"Good. No complications?"

Only if you considered being unmarried a complication. "Everything's fine, Mother."

Anna smoothed her skirt over her thin thighs. "There's still time for a wedding."

"There isn't going to be a wedding."

"Now, Kelsy, of course there's going to be a wedding. You need a partner in this. Someone to stand by you, don't you know."

Kelsy couldn't even bear to look at her mother. "The way your husbands always stand by you?"

"That's really not fair."

"Why do you let them do it? Walk out, treat you like dirt, come back any time they damn well please."

"You don't understand, Kelsy."

"No, I don't. Why don't you explain it?"

A long silence followed. Kelsy finally looked at her mother and saw the pain and confusion in her eyes.

"They do love me, you know. They really do."

All Kelsy knew was that she didn't have it in her to go through the things her mother had gone through.

SEAN DAVENPORT'S PROMISE restored Faith's calm.

He'd said nothing was going to happen to her baby, and the determination in his eyes made her believe it. That was foolish, she knew. He wasn't her father, her big brother or her knight on a white horse. What could he do for her that she couldn't do for herself?

Except maybe punch Walter in the nose. She took a perverse pleasure in creating that moment in her mind, and in reciting it to Ida, Donna and Kelsy. Soon everyone in Hope Springs knew that one of the bigshot attorneys in Richmond had a broken nose, courtesy of the other one, in return for his abominable treatment of Faith. Some of them, in a sign of solidarity and support, jabbed the air with their fists whenever they passed Faith on the street.

"I hope you don't let that macho display go to your head," Chuck Hurd said one day as she stood at the counter with the can of varnish Donna needed to finish a project at Times Square. "All it means is he has a streak of violence in him. That's not exactly something to applaud, you know."

Faith didn't believe for a minute that Sean Davenport had a streak of violence in him. She simply believed that he, like her, had finally had enough of Walter Brickerson.

"I didn't applaud," she said, plopping her money on the counter and preparing to leave. "I laughed."

"You *laughed?*" Chuck sounded appalled. "Faith, you can't let a man like that into your life."

"He isn't moving into the spare bedroom, if that's what you're getting at, Chuck." Her words held a bite and she knew it. But Chuck had no right to pry, no right to give her advice.

Besides, on some level it did trouble her that Sean had tucked her into the front seat of her car, told her to drive carefully, then vanished from her life once again. The confrontation in Richmond had been two weeks ago, and she hadn't seen him since. No, Sean was hardly forcing himself on her.

"Okay, okay," Chuck said, shoving her varnish into a paper bag and holding up his hands in surrender. "Have it your way, Faith."

"Why, thank you, Chuck. I believe I will."

Then she walked out, chin high, wishing she was as clear on the matter of Sean Davenport as she liked to pretend.

When she reached Times Square Crafts, the front door opened with a bang just as she walked up the front steps. Khan raised his head and hissed as a bulky figure stalked through the door and down the steps, almost bulldozing Faith in the process.

Donna's husband, Tom, caught her by the shoulders just in time. "Great day, Faith, I'm sorry. You all right?"

"I'm fine, Tom. What's wrong with you?"

He glared in the direction of the door. "That woman—"

Before he could finish, Donna appeared at the door. Her face was, if anything, more angry and distraught than her husband's. "Hush up, Tom. You've got something to say, you say it to me."

Tom turned toward Donna and placed his hands on his hips. "I've got plenty to say to you, woman."

"Well, not now. I work for a living, you know. I don't happen to be at everyone's disposal twenty-four hours a day for washing and ironing and cooking."

"Oh, I'm well aware of that."

Before Tom finished, Donna had slammed the door.

Faith gave him a weak smile. He shook his head. "I don't know what's gotten into her. All I said was my sister's girl from Charleston might come for the rest of the summer, and she starts pitching a hissy fit."

Faith winced. "Somebody else to take care of, Tom?"

"Now, that's just it. My niece agreed to come up and see to the house while Donna's under the weather. I thought that would be a nice surprise for her." Genuine perplexity showed on his face.

"Oh."

"You'd have thought I offered the girl the deed to the house. I don't get it, Faith. Whatever I do, it's wrong."

Faith gave his hand a squeeze. "She'll calm down."

"Well, I damn sure hope so."

Then he lumbered off and Faith went into the shop. Donna was still fuming.

"He thinks I can't take care of my own house anymore. Did he tell you that?"

Faith hesitated, then decided she might as well speak up whether her partner liked it or not. "He thought you might appreciate the help. That's all, Donna.''

"Well, if I didn't have him acting like another baby himself, maybe I wouldn't need any extra help. You know, I'd be better off without him. I swear, we survived twenty years of diapers and Little League and school suspensions, but I don't know if we can survive twenty more.''

"Try it alone for a while," Kelsy said glumly. "That'll change your mind in a hurry. Right, Faith?''

Faith looked from one of her friends to the other, knowing neither was content with her lot and unsure how much of it had to do with the difficulty of finding emotional balance in the midst of pregnancy. She'd felt it herself. Why, look at her reaction to Sean for a prime example of how a pregnant woman could lose touch with reality. At times she almost trusted him. At times she almost wanted to cling to him, to feel his steady hand on her back, to hear his reassuring voice in her ear.

Little wonder, then, that Donna was ready to call it quits in her marriage and Kelsy struggled daily with whether or not to swallow her pride and get in touch with the father of her baby.

"We're all going to be fine," she said softly.

"Easy for you to say," Kelsy said. "You feel good. You're not having any problems with your pregnancy. You have a house and a nursery. And if worse comes to worst, you can always marry Chuck.''

"Now there's the final benediction," Faith said, putting her bag from the hardware store down beside

Donna's project. "I don't need Chuck Hurd. I have you two, I have Ida, I have Melvin, I have—"

The front door opened again, rattling against the wall. Faith turned to see Clem Weeks stuffing a greasy rag into her overalls, her eyes wide.

"What's wrong, Clem?"

"Guess who I just saw driving into town pulling one of those rented moving trailers behind him?"

Faith's heart lurched.

"That Sean Davenport fellow, that's who."

CHAPTER ELEVEN

BY THE TIME Faith spotted the orange trailer, she had attracted a parade of townspeople, plus a handful of tourists who didn't want to miss out on whatever was going on.

She'd started off in the direction Clem indicated with only Donna behind her. Kelsy had remained on the porch, complaining about her swollen ankles and admonishing her friends to hurry back. Ida heard Kelsy's shouted directions and came out of the tea room, trailed by two tourists still clutching their china cups. Realtor Bama Preston was about to show a young couple from New Jersey a little stone cottage with a nice view of the waterfall, and they fell in step, as well. Then came T.J. from the bakery, a loan officer from Hope Springs Bank and Trust and Reverend Haigler's wife, who had just walked out of the bookstore with a bag full of horror novels, which she did her best to hide. Even Khan weaved his way in and out of the entourage, tail held high.

Faith, however, was oblivious to her following. She had only one thing on her mind: tracking down Sean Davenport and finding out what he was up to.

She spotted the trailer a block off Ridge Lane and zeroed in on it. The back was already open, revealing tidy stacks of uniformly sized boxes, the kind you buy from the people who rent trailers, not the kind you collect from the grocery store and your next-door neighbor's attic. She peered into the trailer but didn't see Sean.

His voice at her back startled her.

"Nice of you to bring help," he said.

She whirled, her heart beginning a wild drumroll. The sensation was different from her usual physical reaction to anger, but she knew that was what this was. It had nothing to do with Sean's voice, his looks, his presence.

"What are you doing?"

He hefted a box from the trailer and nodded behind her. "Who are all these people?"

Faith looked over her shoulder and saw what looked like half the town, all of them waiting eagerly to see what would happen next. She felt her cheeks grow hot.

"This is a cross-examination, Counselor," she snapped. "Just answer the question. What are you doing?"

Sean smiled over her shoulder. "Anybody wants to, grab a box. All help is appreciated."

Exasperated when a handful of people actually did as he suggested, Faith scampered after him as he walked across a lawn toward a wide front porch.

"You're avoiding me, Sean. I want to know what you're doing."

He set a box on the front step and said, "Patience, Miss O'Dare. All will be revealed."

Then he dug into the box, pulled out a wooden

sign and hooked it onto the bottom of the one already hanging in front of the house. Faith read the sign and was certain her heart stopped.

Sean Davenport, Attorney at Law

Speechless, Faith glanced at the sign above it, then back at the house, where a few people were straggling in with boxes from Sean's trailer. She was standing in front of the house where Melvin Guthry had practiced law for the past forty years. The house she'd been in and out of almost daily since childhood. The house of the man she trusted most in this world, after Pop.

Faith gasped. "You can't do this!"

Sean was already moving back to the truck for another box. "Sure I can."

"But Melvin—"

"Can't wait to retire."

"Dolly, we do need some young blood down at the courthouse," said Ida, who passed with a box in her arms.

"Ida! Put that down!" Faith whirled in the yard, discovered that with all the help she'd paraded in, the truck was quickly emptying. "All of you, stop right this minute."

Martha Haigler put a hand on Faith's arm and smiled that serene smile all ministers' wives seemed to have been blessed with. "Now, Faith, it seems to be out of your hands."

Faith was in no mood to hear that divine intervention had anything to do with Sean's invasion of her hometown. She marched after Sean. "Why are you doing this?"

"You said yourself what a great place Hope Springs is." He smiled. He looked serene, too, as if he knew there wasn't a thing Faith could do to stop him and it tickled him pink. "It got me thinking. You know, about the traffic and the crime and everything."

"Where's Melvin? What have you done with Melvin?"

Sean chuckled. "Buried him in the backyard."

"I won't stand for this."

"You'll get used to it."

Bama Preston tucked a business card into the pocket of Sean's shirt. "If you're looking for a place of your own, Mr. Davenport, I do hope you'll give me a call."

Faith retrieved the card and tore it up. "He won't be staying that long."

"I'll be in touch, Ms. Preston," Sean said with that maddening smile of his.

The next thing Faith knew, Martha Haigler was inviting him to Sunday services, the loan officer was assuring him that their mortgage rates were extremely competitive, and even Ida was offering him a free three-berry muffin on his first visit to Sweet Ida's. Melvin himself, her own godfather, was pouring lemonade for the volunteers.

"Traitors," she muttered. "They're all traitors."

Donna slipped an arm through Faith's. "Come on. We'll secede from the town. See how long they can get by without a craft shop. Ha! There won't be a wreath or a ceramic angel in this entire town by the time we're finished with them."

Even her own partner was taking it lightly. "Donna, this is serious!"

"I know it is," Donna said, tugging her away from the crowd that was quickly growing festive. Faith wouldn't put it past Melvin to have doctored the lemonade. "Let's buy ice cream, put our feet up and figure out exactly how we're going to get back at them."

Faith suddenly felt the fight drain out of her. All she wanted was to sit down, close her eyes and pretend none of this was happening. "Can we do that?"

Donna shrugged. "Who knows? At least we'll have fun talking about it."

SEAN WAVED at the last of his new neighbors and paused on the porch long enough to soak up the feel of his new town.

It was midafternoon on a summer day and children were making their noisy way home from the municipal pool. Young mothers pushed carriages and paused to compare notes about baby formula and toddler antics. The delivery truck from Hurd's Hardware rumbled by, and a clergyman smiled and waved to everyone he passed. His white collar remained crisp, despite the July humidity, but his smile was wilting rapidly, Sean noted.

Watching this peaceful world stroll by gave Sean a warm feeling in his chest. He breathed deeply.

"Tired?" Melvin passed him a glass of the lemonade that had flowed freely all afternoon.

"Content, actually."

He'd been moving in that direction ever since he'd gone back to the office the day he'd broken Brick's nose and handed in his resignation to Walt Senior. Senior had been disgruntled and disappointed with his son when he heard the whole story. When Senior had made the offer to help any way he could, Sean knew he meant it.

He wished he believed their relationship could withstand the rift between himself and Brick, but he didn't. Blood really was thicker than water. But somehow, into that void, Melvin Guthry had wandered. And here Sean sat.

He and Melvin went back into the house, where Sean's boxes were stacked in the parlor on the right, the one with the bay window overlooking the rosebushes. Melvin had insisted he take it. Best view in the house, he'd said, and Sean might as well get used to it.

"You made a lot of friends today," Melvin said, leaning against the open French door as Sean opened a box and wondered where to begin.

"Did I? Or was I just a curiosity?"

Melvin's bright eyes crinkled at the corners when he smiled. "Oh, certainly that. But you'll find Hope Springs a very welcoming town."

Sean hoped that would turn out to be true. He didn't know much about small towns. But once he'd talked to Melvin about buying out his practice, he'd been consumed with pleasant images of living and working in Hope Springs. He'd already imagined finding a little house for his mother, because she refused to consider moving into the house where he would be practicing. Sean had said he would live upstairs, where the rooms were spacious, but Lucy Davenport was adamant that she would not intrude on her son's life.

So he would find her a nice little house and help her fix it up on weekends. He would help the people he'd seen walking the town's quiet streets with their wills and their trust funds and their contracts. He would grow not rich, but happy.

He would find out if the words on the town's welcome sign were true: You'll Need No Other Medicine but Hope.

He believed it already. There was only one little hitch in the perfect world he envisioned.

"But they're really Faith's friends," he said, taking his framed diplomas out of a box and stacking them on a polished desk. "If Faith resents my presence, how long will it be before everyone else shuts me out, too?"

"I think you underestimate the town. And Faith."

Sean studied the old man, who looked so dapper and old-fashioned in his seersucker suit and bowtie. "Do I?"

"Faith will come around when she realizes your intentions are good. And we do have an agreement, do we not?"

Melvin had agreed to Sean's generous offer with only one condition—that Sean keep an eye on Faith and make sure his old partner did nothing to hurt her. Sean was only too happy to comply.

"That we do," he said. "But we don't need an

agreement, you know. That's part of the reason I'm here in the first place.''

''That's what I'm counting on, young man. That's what I'm counting on.''

When he settled into his bedroom that night, Sean sat by the window and watched lights go out in houses up and down the block. Yes, if hope was good medicine, Sean already had a full dose.

But his hopes went farther than practicing law here and buying a new home for his mother. Sean had other aspirations, as well. He could see himself pushing a baby carriage and holding hands with the baby's mother. He could see himself learning how to coax that smile he'd fallen in love with out of the mother, then the baby. He could see himself working in the garden with her at his side. Holding her close at night.

Don't push your luck, Davenport. Draw up a few wills, handle a contract or two and let things evolve naturally.

And they would. This time things would surely fall into place with no problems, no crises, no tragedy.

BY THE END of Sean Davenport's first week in Hope Springs, Faith felt like a woman under surveillance. Everywhere she went she looked over her shoulder. She glanced around corners before she made turns. Sometimes she even crossed the street to avoid being seen.

She was standing in line with the deposit from Times Square when she saw him sitting across the bank lobby, chatting with the loan officer he'd met the day before. He was wearing jeans and a cotton shirt right in the middle of the workweek, as if he'd already made himself at home in Hope Springs. As if he already knew he wouldn't impress anybody here with his pin-striped suits.

Faith turned her back on him, resenting his presence, his ease, in *her* town. *Her* haven.

He said good morning to her on his way out, his low voice as relaxed as the rest of him. She felt a shiver begin somewhere deep inside and told herself it was anxiety over his presence.

She saw him at the grocer's the next day. He'd paused in the frozen-foods aisle, his cart at an angle that made it impossible for her to pass. A fine coincidence, she thought, her irritation growing.

She gave his cart a little jab with hers. He looked up, startled, then pleased.

"Well, hello," he said, tugging his cart out of the way.

"This is a small town and we have a small grocery store," she said. "You can't sprawl out all over the aisle."

"I'm learning."

He had two packs of frozen vegetables in his hand, but he seemed to have forgotten them. He was staring at her, and she was losing her patience. *Then keep moving,* she told herself. But she couldn't seem to budge.

"You'll hate it," she said, hoping she was right.

He leaned across his cart, smiling. "Did you know the house where I'm living is exactly one block away? One short block down Old Dominion and I'm home with my milk and bread. And they'll let me push the cart home if I want to."

He'd won over the whole blasted town. "They will."

He nodded. "Said they trust me."

"They trust you."

"Only on Melvin's say, I suppose."

The traitor.

"You haven't been putting out the good word on me, too, have you? I mean, so many people seem to know me already, and I just wondered if you had anything to do with it."

"You're not funny, Sean." She pushed past him, but his hand caught her arm.

"I wish you'd talk to me," he said softly.

"I wish you'd go back where you belong," she retorted.

But she didn't feel as sharp and certain as she forced herself to sound. She felt unsure of herself, her feelings a knotted web of emotions. Sometimes she felt threatened by Sean's presence, certain he was here to keep tabs on her for the man who wanted to take away her baby. Mostly she knew that wasn't so but still didn't feel comfortable having this particular man waltzing into her hometown and into the hearts of her friends.

Hadn't she been down that path before? Hadn't it turned out badly?

And didn't she want to be won over this time, too? At least part of the time she knew it was so and had to admit it to herself. Especially late at night, when she sat in the nursery and looked out over the treetops and thought about him sitting a few blocks away in a house that was as familiar as the one she'd grown up in. She imagined him shaving in that narrow upstairs bathroom with the clawfoot tub and the pedestal sink. It had a tiny oval window with etched glass, and as a child she'd always thought what a lovely place it was to hole up in and pretend no one could find her.

And now Sean was there, too big for the room, his shoulders getting in the way when he turned to retrieve a towel, too tall to shower in the raised tub.

No matter where she hid, images of Sean could always find her these days. And her only defense against her unruly thoughts was to mistrust him. So she clung to that, desperately but unconvincingly.

She saw him on her way to church, at the post office, even the night she reluctantly agreed to have dinner with Chuck Hurd at the Ole Virginny Diner. Chuck had wanted to take her to the restaurant at Towering Pines Bed and Breakfast, considered by many to be the best food and the toniest atmosphere in town. But Faith didn't want to elevate their get-together to that kind of status.

Besides, Towering Pines was right next door to Melvin's—or should she say Sean's—house.

So there she sat at the diner, listening uncomfortably and without much interest to Chuck's rundown on the bright future of the hardware store, when Sean walked through the front door.

Faith almost choked on her smothered cabbage.

"But this area is way too small for one of the big chains to be interested," Chuck was saying, oblivious to Sean's presence or Faith's distress. "So we're secure. Know what I mean?"

Faith tried not to stare, wished she could pretend she hadn't noticed Sean. But it was too late for that. He saw her, and he'd no doubt seen the way her gaze stalled and froze when he arrived. He smiled.

"Faith?"

And now Chuck was going to notice that she couldn't take her eyes off Sean. "What? I mean, that's good, Chuck."

"I don't think you see what I'm getting at, Faith."

"I do, Chuck. I do."

"What I'm saying, Faith, is that it's a good business for a family man."

That dragged Faith's attention back to her would-be suitor. "Oh, Chuck, don't start that again."

"You're just being stubborn, Faith."

"I am not stubborn. I just—"

"She can be stubborn, can't she?"

That was the voice of Sean Davenport, tableside, injecting himself right into their private conversation as if he owned the blasted town.

Chuck was apparently no happier with the development than Faith.

"Who asked you, Davenport?"

The challenge in Chuck's voice was unmistakable.

"Oh, don't let me intrude," Sean said, backing away with a good-natured smile. "I was just passing your table on my way to—" he looked around "—this table."

Then he sat at the empty table next to theirs.

Faith wadded up her napkin. "I'm finished."

"You must want me to punch your lights out," Chuck said, rising.

Sean's eyes twinkled. He winked at Faith. Chuck didn't miss it.

"Oh, I'm afraid I'm not a fighting man."

Chuck looked at Sean, then at Faith. "So what does that mean? Did you make that whole story up, Faith? About him breaking Walter's nose?"

"Oh, for... I'm leaving now. You two play schoolyard bullies if you like. I'm not interested."

Chuck caught up with her before she reached the corner. "I'm sorry, Faith. He pushes my buttons, that's all."

Mine, too, she wanted to say, but didn't. She was afraid the buttons Sean pushed in Chuck were entirely different from the buttons he pushed in her.

By the time the folklore festival rolled around two weeks later to celebrate the grand opening of the town's new Southern Folklore Museum, Faith's initial reaction had begun to subside, mostly due to conversations with Melvin and Ida.

"My dear girl, I can assure you the young man has no ties to his former firm or anyone in it," Melvin said after church. "Surely you know I wouldn't be a party to anything that held even the remotest possibility of hurting you."

"I know that. But—"

"You worry I've been taken in."

"It's happened before."

Melvin shook his head. "Not when you've shared a cigar with another fellow."

"But Walter—"

"My dear, Walter never took me up on my offer. Not for cigars or brandy. That should have told me right there he had something to hide."

"But Sean—"

"In the case of Sean Davenport, please allow me to set your mind at rest."

"You've offered him a cigar?"

"Oh, almost every night we share a smoke on the porch. I don't think he's extremely fond of cigars, but he is kind enough to indulge an old man."

Faith heard the appreciation in Melvin's voice, and she felt a moment of involuntary gratitude. Anyone who indulged Melvin deserved a few good marks in her book.

Then there was Ida, worldly-wise Ida. She and Faith were setting up a booth in the city park, where many of the folklore-festival activities would be taking place. They were draping folding tables in pink-and-white crepe paper under a pink-and-white-striped tent. The little round iron tables from Sweet Ida's would be brought over later, along with plenty of scones, muffins and iced drinks.

"Raspberry-mint tea will be the hit of the day," Ida predicted, talking around the straight pins she held in her mouth.

Faith couldn't get very concerned about raspberry mint versus licorice whip. She wondered if Sean would show up. And that, of course, was foolish to even ponder. Naturally he would. Since arriving in Hope Springs, hadn't he been more visible than the mayor a week before election day?

"He'll probably give the mayor a run for his

money next November," she grumbled around her own mouthful of straight pins.

"What's that, dolly?"

"I said Sean Davenport is as sleazy as a politician."

Ida laughed. "Careful, dear. You don't want me swallowing my pins."

"I wasn't being funny."

"Well, you couldn't have been serious."

"And why not?"

"Why, you might as well call Reverend Haigler sleazy."

Faith stood, all her pins jabbed into place, and stretched her back. "So he's won you over, too?"

Ida peered at her. "And I suppose you'd like me to believe he hasn't won you over?"

Faith glanced to her left, where a man and his wife were setting up their own display of hammered dulcimers. They didn't seem the least bit interested in the conversation between Faith and Ida.

"Wouldn't I be crazy to fall for a man like that twice?"

Ida's eyes grew wide. "Twice? Why, who was the first, dolly?"

"You know darn well I'm talking about Walter."

Ida waved a dismissive hand. "Oh, him. You shouldn't even talk about those two men in the same breath."

"You're so sure of that, are you?"

"I know people."

"Then why didn't you know Walter?"

Ida struggled to her feet and stepped back to study their handiwork. "Your side drags, dolly."

"Come on, Ida. I want an answer."

"Okay. I didn't know Walter because some people have told their lies so often they come to believe them. And that makes it easier for them to fool the rest of us. Walter was like that."

"And you're sure Sean isn't?"

"Positive. Besides, I talked to Sister Margaret last week."

Sister Margaret was Margie Fortier, who wore a turban and foretold the future from a mobile home on the highway. Faith had always wondered, if Sister Margaret could foresee the future, why she hadn't known that Abe Fortier was going to run away with their teenaged baby-sitter the minute she graduated from high school. Faith wasn't the only one in town who wondered that, either.

"Sister Margaret said not to worry, that you'll have a very tiny problem but Sean will stand by you."

"Oh, if Sister Margaret has faith in Sean, that's all the reassurance I need."

Ida walked around the table and began straightening the crepe paper. "You know who Sean reminds me of, dolly?"

"Who?"

"Your pop."

"You're too young to be getting senile, Ida."

"Oh, he doesn't look like Patrick of course. But he's got that gentle way about him. And he smiles right up to his eyes. I'm surprised you haven't noticed.''

Faith had noticed, and she noticed it again when he walked up later that day when the festival was in full swing. Faith was watching a basket weaver, wondering if she could learn the technique herself to teach at Times Square Crafts.

Then she felt someone behind her, someone whose presence felt different from everyone else's. Faith looked over her shoulder and right away thought of what Ida had said. Sean did have a gentle way about him. And he smiled with his eyes, even when his lips weren't participating.

"I found the most wonderful thing," he whispered. "I wanted to show you." He extended his hand. "Come with me?"

And Faith knew that, despite her doubts, she would do exactly that. Because Melvin trusted him; Ida trusted him. And in that place in her heart that refused to be warped by what Walter had done to her, she trusted him.

She took his hand.

He led her to a tiny booth where a woman from the mountains used scrap wood and straw and strips of fabric to make little dolls. The dolls, she said, had been hung over cribs in the old days to keep babies safe. The little dolls were primitive but sweet, and Faith ran her fingers over one of the tiny calico aprons.

"Oh, you can call it an old wives' tale," the woman said. "Unless you know something about herbs.''

Tied up in the bundle of apron, Faith learned, was a collection of herbs that people had relied on for generations to soothe a cough, ease digestion and keep fever down.

"Can I buy you one?" Sean said. "After all, I did promise I'd keep an eye out for your baby."

Faith let him buy the doll.

She liked the feel of him at her side so well that she let him stay there the rest of the day. He felt solid and strong and solicitous. He watched where she was placing her feet when she forgot and urged her to sit and rest before she even realized she was tiring. He sat beside her, mesmerized, as they listened to traditional storytellers recounting tales generations old that had never been captured on paper. He walked through the photo exhibit in the new museum, reading the captions.

"Mom's going to love this place," he said.

"Your mother is coming?"

He nodded. "I'm bringing her up next weekend. I want her to look at a couple of houses."

"Houses?"

"She doesn't want me buying her a place, but I usually manage to get my way."

"I'm not surprised."

"She's not as hardheaded as some. And she likes me better than some do, too."

"Oh, you're managing to win over plenty of people right here in Hope Springs."

"Am I?" He looked pleasantly surprised.

"Ida. I was thinking of Ida. And Melvin."

"Ah. But not you."

"I'm a hard case."

He seemed to believe it, but Faith feared it wasn't true. How long could you hold out against a man who was buying his mother a house, bringing her to live close to him? He couldn't have many wives stuck away in other cities if he dragged his mother with him wherever he went.

"You're close to your mother," she said later, when they had wandered away from the crowds to one of the dozens of waterfalls gushing and babbling and trickling through the woods.

"It was just the two of us when I was growing up," he said. "I guess you know how that is."

They paused on one of the old bridges at the foot of Silver Lady Fall. The spray reached them, cooling Faith's face. Most summer days they wouldn't be alone on the path, but today the festival was keeping people in town. They could have been a million miles from the rest of the world.

"What happened to your father?"

"My... I never knew my father. He left before I was born. They were never married."

Faith felt a chill and hugged herself against it. An abandoned woman, giving birth alone, raising a son alone. A son who grew up to be Sean Davenport, worrying about another abandoned woman, giving birth alone.

"Is that it? You pity me because of what your mother went through?"

He got that hard look she had seen only a couple of times, a look that said he'd heard something he didn't like. "I never pitied my mother. I admired her."

She nodded, but she wasn't sure. She turned back toward the waterfall, but its magic failed to capture her for the moment. "You can't make it up to her through me."

He turned her to face him and lifted her chin so she was looking into his eyes. "I know I can't make it up to you, period. This is just something I need to do for me."

"Why?"

He didn't answer. Instead, he lowered his mouth to hers, slowly, almost as if he was giving her a chance to back away, to protest, to stop it before it was too late. But Faith did none of those things. She let her eyes drift shut and held her breath as she waited for his lips to touch hers.

When they did, Faith could no longer fool herself that this was a friendly kiss, a consoling kiss or even a reassuring kiss.

For, as gentle as it was, it was also a kiss tinged with passion.

CHAPTER TWELVE

THEY WALKED BACK to town, Faith's heart pounding, her skin tingling. She felt things she wasn't sure a pregnant woman was supposed to feel, but she didn't want to have to figure out what her emotions should be at this moment.

"You see," Sean said as the first sounds of the festival—fiddlers and children and hawkers of fudge and lemonade—reached them on the edge of town, "this has nothing to do with pity. And it has nothing to do with Walter."

"I don't want to talk about Walter again. Ever."

He smiled. "That suits me."

"Would that be wrong? For the baby, I mean?" She asked because she thought he might know, having grown up without the man who helped give him life.

"I can't answer that for you," he said.

She pressed. Having his opinion, knowing his experiences, seemed vital right now. "But you know how you felt."

He paused beside a shallow gully that was sometimes a creek, sometimes not, depending on rain or drought. This summer it was bone-dry.

"Sometimes not knowing left me feeling empty.

Incomplete.'' He looked into her eyes, his expression intense. ''Not because my mother failed me in any way. It wasn't that at all. Just because, when you're a kid, there's so much you can't understand about the things grown-ups do. So you always think it's about you, that it was something you did or didn't do.''

Faith took a deep breath. ''So you thought not having a father was your failing.''

''Something like that.'' He took her hand in his and she drew reassurance from it. ''But that was just me. You'll know what's right when the time comes.''

She didn't tell him that his answer would no doubt sway her when that time came. Because someday her son would be a man and she could do worse than to have him turn out like this man, she suddenly realized.

But could she do that alone?

Ah, girl, you can do whatever you make up your mind to. But you can't do it alone. We all need a little help along the way.

How many times had she heard Pop say that? She wondered for the first time in her life if he'd ever been afraid of raising a daughter on his own. If so, she'd never seen it.

Faith had arranged to meet Kelsy, Donna and her family on the grounds at the Heritage Manor for the grand finale, a concert at dusk. So she and Sean walked toward the manor. It would have seemed so natural to hold hands, she thought, but she looked around and knew she'd just be asking for trouble. Half the town would run to her with advice, and the other half would run to Chuck with the news. And all of them would spend more time speculating and giving commentary on Faith's love life than on whatever made the front page of next week's *Courier*.

So she walked beside him and felt the aftershock of his kiss and wondered what it all meant.

A blanket of lush grass curved and rolled in front of Heritage Manor. The imposing brick hotel had been built long before the Civil War, a four-story edifice with turret windows and gables peeking out from the oddest spots along the red-tile roof. Wings had been added sometime early in the century, and the sweeping drive up the hill from the highway had been widened to accommodate luxury cars, instead of horse-drawn carriages. Today, the lawn—which had been spared the effects of the drought that was causing grass to curl up and turn brown all over town—was dotted with quilts and lawn chairs and the brightly striped umbrellas shading vendors of hot dogs and ice cream. Faith smelled popcorn and sunscreen and the sizzle of smoky bratwurst. The squeals of children clashed with the sounds of the musicians tuning up for the concert.

Faith spotted Donna amid the throng of people who had brought quilts and lounge chairs for the final entertainment of the day. Donna's pregnancy was already more pronounced than Faith's, as was Kelsy's. Faith could also tell even from a distance that a squabble had already begun. But before she could veer away, Donna waved her over.

"Explain to this big ox why he was supposed to bring folding chairs today," Donna said. "Tom, you know pregnant women can't sit on the ground. Not without a forklift to get them up.''

"I'll give you a hand,'' Tom said. Impatience gave an edge to his usually gentle voice. "What's the big deal?''

"The big deal is I weigh a ton. You'll put your back out, and then who'll have to listen to you complain?''

"Oh, and I guess I'm supposed to feel sorry for you if you have to be the one listening, instead of the one complaining for a change?''

Donna threw up her hands and looked at Sean. "Do you do divorces? You know, those really ugly ones where both parties are out to cut the other's throat?''

"Now, Donna,'' Faith said, putting a hand on her friend's arm.

"Actually I recommend mediation before you get to the throat-cutting stage,'' Sean said, and Faith was grateful for the light tone he used in an attempt to deflect the hard feelings, which were escalating into more than a squabble at the end of a long hot day. "Tom, why don't you and I walk back to Melvin's and get a couple of folding chairs and I'll explain about mediation.''

"Oh, no, you don't,'' Donna said. "He goes with you and he'll know all about how to get cut-rate child support.'' She turned to Tom, shaking a finger at him. "If you leave me, you'll never have beer money again, do you hear me?''

"If *I* leave *you*? I'm not the one always talking about divorce,'' Tom said.

While the argument continued, the Washington family arrived with their folding chairs and overheard what was going on. They offered to swap folding chairs for the quilt, and the dispute ended before there was bloodshed.

The community band played valiantly, despite the fact it had lost its percussionist to summer term at the University of Virginia. Popular show tunes and light classical music, along with a Souza march just to get the blood pumping, filled the air until dusk had settled softly and turned to dark. But the music didn't ease Faith's tension. She remained alert to Sean's presence, starkly aware of the fresh intimacy passing between them, drawing them closer. Her skin felt alive, seemed to cry out for his touch. They had already touched in ways that went deeper than flesh to flesh, and Faith didn't know where to go from here.

When the music ended, they called out goodbyes and he walked her home surrounded by others leading sleepy-eyed children and rambunctious puppies. Again Faith found herself thinking how natural, how easy it would be to slip her hand into his.

But she didn't. She even kept a careful distance between them so their shoulders didn't brush, their warmth didn't mingle. They were quiet, making only occasional chitchat about the concert and the weather and the successful grand opening for the folklore museum until the crowds thinned near the south end of Ridge Lane.

"So, what do you have to do to get into the community band?" he said, playing a tattoo with a pair of imaginary drumsticks. "Bring a note from Juilliard? Rigorous auditions?"

"Show up with your drums every Thursday night for practice, I believe." She laughed at the surprise on his face. "This isn't exactly the Richmond Symphony. Do you play?"

"Well, I always wanted to."

"Why didn't you?"

"No time for it. My spare moments in high-school days were spent flipping burgers. By the time I made it to Harvard, I'd graduated to waiting tables, but there was still no time for a budding musical genius. Not for a kid on scholarship—need-based scholarship, I might add, not academic."

"Are you telling me you weren't a genius?"

He made a funny face that said his feelings were deeply wounded. "Not at all. But my lack of money justified special attention. I'm afraid my brains didn't."

They turned the corner onto Timber Gap Lane. Her house was nestled in a dark pool of shade beneath a half-dozen oaks and elms. The sight of it leeched some of the tension out of her shoulders. She did have a haven, a place to escape from the feelings she couldn't fight, couldn't control.

"You really were poor?" she asked.

"Mom was a telephone operator," he said. "That covered the basics and not much else."

No wonder he believed so fervently that she needed his help if he'd seen his own single mother struggle.

"But we were happy."

They walked onto her porch.

"That's better than ten-speed bikes and a pocketful of spending money," she said, wondering what would happen now that she was alone with him in the dark.

"Yes, it is."

He moved closer and Faith wished she had locked her door. Then, at least, she could fumble with a key. She put her hand on the doorknob.

"This is better than money," he said softly.

"What is?"

She could barely see his face. Soft shadows fell into the crevices beneath his cheekbones, the valley between his strong nose and his prominent chin. Only the glint in his eyes showed in the dark, and that glint was focused on her. She wanted to look away but couldn't.

"This town, a day like this, that's worth more than a million in the bank," he said. He tucked her hair behind her ear and his hand lingered almost imperceptibly along her neck. Faith's pulse once again began to race. "Being with you in the quiet, in the dark."

"Sean—"

"I'm going to kiss you again."

"I know." She barely had breath to get the words out.

"In court we call that discovery. I tell the judge and the other attorney what I plan to do so nobody gets surprised."

"I can tell you're an attorney," she said.

"You can?"

She nodded. "You talk too much."

He came closer. His voice grew softer, more intimate, each time he spoke. His fingers brushed along her neck to the base of her skull. She shivered.

"I can be rehabilitated."

"I don't know. You're beginning to sound like a chronic offender to me."

"I'll throw myself on your mercy."

She might not have heard him at all except that his lips were so close, so close his breath mingled with hers. Then, before he kissed her, he put his free hand on her back and drew her body against his, slow and sweet. He felt lean and hard. Sensations rippled through her, then washed over her in ever stronger waves as his lips teased and played over hers. His kiss was like him, tender but assured, taking her willing prisoner.

She twined her arms around his neck, running her fingers through the soft hair that never quite did what it should. Her thumbs ran along the sides of his face, exploring the set of his jaw, the rasp of day-old stubble. She sighed, then gasped when she felt the hand at her back slide forward and brush the side of her breast.

He pulled away abruptly. "Sorry," he whispered.

She stood there, confused, unanchored by his sudden retreat. She ran a trembling hand through her hair, touched her lips. "No, I... It's nothing. I..."

"I should go."

She started to protest, but he was already backing toward the steps.

"I'll see you...soon."

He was gone before she could say good-night, and she couldn't help but wonder if she would, indeed, see him soon.

SEAN SHOULD HAVE BEEN paying close attention to Tood Grunkemeier's instructions for his final will and testament. Instead, he kept thinking about his final kiss of the night before. He hadn't even dug out his reading glasses, which showed how serious he was about the notes he was pretending to make on the legal pad in his lap.

He was aware that silence hung over his office and looked up. The farmer, as lumpy and unformed as a sack of potatoes, stared at him expectantly. Sean ordered his mind back to the moment, reached for his glasses and said, "Yes, well, so you have no relatives to inherit."

Tood looked disgusted. "Not any that I can *find*," he said, and Sean had the distinct impression his new client was repeating himself. And none too happy about it.

"None you can find. I see. So what would you like to do about your estate?"

It wasn't that Sean meant to let his mind wander. It's just that the kiss had frightened him. Well, not so much the kiss itself. The kiss itself had been sweet, ripe with untapped passion. He had felt the pulsing at her neck, the rush of her heart, the soft thrust of her breasts against his chest. But—

"Find 'em."

"I beg your pardon?" Woolgathering again. Melvin Guthry probably never drifted off while his clients were explaining what they wanted from him. "Find them?"

"I want to find my niece. She's my only living relative, the best I can figure. So I want to find her. And then leave it all to her. So it can be passed on. To the next generation, you see."

The next generation. Actually that was what had bothered Sean about the kiss. Not the heat he'd felt in Faith's response or the urge to touch her he'd been unable to stop. What had bothered him about the kiss wasn't Faith at all, but the baby. "Yes, I see exactly what you mean. But, Mr. Grunkemeier—"

"Tood. Folks just call me Tood. Some of 'em call me Grunk, and I don't mind that a bit. Folks called my daddy Grunk, too, you see."

"Fine...Grunk. But I'm only an attorney. I'm not really in the business of finding people. Have you filed a missing-persons report?"

"She's not missing. I just don't know where she is. She went off with her pa, that was my brother's only boy—I practically raised Bill myself after his ma and pa passed away. Anyway, Bill and his second wife and the girl took off. But I heard Bill died out West somewhere and nobody ever said a thing about the girl. My niece. Great-niece, I reckon you'd say. Emily, that's her name. Seems to me she ought to be with blood kin, don't you reckon?"

Sean nodded absently, more than half his mind still on his reaction to kissing Faith. He hated admitting it, but fear had reared its ugly head, blotting out his desire. Because about the same time Sean had touched Faith's breast, about the same instant he heard her gasp, Sean had felt another response that wasn't hers at all.

He'd felt her baby move.

"Still," Sean said, plunging back into the welcome distraction of Tood Grunkemeier's missing great-niece, "I'm not in the business of finding people."

"But you know people who are," Grunk said. "Private detectives and such. I saw that on TV. Lawyers always have private detectives finding out things for them. So I figured you could set me up with a private detective, then we'd know where to find my niece and you could do the will for me."

Sean decided then to help the farmer find his niece. He did, indeed, know investigators who could probably track down the girl. And the footwork would give him something to think about for the next few hours besides the reality of Faith's pregnancy. Sean's experiences with pregnancies weren't good. He'd been around four of them, four of them that ended tragically. And here he was tempting fate again.

What if he was a jinx?

He knew, even as he had the thought, how irrational it was. But he couldn't help it. He couldn't seem to get a grip on his emotions. Not when it came to Faith.

He'd lain awake half the night thinking about all the possibilities. And even when he'd tried to direct himself to good outcomes, the bad ones always crept into his mind and took over. His head had been a black hole of misery.

The coming of daylight hadn't helped, either. The

black hole was still with him, taunting him with fearful possibilities.

What would happen if Faith ran into problems? What would happen if she needed the kind of protection he couldn't provide? He could go to court with her and fend off dragons. He could sharpen his sabers and protect her from the likes of Walter Brickerson. But there were other dangers against which he was powerless. He knew that all too well. And he couldn't go through that again. He simply couldn't.

But he'd made a commitment to Melvin and to Faith. And Sean knew he'd keep that commitment, even if it scared the hell out of him.

"Then you won't let me down, will you?" Tood Grunkemeier said as they shook hands on the front porch a half hour later, all the arrangements made.

"I'll do the best I can, Grunk."

He didn't tell the farmer that sometimes his best wasn't good enough. Some things were too big for any one man to take on. All a man could do was fight the good fight, get bloodied and try to find a way to live through the pain.

"A TRIPLE BABY SHOWER is a bad idea."

Kelsy sounded gloomy as she and Faith stepped out of the pool at the fitness club and dried off. Water aerobics turned out to be the only exercise Kelsy could handle, and Faith gladly came along twice a week in a show of support.

"It'll be fun," Faith said, more to cheer up Kelsy than because she actually believed it.

A baby shower for all three women had been Ida's

brainchild. She'd discovered they could use the grand art deco lobby of the old Bijou Theater, which stood empty these days. Barely waiting for a reply from Faith, Donna and Kelsy, Ida had begun working on invitations, guest lists and a theme.

The social event of the autumn season was what Ida was calling it. And, in fact, it was shaping up that way.

"It's getting out of hand, that's what it is," Kelsy said, wrapping her towel around her expanding waist and sitting on a bench until she stopped huffing and puffing. "Clem told me Chuck Hurd has volunteered to dress up like some cartoon character."

Faith groaned and joined her friend on the bench. "I'll talk to Ida. See if she won't rein things in."

"There's a waste of good breath."

"You're just feeling down in the dumps," Faith said. "It really could be fun, you know."

Faith didn't realize at first that the water trickling down Kelsy's cheeks wasn't dripping from her hair. She put her arm around Kelsy's shoulders. "Oh, honey, don't worry. Everything's going to work out."

Kelsy leaned against her and sniffled. "I just feel so alone. So scared. How can you be so brave?"

"I'm not so brave."

"You are, too."

Faith didn't know how to tell her friend that her fears had little to do with finding herself alone. Her fears these days all centered around Sean Davenport and making the same mistake all over again—falling for the wrong man. Sometimes it seemed to her that

Sean wasn't the wrong man, after all. Sometimes he seemed like a million light-years away from the man who had ensnared her with his lies and his charm.

Then something would happen and she would wonder all over again. After all, it was too much to expect any man to step in and willingly take over another's responsibilities. Sean had proved that the night of the folklore festival, hadn't he?

She'd let go of her fears long enough to spend the day with him, to talk to him about some of her deepest insecurities. She'd kissed him, not once but twice, and allowed herself the wonderful luxury of melting into his embrace.

And as soon as she had given away that much of herself, what had he done?

Run.

And she was foolish enough to be hurt.

"I've been thinking," Kelsy said. "Tell me if this is dumb, okay? But maybe I should try to call Steve. After all, he doesn't know about this baby. And he is the father. He has a right to know. I mean, it's probably only fair to call him. What do you think?"

Faith wondered if the father of Kelsy's baby would run, too, and hated herself for the new cynicism in her thoughts. She hadn't been raised to be a cynic.

Still, she wasn't about to be Pollyanna at Kelsy's expense. "I think you ought to be sure why you want to call him before you do a thing."

"What do you mean?"

Faith knew she was practicing her Pop routine and plunged ahead. "I mean if you're calling him because you think he deserves to know about his baby, then do it. But if you're calling because you think he'll come running to the rescue, you could be setting yourself up for disappointment.''

"I suppose it's a little bit of both." Kelsy smiled. "Well, maybe it's a lot of the latter.''

"We don't need men to rescue us, Kelsy.''

"Oh, but it would be nice, wouldn't it?''

And someplace deep inside of Faith, when she lay in bed alone at night in her empty house, thinking about juggling diapers and midnight feedings and running her own business and finding new crafts to teach and toilet training and being everything a little boy needed in a mother and a father, Faith had to acknowledge that having someone else to turn to for help *would* be such a relief.

But the only man she could think of she would really want to turn to was Sean Davenport.

And that frightened her so much she found herself at Hurd's Hardware the next morning under the pretext of looking for upholstery tacks. She'd finished the upholstery project a week ago and didn't really need any more tacks. But she did want to take another good look at Chuck. After all, Chuck was dependable. There would be no surprises with Chuck. Her common sense wouldn't be clouded by foolish notions of a grand passion that would make her life complete.

Maybe she ought to marry Chuck, after all, just to make sure she didn't make another colossal mistake.

CHAPTER THIRTEEN

SEAN WASN'T CRAZY about the idea of a small-town church supper, but Melvin had assured him it was the best way to introduce his mother to the people of Hope Springs.

"They're going to judge her, because that's what small-town people do," Melvin had said after a Saturday afternoon in which he'd tried unsuccessfully to introduce Sean to the joys of creek fishing. "But if they meet her at church, they'll judge her highly. And your rating will go up a point or two for bringing her."

So here he was.

There was nothing small-town about the church Fellowship Hall. The building was new, an addition to the quaint-looking stone church on Old Dominion. The vaulted ceiling overlooked gleaming hardwood floors and a half-dozen arched windows. At one end of the room was a stage, at the other end an open counter into the kitchen. Dozens of folding tables and chairs filled the floor.

"I'll never keep all these names straight," Lucy Davenport whispered as they circled the buffet table. She sounded nervous and unsure of herself, something Sean wasn't used to seeing in his independent mother.

"Nobody expects you to, Mom." He picked up a glass of tea for each of them. "Come on, let's go sit with Melvin."

She stopped. "I'd rather sit with Faith."

He looked at his mother, who had quickly reverted to her usual determined self. Her dark hair, barely silvered at the temples, was immaculately but simply styled, and her summer dress fit her trim figure nicely. No wonder Melvin had looked at her with such surprise when he'd introduced them earlier that afternoon.

He hadn't, however, introduced her to Faith. Things weren't going well with Faith. He wasn't sure which of them was going farther out of the way to avoid the other.

"You don't even know her," he said.

"No, but I intend to." Lucy gestured with her plate across the Fellowship Hall. "I'm betting that's her."

Sean looked in the direction she'd gestured, and sure enough, there sat Faith at one of the long folding tables. He hadn't seen her for days, and the sight of her made him want to talk to her, to watch her face, hear her voice.

"How did you know?"

"Because she looks frail and in need of rescuing," Lucy said, starting off in the direction of Faith's table. "I doubt that's the case, but you men are hard to convince. Besides, she's pregnant."

"Mom…" He gave up and followed her.

"I'm Sean Davenport's mother, Lucy," she was saying when he reached her side. "Mind if we join your table?"

Faith, Ida and Kelsy looked up, each of them apparently momentarily stunned into silence. Faith in particular stared at Lucy Davenport as if she were speaking Norwegian.

"N-no," Faith said. "Of course not. That would be...lovely."

Lucy smiled at her son over her shoulder as they sat. Sean made the introductions, noting that Faith focused all her attention on his mother.

"I hope you don't mind, but I've been eager to meet you," Lucy said to Faith.

Faith's translucent skin grew pink. "You have?"

"Yes. I thought it would be interesting to find out how you're reacting to my son's white-knight routine."

Sean sighed and began working on his fried chicken. "I should've left you in Richmond."

"White-knight routine?" Faith said.

"He's been trying to rescue you, hasn't he? Sean has an overdeveloped sense of responsibility. I know that's my fault. I let him grow up too fast."

"Did you really?"

Now Faith looked at him. Sean smiled at her and shrugged.

"Oh, yes. I was a single mother, you know. I'll bet he's mentioned that, hasn't he? I never could convince him he didn't have to be the little man of the house. We all make our mistakes with children."

Kelsy put down her plastic fork and stared at Lucy. "You were a single mother? Golly, was it hard?"

"Oh, yes. But you manage. Of course I was blessed. Sean was a good boy. If he'd been a problem, I'm not sure I could have coped."

Kelsy shrank back in her chair. Faith looked undaunted.

"I'm sure it must be harder in the city, where you don't have a community to fall back on," she said.

Lucy looked closely at Faith, then smiled. "You seem very independent."

Ida chuckled. "Oh, she is. She climbed the highest tree in town when she was six just to show up the first-grade boys. Of course, she couldn't get down and she wouldn't let the fire department come up with their ladders."

"Ida, I don't think anyone's interested in that."

"I am," Sean said, grateful for anything that took the focus off his own immaculate boyhood.

Lucy smiled into her plate. "This is going to be very interesting."

"Isn't it, though?" Ida replied.

At that moment they were distracted by the appearance of Donna, who managed to create quite a bit of noise with a foam plate, plastic cup and plastic utensils. Even her paper napkin seemed to hit the table with a resounding thud.

"I think I'm going to divorce my kids, too," she announced without preamble. "Can I do that, Sean?"

"Well, there is some precedent for that these days."

Donna's chin began to tremble, but she held her voice steady. "They all hate me."

Faith put a hand on Donna's. "I don't believe that."

"Well, they all think I'm wrong. It feels like the same thing." A tear trickled down her cheek.

Sean heard his mother murmur, "Oh, dear." He wondered how long it would take her to get used to the way private dramas were often played out in public in a small town like Hope Springs.

For the next few moments Donna and Faith might have been the only ones at the table as Faith reassured her friend. Sean paid little attention as Donna talked about the way her four adult children had lit into her. He was too absorbed in watching Faith. Her soft voice was soothing, and the platitudes she spoke held a conviction that rang of truth.

"That's her father speaking," Ida whispered. "He was a wise man. She doesn't realize how much like him she is."

Lucy leaned across her son and replied to Ida, "She's going to be a wonderful mother, isn't she?"

Ida smiled. "The best."

Sean's heart swelled, then settled into a lonely ache. He missed Faith. He hated the distance he'd allowed his fear to create. He had to find a way to bridge that distance.

Donna had sniffled away the last of her tears when Kelsy said, "Uh-oh," and everyone looked in the direction of her gaze. Donna's husband, Tom, was stalking toward them, black rage in his eyes. Donna began to rise, but Faith put a hand on her arm to stop her.

"Calm down," Faith said. "He can't make a scene all by himself. If you don't catch the ball, there's no game."

When Tom reached their table, he surprised them all by nodding curtly, then kneeling beside Donna's chair.

"Are you okay?" he said, touching her hair with the tips of his fingers.

The big man's proprietary tenderness stirred a feeling of envy in Sean. He wanted that right, too, the right to intimately touch the woman he loved in front of God and everybody.

"No, I'm not okay," Donna replied. "My own children think I'm some kind of wretched beast."

"They're rotten kids," Tom said. "We'll sell 'em to Gypsies."

"Gypsies don't buy grown kids," Donna said, a small smile touching her lips.

Sean glanced around, wondering if anyone but him thought they should all sneak off and leave these two to talk in private. Kelsy, he noticed, had tears glistening in her eyes. His mother looked openly fascinated. Then he caught Faith's eyes and had to look away. The emotions he saw there were too intense for him to intrude.

Tom said, "Then we'll disinherit the ingrates. That'll teach 'em."

Donna laughed, then grew sober. "They're right, though, aren't they?"

"Only half-right."

"Which half?"

"Well, they said you don't appreciate their father nearly enough. Maybe that part was right."

"Maybe. Then the part about making everybody miserable over what should be a joyous occasion for the family—that part wasn't right."

"Well, there's something to that, too, I suppose."

Donna cuffed him lightly on the arm. "Oh, you. Then you think they're all right."

"Nah. Only half. 'Cause they left out the part where I'm guilty of the same stuff."

"They did? You are?"

"Yeah."

"Oh, Tom."

A longing to have what this couple had struck Sean like a blow to his chest. Despite their squabbling, these two were clearly of one mind, of one heart. Sean had never felt so empty, so needy.

"Tell you what," Tom said. "Let's make 'em eat their words."

"Well…"

"I'll start treating you like a queen and…uh, you don't have to start treating me like a king until after the baby's born. How's that?"

"You mean it?"

Tom shifted his weight. "Woman, this knee's gonna give out soon. Can we maybe get a move on this making-up business?"

Sean held his breath, wondering if Tom had broken the mood. But Donna just laughed, stood and tugged her husband to his feet.

"I love you, you old fool," she said, putting her arms around his waist.

When he put his arms around her and kissed her, applause broke out in the Fellowship Hall. Someone started pounding out a rousing rendition of "It Had to Be You" on the piano in the corner.

Lucy Davenport released a sigh. "Well, that's a relief. Is life always so...dramatic here in Hope Springs?"

Sean looked across the table. Faith was smiling, but there seemed to him to be a wistfulness in her eyes. And he wanted to do something about it, even more than he wanted to do something about the longing in his own heart.

His mother was right. White-knight syndrome, indeed. He supposed he could learn to change if he wanted to. But when it came to Faith O'Dare, he didn't want to change.

THINGS WERE CHANGING too fast for Faith. First there'd been the week Donna and Tom went off to New England for a second honeymoon. That had been the same week Kelsy had started trying to reach her baby's father, so far with little luck.

And now, this morning, more changes in her body. This morning's change didn't feel pleasant, but as Faith went downstairs for her morning coffee, she told herself that was bound to happen. After all, look at how miserable Donna and Kelsy had been in the early months of their pregnancies. Kelsy said every day that she felt like one of the black bears the Virginia mountains were infamous for—huge, clumsy-looking and ready to snap at anything in her path.

Faith poured her decaf and glanced out her kitchen window, grateful these twinges of discomfort were the first physical problems she'd had to contend with. Maybe she should call Sarah just to reassure herself that everything was fine. But as the next little spasm nipped her, she was distracted by the sight of a man in her backyard.

Sean.

He was checking her tomatoes and her pole beans, probably to make sure they weren't being nibbled by critters. He turned on the sprinkler, then stepped back, nursing a mug of coffee, to watch the water soak into her thirsty garden. A smile crept onto her face.

He'd been on her mind too much to suit her. She hadn't liked seeing him with his mother. That had made it difficult to keep wearing her skepticism like a protective armor. How evil could his intentions be if he was willing to expose them to his mother?

She opened her back door and stepped out. "So that's why I have the only garden in town that isn't dying in the drought."

He turned toward her. His eyes over the rim of his coffee mug were the wary eyes of a little boy caught doing mischief. "You're up early."

"Couldn't sleep."

"Are you feeling okay?"

"Fine," she said, realizing that the tiny aches and pains she'd felt upon rising were gone. She felt silly for even worrying. What a wimp Donna and Kelsy would think she was. "But Patrick wakes up with the sun most mornings."

"Patrick?"

She patted her tummy. "That's his name."

"Patrick?" He looked and sounded startled.

"I finally picked a name," she explained. "Patrick was Pop's name."

"I see."

"Anyway, you shouldn't be doing this," she said.

"If I want fresh vegetables, I guess I'd better," he said, walking toward her. "Melvin's thumb isn't very green. And you really aren't in any condition to tend a garden."

"So I'll owe you half my crop?"

"What a nice offer, Faith O'Dare."

She smiled again. She liked the idea of him tending her garden. She liked the idea of sharing the harvest with him. Sometimes it was scary to realize what a dreamer she could be, even after all that had happened.

"We'll check when you turn off the sprinkler," she said. "See how far along the corn is."

"We have corn?"

She laughed. "What kind of boy did your mother raise?"

"A city boy."

When he turned off the sprinkler, they walked out into the wet garden and she showed him the tall stalks of corn. She peeked beneath the beard of corn silks to see if the largest ears were ready.

"Another week," she said.

"We couldn't sneak a couple of ears now?"

She shook her head. "No, we could not."

"Oh. I guess I'm not very patient."

She rested a hand on her tummy. "I understand."

His dark eyes, which were usually so piercing, seemed to soften. "Patrick, huh?"

She nodded. His gaze held her, mesmerized her. Humidity rose off the damp earth, mingling with early-morning heat. He touched her arm where she'd brushed against the cornstalks; his fingers slicked over her moist skin. Arousal ruffled her, filling her chest, softening her loins. Restless, she wondered if he would kiss her. It had been weeks now, a lifetime. She felt, at this moment, as if she'd been holding her breath ever since. Waiting.

Wanting.

"I'd better get back," he said, "before Melvin misses me."

But he didn't step away, didn't move at all. Now Faith held her breath in earnest. She had forgotten the discomfort of moments ago. All she knew was Sean, the drift of damp heat and the pounding of her heart.

"Well, Counselor?" she said when she could stand the silence and uncertainty no longer.

Sean leaned across the scant distance between them and touched his lips to hers. Faith sparked to life. He caressed the seam of her lips with the tip of his tongue, and she opened to him, inviting him in, moving into his embrace. He tasted of black coffee and white-hot need. She ran her fingers through strands of hair that were always too long, always out

of place. He hadn't shaved. His chin abraded hers.
A low moan of satisfaction rose from her chest.

For months she had allowed herself to forget this
part of being a woman. She found she wanted it back.

But here and now was not the time. She knew that.
She struggled to bring that thought to the forefront,
to give it precedence over the way her body yearned
for a man.

This man. This man who couldn't possibly be the
right man.

She put her hands between them, on his chest. Reluctantly they ended the kiss.

"We don't want Melvin to come looking for
you," she whispered.

He nodded. "Later."

She nodded.

"Maybe tonight," he said.

She hesitated. "Later."

He brushed her damp lower lip with his thumb.
His voice was raspy when he spoke. "Definitely tonight."

She watched him leave, and shivered in the steam
off the garden.

CHAPTER FOURTEEN

DONNA WAS REGALING them with stories of her second honeymoon when the telephone rang. Faith was barely listening. In fact, she'd thought of nothing but Sean and the promise implied in his words when he'd left her standing in her garden an hour earlier.

"Not another word," Kelsy said, reaching for the phone on the desk. "This might be Steve." She'd said that so often no one paid much attention.

Donna yawned. "But now I'm exhausted. You guys won't mind if I take another week off just to—"

"Steve!"

Faith looked up at Kelsy's exclamation. Kelsy nodded at them, her freckled face excited. The ex-fiancé had finally called back. Faith smiled.

"I'm so glad you got my messages," Kelsy was saying. "You know, I was thinking..."

Then she began nodding in response to whatever Steve was saying. Each time her head dipped, the excitement in her face faded a little more.

"In Spain," she said at last. "For the European tour. How nice."

Donna groaned. Faith felt another twinge of discomfort, and this time tried to label it an empathetic response to Kelsy's disappointment. She'd forgotten her intention to call Sarah just to make sure the twinges were nothing to worry about. She glanced at her watch. By the time Kelsy got off the phone, Sarah would be in and she could call. Let Donna call her a fraidy-cat.

"For a year." Kelsy dropped into a chair. "Well, Steve, that's wonderful. Exciting."

They talked for a few more minutes, but most of Kelsy's replies were monosyllables. Finally she said. "Yes, you do that. Bye, Steve."

"You didn't tell him!" Donna wailed when Kelsy hung up.

Kelsy's face was distressed, as was her voice. "He says he'll drop by when he gets back from Europe. For a visit."

Trying to ignore the twinge that was becoming more of a gripping pain, Faith put a hand on Kelsy's shoulder. Sarah would surely say this was nothing to fret over. "Oh, Kels, why didn't you go ahead and tell him?"

"He's got this big plan," Kelsy said, starting to sniffle. "He's going to get his game in shape on the European tour, then… Oh, what difference does it make? The point is, I can't just drop a bomb in the middle of his lap like that."

"That's okay," Faith said. "When he gets back, you'll have a chance to—"

A gasp cut through her words. She put a hand to her belly. Donna was at her side in an instant.

"Faith, what's wrong?"

Faith shook her head. "I'm sure it's nothing. Indigestion maybe?"

"Tell me what you're feeling."

"Oh, Lord," Kelsy whispered.

Faith described the sensations.

"For how long?"

"I'm not sure. Since early this morning, I think. They woke me up."

"And the baby. What's the baby doing?"

Faith straightened and frowned, angry at the fear creeping up her spine. "Donna, nothing's wrong. You know that. I've felt so good. There can't be anything wrong. I'd know it."

She recognized how hard she was fighting the idea that her discomfort had anything to do with her pregnancy. Realized she hadn't even been willing to call what she'd been feeling pain.

"Tell me what the baby's doing," Donna said, her voice steely.

"Nothing. He—" Faith gasped again. "Oh, God, Donna. He hasn't been moving. Oh, please, no. Nothing's wrong with my baby. It can't be."

IN THE NEXT HOURS, Faith's world tilted on its axis. Her nice, comfortable pregnancy turned into a nightmare.

She lay in Labor and Delivery at the county hospital, hooked up to monitors and holding Ida's hand in a death grip. Sarah's insistence she be taken by ambulance straight to the hospital had terrified her. To save time, Sarah had said, just in case. Since then, she'd heard a lot of talk about effacing, about her cervix thinning. But Faith couldn't focus on the words or make sense of them. All she wanted to hear was that her baby was fine.

"Why won't she tell me something?"

"She'll tell you as soon as she knows something, dolly. Your job is to stay calm."

Faith squeezed her eyes shut against Ida's unreasonable suggestion. "Stay calm! How can I stay calm?"

"Now you know that when you're upset, so is little Patrick. And whatever is going on here, I suspect the little fellow needs to stay calm, wouldn't you say?"

Faith had no patience with rational people. She was terrified and she wanted answers, and all anybody could say to her was to be calm. She drew a long deep breath. It didn't help. She was ready to crawl out of her skin.

The door opened and Sarah came in, smiling the reassuring doctor smile that Faith was beginning to hate.

"This happens sometimes," Sarah began, then paused to check all the monitors, including the one attached to the band circling Faith's belly. "We call it an incompetent cervix, and all it means is that your uterus wants to open up early."

Medical mumbo jumbo, irrelevant at the moment. "But is Patrick all right?"

"He's fine. He was just getting ready to make his appearance, that's all."

Faith wanted to deny the import of the words. "What? But it's too early. Only..." Faith paused to calculate, but her mind wouldn't operate well enough to figure.

"You're twenty-eight weeks along," Sarah said with crisp efficiency. "Normal gestation is forty weeks. So, yes, Patrick did get a little ahead of himself."

Fear made Faith's heart race. "But why?"

"We're not sure why. We just know this happens sometimes, and most of the time we can't find a good reason for it."

Faith didn't like things that couldn't be explained, because what she couldn't explain she certainly couldn't control.

"But it won't happen again." It wasn't a question, it was an order.

"Not if we can help it. Not if you cooperate."

"Of course I will. I'll do whatever you say. I'll take more vitamins. I'll drink more milk. I can get more exercise. Anything."

Sarah glanced at Ida and smiled. "Good. Here's what I'm going to need you to do. You're going to have to go to bed."

"Okay. For how long?"

"For the rest of the pregnancy."

Suddenly Faith found she could calculate again. "The rest— That's twelve weeks! You don't mean you want me to go to bed for *twelve weeks.*"

"All day," Sarah said, ignoring her protests. "Every day. We're going to put you in the hospital for a couple of days, get some medication into you to stop the contractions, make doubly sure that everything looks normal. Then we'll give you some oral medication to take every day and send you home."

"To *bed?*"

"Ida, is there any chance we can get some help moving Faith's bed downstairs for the next few weeks? That should simplify everything and eliminate any need for her to go up and down stairs."

Faith imagined her house being overrun with strangers, robbing her of control and treating her like a helpless invalid. There had to be another solution. "Now, hold on a minute—"

"Consider it taken care of," Ida said.

"And maybe someone could put together a roster of people to check on her, bring her meals, that kind of thing?"

"Oh, no, you don't. This isn't—"

"No problem," Ida said.

They were ignoring her. "Listen, both of you—"

But they were out the door, leaving her lying here, hooked up to monitors and wondering how she had lost control of her life.

SEAN HEARD about Faith when he dropped by the bank that afternoon. He saw Bama Preston across the lobby, and when she waved, he figured she'd found the perfect house for his mother.

Instead, she said, "Have you heard about poor Faith?"

His anxiety went into overdrive as she explained that Faith had been rushed to the hospital, that no one was exactly sure what had gone wrong, but that the entire town was being mobilized to care for her.

Sean barely heard the details for the roar of fear in his head. He had to work to catch his breath.

"The poor dear," Bama said. "I even heard some-one say it might be for the best."

"For the best?"

"Well, you know how it is. Her being all alone."

Sean grabbed the woman by her amply padded shoulders and fought not to shake her until those gi-gantic gold disks dislodged themselves from her ear-lobes. "It's not for the best. Do you hear? Faith is not going to lose this baby. I swear she's not."

Then he dashed out, forgetting about the check he had intended to cash, forgetting his two-o'clock ap-pointment, forgetting everything but Faith.

She needed him. He had to be there.

He dashed around town like a madman. Things were locked up tight at Times Square Crafts. No one was at home at Faith's or next door at Ida's. He was standing in the middle of Ridge Lane, frantically wondering what to do next, when the editor of the *Courier* led him to the corner and gave him direc-tions to the county hospital.

His hands were shaking so badly he couldn't write down the directions himself. He assured Melvin he could make the drive safely, then ran two stop signs on the way out of town. The delivery truck from Hurd's Hardware had to screech to a halt to keep from hitting him, and three bales of pine needles flew off the back of the truck and landed in the intersec-tion of Ridge and Presidents' Drive.

He calmed himself only slightly on his way down the mountain, although he did try a prayer that actually sounded more like a direct order. *God, don't do this. Don't you dare do this.* The drive to County Memorial Hospital took twenty-five minutes, according to Melvin. Sean squealed into the parking lot seventeen minutes after getting into his car.

When he finally found Faith's room, she was surrounded by people from Hope Springs who obviously hadn't stood around in the middle of the street wondering what to do next.

"If you'll just sign up in my appointment calendar," Ida was saying to a group of older women who had church auxiliary written all over their neat print dresses, "we can make sure Faith has everything she needs."

Sean couldn't even see the hospital bed for the throng of people. He stood on tiptoe, needing to see her, dreading what he might see. He tried elbowing his way through the crowd, but a very determined-looking nurse caught him by the arm.

"We *must* clear this room." Her tone said she held him personally responsible for the disruption. "Immediately."

"I agree," he said, and turned to resume his own journey.

"Starting with you," she said.

"But I'm…" The expression on her dour face told him that nothing he could say had a prayer of winning her sympathy. So he took desperate action. "The father."

She arched an eyebrow. "Oh, really?" It incensed him that she obviously didn't believe him. "Then you may want to step down the hallway to the waiting room with the rest of the fathers.''

"The... *What?*"

She jerked a thumb toward the door. ''Out, Papa.''

Sean had always prided himself on being the kind of poker player who knew when it was time to fold. So he gave in and left Faith in the care of the drill-sergeant RN and Ida's motherly brigade. He hung out at the door for a moment, then curiosity got the better of him. He found the waiting room down the hall and peered in.

A half-dozen familiar faces peered back at him. The cook from Luisita's, the fellow who ran the Southern Folklore Museum, a couple of regulars from the barbershop. And Chuck Hurd. He frowned at Chuck. Chuck frowned at him.

''What's happening?'' Sean asked, hoping someone knew something that would reassure him.

Chuck looked reluctant to part with information that marked him as an insider, Sean as still on the outside. ''She started going into labor.''

Sean thought of the slight swell of Faith's tummy, pressed against him that morning, and knew it wasn't the tummy of a woman ready to give birth. ''But why? It's too soon.''

''They don't know why.''

''Or ain't tellin','' said Fudgie from the barbershop.

''Doc said it happens sometimes,'' said the other barbershop regular. ''No particular reason, just happens.''

''But if the baby came now—'' Sean stopped,

wondering just how slim the possibilities of surviving were for a baby born this early.

He listened as attentively as he could while the other men from Hope Springs told him all they knew—that Faith would be given medication to stop her contractions, that she and the baby would be monitored at least overnight to make sure everyone was healthy, then Faith would be ordered home for complete bed rest for the duration of her pregnancy. But as much as he wanted to hear every detail, Sean had trouble concentrating. His thoughts kept wandering off to explore every possible tragic scenario.

He wanted to help—needed to help—and they wouldn't even let him see her.

He sat in the waiting room, shifting from uncomfortable couch to uncomfortable chair the rest of the afternoon and into the evening. He signed Ida's appointment book when she came through, vying with Chuck for all the hours that hadn't yet been filled. He made Ida repeat all the details he'd already heard and didn't feel a bit better. He bought bad coffee and ham-and-cheese sandwiches from a machine in the basement. He watched everyone else go home as the evening wore on. Everyone else but Chuck. He and Chuck kept jealous vigil, neither willing to concede turf to the other.

At last Chuck fell victim to the boredom of the repeat of a bowling championship on the sports channel. He slept. He snored, Sean noted with satisfaction, a real window rattler. Convinced he'd proved himself the better man, Sean sneaked down the hall and into Faith's hospital room.

He'd expected her to be asleep. The lights were off except for a dim bulb over the sink and the greenish glow of monitors. But Faith's eyes weren't closed. They stared out the window, wide and troubled. Her hand rested on her belly.

"You should be sleeping," he said.

She turned toward him, but there was no real welcome in her eyes and the crease between her eyebrows didn't smooth. "What are you doing here?"

"I heard the coffee was good."

"It's a good thing you're not under oath."

He smiled, but her bleak expression didn't change. "How do you feel?"

Her chin quivered and she worked to regain control of it. "Is this a cross-examination, Counselor?"

"It's going to be okay, Faith." He didn't believe it, but maybe she would.

"You don't know that. Nobody knows that." Her face crumpled. "I don't know what I did wrong. Nobody's telling me anything. I don't even know why this happened."

Sean sat on the edge of the bed and pulled her into his arms as best he could without disturbing the monitor and IV needles. Her face rested against his chest and he felt her chest heaving with sobs. He was determined to do something to help, and right now it seemed the only thing he could do was hold her while she cried.

It wasn't enough, dammit. Not nearly enough.

FAITH LAY IN THE BED that had been set up in the family room, every pillow in the house propped up behind her and around her. She was growing accustomed to the fact that, even with the medication she was on, the contractions hadn't completely stopped. But they were fleeting and irregular and she knew to pay attention if that changed. She had also grown accustomed to the way her heart raced from the medication and to lying mostly on her left side so Patrick could get more oxygen. What she hadn't grown accustomed to was the boredom.

Faith looked at the color of her nails and decided she didn't like Ripe Raisin, after all.

"No problem," she muttered. "Change it."

What else did she have to do?

In the week she'd been home from the hospital, Faith had learned that daytime television irritated her, that books only made her impatient to know how her own story was going to turn out and that quilting and knitting weren't easy from a prone position.

And Sarah had had a fit when she'd popped in to find her patient actually sitting up in a chair.

"We call it bed rest for a reason," Sarah had said, standing guard as Faith toddled back to bed. "Because we want you in bed. Lying down."

Bed rest was boring, despite the steady stream of people who came by with magazines, movies on video, library books, hot casseroles and hotter gossip. Faith found herself growing restless, then irritable. She'd had Kelsy bring her a calendar from the drugstore so she could mark off the days.

The days slowed to a muggy crawl.

Only her temper got quicker.

She'd decided to pin up her hair to get it off her

neck when the screen door opened. Whose hour was it now? she wondered, thinking if it was Bertie Newsome and her four grandchildren again, she might have to barricade herself in from here on out.

It was worse than Bertie Newsome. She heard their voices in the entrance hall.

"This is *my* hour."

Chuck Hurd sounded huffy and possessive. Faith didn't have to hear the reply to know who was with him.

"Well, I had a few minutes and thought I'd drop in," Sean said. "Melvin wanted me to bring tea cakes."

"You *knew* it was my hour. You always horn in when it's my hour, Davenport."

Faith smiled. At least she would get Melvin's tea cakes in the bargain. Buttery and sweet, they were almost worth an hour of listening to Chuck and Sean try to outdo each other.

"Get in here and quit bickering," she called out.

Chuck stuck his head through the door first. He waved a casserole dish wrapped in a peach-and-green-flowered kitchen towel. "Brought you some of Mama's gelatin salad. The kind with pineapples and cream cheese."

"Perfect with tea cakes," Sean said. He eased past Chuck and stood at the foot of her bed with a covered plate in his hands. His arms were bronze against his white shirt and his smile turned her insides on end. He looked more delicious than any of the covered dishes that had been stashed in her refrigerator the past week.

And that irritated the pure-T heck out of her.

"I'm going to have to start selling plate lunches out the back door if you people don't stop bringing food," Faith said, trying for a smile. "Do I look malnourished?"

"You look sensational," Chuck said so enthusiastically that Faith considered throwing her hairbrush at him.

"I look like somebody who's been wallowing around in bed for months," Faith grumbled.

Sean handed his plate to Chuck. "Here. Why don't you take this stuff into the kitchen?"

Chuck stood there with his hands full and looked disgruntled. "Why don't *you* make a kitchen run, Davenport?"

"I thought this was your hour to help out, Hurd."

Sean smiled, unperturbed. Faith found it hard not to smile with him as Chuck stomped off to the kitchen.

"You're not very nice to Chuck," she said.

"I'm working on improving my disposition." He sat in the armchair that had been pulled close to the bed. "How are you feeling?"

"Bored."

"A marked improvement. Yesterday you were feeling like killing the next person who walked through the door with a basket of corn bread."

"I'm working on improving *my* disposition."

She heard the sounds of water running and dishes rattling in the kitchen.

"I'd play it for all it's worth if I were you. After all, how many chances do we get to lie about and be catered to and still get excused if we aren't all sweetness and light?''

"Not many chances, I hope.''

"Can I help you with your hair?''

She realized her hair was half up, half down. She opened her fist to reveal a palmful of bobby pins. "I thought it might feel cooler.''

He nodded and picked up her brush. "Turn on your side.''

"But—''

"Come on, you're letting Chuck wash your dishes.''

"That's different,'' she mumbled, but she did as he asked.

She felt the whisper of his fingers as he slipped out the pins she'd already jabbed into the tangle of hair. Then he brushed through it gently. He began to talk in a low voice and she realized he was telling her a story, the story of a princess with long hair locked in a tower. Faith smiled. The easy rhythm of the brush strokes soothed her. His voice lulled her. Long before the princess lived happily ever after, Faith's eyes grew so heavy she could barely keep them open.

SHE HALF AWOKE long enough to hear them leaving, still bickering. She smiled and kept her eyes closed. She hadn't felt so safe, so cherished, in a long time. She wondered when Sean would be back.

She hoped it would be soon.

CHAPTER FIFTEEN

KELSY HADN'T BEEN the same since Faith had almost lost her baby, she realized as she and Donna tried to convince their friend how much fun it could be getting beaten at cards.

"Rummy," Donna announced for the fourth time in an hour, leaving Faith and Kelsy with a handful of cards that would score against them.

Faith groaned. "I quit. I thought it was understood that you go easy on invalids."

Donna shook her head. "Not a prayer. I *always* go for the kill. Always."

Kelsy swept the cards up and began to shuffle.

"So how are you guys feeling?" Faith asked.

Kelsy glanced at Donna. They had agreed before coming this evening not to regale their partner with how much better their own pregnancies were going these days. Both of them were actually farther along than Faith and it seemed the closer they got to delivery the easier it grew. Even Donna admitted that once she'd accepted her pregnancy, things settled down.

And Kelsy, having witnessed Faith's difficulties, had come to cherish the life growing inside her. These days it seemed all she had to do was be still, close her eyes and wait for movement, and she was filled with something close to peace of mind, a commodity she'd rarely had in her life. She resisted the impulse to put her hand on her belly.

"Good," Donna said. "Like a horse, but good."

"Okay," Kelsy said, dealing out another hand.

"What about the blood pressure?" Faith said.

"Better."

"She's calmed down and quit fighting it," Donna said.

"Look who's talking," Kelsy retorted. "Speaking of which, Faith, when are *you* going to quit fighting the inevitable?"

Under her breath, Donna muttered, "Asking for trouble."

"The inevitable what?" Faith asked.

"Sean Davenport."

"Sean Davenport is not inevitable."

Kelsy drew from the discard pile. "He's awfully attentive. I think he'd make a wonderful father, don't you, Donna?"

"Deal me out of that conversation," Donna said.

"The last time we talked about the potential-father pool in Hope Springs, you were advising me to marry Chuck Hurd," Faith said.

"I was wrong. This time I'm right."

Faith ignored her. Donna ignored her, even though Kelsy knew for a fact that Donna and Sean had had their heads together over some kind of surprise for Faith.

"You know, Faith, you can't let the past rule the present," Kelsy said. "Just because some men are jerks doesn't mean they all are."

Faith threw down her hand. "How about dessert? Ginny Bryant's sweet-potato pie or Esther Hurd's tunnel-of-fudge cake."

Kelsy gave up on her attempts to get Faith to think twice about Sean Davenport. But as she dished up dessert for them, the words she'd just spoken to her friend lodged somewhere in her chest.

Faith wasn't the only one letting the past rule the present. Not all men were jerks. And all women didn't have to be doormats just because they were in love. Maybe it was time she listened to her own advice and left the past behind.

FAITH HEARD the racket on the front porch. Khan jumped into the window and peered out.

"What are they up to now?" Faith asked the cat, who had grown as irritable and restless with the confinement as Faith. Her partners had brought her the cat for company, admonishing him to keep an eye on Faith, and he apparently took the job seriously. Faith had considered telling Donna to take him back to Times Square Crafts, where he could enjoy his freedom again. But apparently misery did love company. She hated to let him go.

He let out a throaty yowl and swished his tail briskly.

"That's not very helpful information," Faith said.

The waiting had stretched to almost three weeks, and Faith's nerves were wearing thin, despite the best efforts of everyone in town. She took her medicine and Sarah stopped by at least once a week. She kept hoping her friend would tell her that the bed rest had done its job, that she was free to go back to work, to start living, to take charge of her life again.

It hadn't happened. It wasn't going to happen. She knew that. But she kept hoping. Because she was slowly but surely going stir-crazy.

And all the well-meaning folks in Hope Springs didn't make it any easier.

Especially Sean.

He'd brought her a new oscillating fan on a stand the day after she complained about the heat. He was reading a book to her, sometimes acting out the dialogue with such gusto she felt as if she was watching a stage play. He brought a litter of kittens from a neighbor just so they could play on her bed and amuse her with their antics for an hour. Khan had watched from the mantel, his blue eyes narrowed to unfriendly slits.

Sean always managed to make Faith laugh, but the good feelings wore off quickly once he left, because the lonely hours stretched so far into the future she couldn't see the end of them. And her frustration only grew, because it disturbed her to realize that, of all the people in town, only Sean seemed to have the power to make her feel better.

The sound of furniture dragging across her porch almost prompted her to get up and peek out the front window. But before she could make up her mind to do so, the front door opened. Sean came in, a smile on his lips.

"What was all that racket?" she asked.

"A surprise."

"What kind of—"

He pulled back the sheet.

"Hey!"

He slipped one arm beneath her knees, the other around her back and lifted her.

"What are you doing? Besides giving yourself back strain."

"Back strain? With a little thing like you?"

He carried her through the entrance hall, shoved the screen door open with his foot.

"We're going outside," she said. The first hint of fresh air on her face made her smile. "Oh, Sean, I can't..."

He was setting her down in the place where one of her rockers usually stood, but she wasn't in a rocker. She was reclining, legs up, sinking into soft cushions. She glanced around. She was sitting in the antique chaise longue from Cookie's, the one she'd coveted the day she and Donna shopped for a cradle. Someone had made fluffy chintz cushions and extra pillows for her back.

"Sean, what is this?"

"Just a little something I heard you might like."

"But it's..." Being on her shady porch, looking out on the dappled sunshine in her yard, felt wonderful. The spire of the Episcopal church across the street rose into the clear blue sky like something on a postcard. The smells of summer crept into her nostrils. She felt like a prisoner set free. "I can't afford this. Not now."

"It's a little gift."

She shook her head even while she fought the giddy excitement of simply being outside.

"You have to take it back," she forced herself to say.

"I think Cookie said all sales are final."

"Then I guess you and Melvin have a new chaise longue for *your* porch."

He didn't say anything for a moment, just leaned against the railing and stared at her with that completely unflappable gaze of his.

"The kittens will be old enough to leave their mother next week," he said. "I was thinking of adopting one."

"Changing the subject doesn't get you off the hook, Counselor."

"The little tortoiseshell with the noisy meow. I liked her attitude."

Faith remembered the one he meant. The other four kittens were docile and sweet, but the tortoiseshell let you know right away—and very vocally—when she wanted your attention. "A noisy meow comes in handy when people aren't behaving the way you want them to."

He grinned at her. "You didn't learn that from the kitten, did you?"

"I learned that a long time ago. So if you think I'm going to let this go, you don't know me very well."

"I found a house I think will be perfect for my mother."

That did shut Faith up for a moment. She'd thought maybe he was just bluffing when he mentioned moving his mother to town. "Oh."

"Bama called it the old Harrilson place."

"Near the high school." She knew the old Harrilson place, a quaint little cottage with a rose arbor over the front gate. Mayrene Harrilson had tended her roses with the attention of a fussy, overprotective mother. "You are settling in, aren't you?"

"Putting down roots. You know, I spent my whole life in Richmond, but I never had roots there."

Why here? she wanted to ask him. *Why my town?* But she didn't dare ask because she was afraid of the answer.

"I never had a future there," he continued, leaning against a column and putting his foot on the railing for balance. He looked so good there, so perfectly at ease, nothing like the rigid-shouldered man who had walked into Times Square Crafts four months ago. He did seem to belong here, and the idea made her darned uneasy. "I spent my whole life desperately wanting to fit in. I thought I could fit in with Brick and his crowd, but it never worked. I felt like a fraud, expecting to be found out any minute.

"I've been here six weeks and I already belong." He smiled. "And I haven't had a single headache the entire time. Not even a twinge."

She wanted to dispute his conclusion, but she couldn't. She'd seen it happen to others. Hope Springs didn't attract many new residents, but occasionally people drove into town for a week at the spa and before it was over knew they would never again feel at home anywhere else.

"I thought at first it was the town," he said. "But it's more than that, Faith. It's you."

"Sean—"

"When I think about the future here, only one picture comes to mind."

"Don't."

"Love can heal a lot of things, Faith. I know we got off to a rocky start. But that's all in the past now."

Faith swung her legs off the chaise. "Sean, I want you to take your chaise longue and go home. This isn't a conversation I want to have."

He pushed away from the column and knelt beside her, a position that evoked images she had no intention of entertaining. "I know how I feel, and you won't make that feeling go away by pretending it doesn't exist. Doing things for you, being with you, gives me such peace. I've never felt that before. It's simple. I love you, Faith. And I think if you'll search your heart, you'll find you love me, too."

She stood up, angry—and so afraid of trusting the feelings his words of love stirred. "Go away, Sean. I mean it. And take your damned chair, too."

She shoved the chair aside so she could pass him without touching him. He called her name, but she marched to the door on legs that were wobbly from disuse and something else besides. "If I see that chair on my porch in an hour, I swear I'll throw it in the yard myself!"

FAITH PACED. Back and forth. Up and down. She'd locked the front door and ignored more than one knock in the past hour.

Khan paced with her, yowling his protests over her mood and activity.

When she'd finally been able to resist no longer, she'd peeked out the front curtains. The lovely chaise longue was gone and her rockers were back in place. Disappointment had a bitter taste, but it was just as well. Sean's gift came with strings attached, strings that were sure to strangle her.

"Love!" She looked at Khan for his reaction. "How *could* he talk about…that? Now, when I'm so…stir-crazy I might believe anything."

She was so agitated she couldn't lie down, couldn't even make herself sit down. After the third knock on her locked front door, she wandered back to the kitchen and found nothing she wanted to eat. Of all the food that kept pouring into the house, she didn't find one thing that sounded like comfort to her.

But she knew what did, and she could make it without a bit of help from all the busybodies in Hope Springs.

Khan rubbed against her ankles while she searched for the recipe. It was on a yellow egg-stained card in Pop's messy scrawl. Peanut-butter-oatmeal cookies, the ones he always made when she was sick or upset. As she started creaming the butter, she began to calm down.

"I know," she said to the heavyweight Siamese, who seemed to sense that food might be in his future. "I overreacted. That's nothing new."

Sean's words had frightened her because they asked her to do the one thing she wasn't sure she could do right now—trust her own judgment. Her confidence in her judgment had been shaken by what happened with Walter, and shaken again when her body began to betray her. No matter how often Sarah reassured her, Faith had the nagging feeling that something she'd done had caused this problem with her baby.

And Sean wanted her to have faith that everything would work out perfectly. With her baby. With him.

She simply couldn't do that.

But she didn't have to overreact, either. She'd done a lot of that lately. Maybe when she finished her batch of cookies, she would have someone take half of them to Sean. With a note. That was it. She could write a note and explain, in the calm rational way she couldn't seem to muster when he was nearby, exactly how she felt and why.

"Then I'll lie back down," she promised Khan.

She had just put the cookie sheet into the oven and gone in search of notepaper when the pain gripped her.

RELUCTANTLY SEAN had loaded the chaise longue back into the truck he'd borrowed from Cookie and delivered it to Melvin's front porch. Then he returned Cookie's truck and walked back to Melvin's via the back streets of Hope Springs.

He skirted the edges of the cemetery, taking in headstone after headstone bearing names he now recognized. He passed the elementary school, waved at the workers who were sprucing things up for the new term that would begin in mid-August. He passed a couple of churches, the municipal pool, even the picture-perfect cottage he had been so certain he should buy for his mother.

Maybe he was wrong, he thought as he looked at the tiny patch of lawn and the cobblestone walkway. Maybe he shouldn't be trying so hard to work out everyone else's life to suit him.

Maybe Faith would never trust him enough to give her heart to him, and he would only make them all miserable by working so damned hard to convince her otherwise.

He closed the gate beneath the rose arbor and headed up Loblolly to Ridge Lane. He would pick up the weekly paper, then go back to the house. He could find someone else to take his next shift at Faith's. Chuck maybe.

He was so absorbed in his thoughts he almost missed the shriek of the ambulance as it zoomed past him on Ridge Lane. He looked up, wondering where it was headed, already understanding that in such a small town it was doubtless headed for someone he knew. He watched, uneasy.

Then he saw a car zoom past, hard on the heels of the ambulance. He took his copy of the paper from the rack, then glanced back in the direction of the car, which had already disappeared around the bend in the lane.

Had that been Ida's car?

He began to walk in the direction of Faith's house, coaching himself to remain calm. But it wasn't long before he was walking too fast for comfort. And by the time he rounded the corner of Timber Gap Lane, he was running, the *Courier* wadded up in his hand.

The cold fist of fear clutched his heart when he saw the ambulance parked in front of Faith's house. He stumbled, lurched to a stop.

He caught a glimpse of Faith's pale face as the ambulance door closed. The ambulance sped away, ignoring him when he ran after it, calling her name.

CHAPTER SIXTEEN

IF FAITH'S BABY DIED, Sean was convinced that he was to blame. He looked around the tension-filled hospital waiting room and wished there was someone to whom he could confess.

The room was long and narrow, lined with uncomfortable chairs in dingy colors and couches with flattened cushions. There were no windows and the lighting was bad. A TV eavesdropped on the trials and tribulations of teenagers who wanted to date their high-school teachers, but no one seemed to be watching. At one end of the room were family members whose waiting was tempered with excitement and anticipation.

But the end Sean occupied was standing room only with people from Hope Springs, people whose drawn faces held little hope. This end of the room was silent.

Sean propped his elbows on his knees and dropped his head into his hands. His forehead throbbed. He was wrung out. Six hours of sitting vigil while Faith labored to birth a baby who had only a slim chance of survival had exhausted him, emotionally and physically.

He felt a hand on his shoulder and looked up. Ida

sat on the arm of his chair. She looked as if she'd aged ten years since the last time he'd seen her.

"This isn't your fault," she said.

Her gentle voice tore at him; he looked away. "I shouldn't have argued with her. If I hadn't been trying to tell her things she didn't want to hear..." He ran his hands through his hair.

"Faith's temper has been her downfall more times than she can count," Ida said. "She knew better than to be up and about."

Ida's reassurance did nothing to alleviate his guilt, but he didn't say any more. What was the point? He had promised himself—hell, he'd promised Faith— to protect her, and look what had happened. She lay in a delivery room down the hall, giving birth to a baby who needed more time in the womb to be strong and healthy.

It was like history repeating itself, only worse. He'd survived four miscarriages during his marriage, each one harder than the one before, each one destroying a little more of the fabric of his marriage. Each time he and Rachel had left the hospital, she had been a little more distant and he had felt a little less equipped for the role of husband, provider, protector. He had failed her, and her attitude toward him had reinforced that judgment.

And now here he sat in another hospital, waiting for another woman he loved to emerge brokenhearted.

At least she had no faith in him to lose. She'd had none to start with. That irony didn't ease his despair.

Sean felt Ida tense at his side and glanced up. Doc

Sarah stood in the doorway in her scrubs, looking strained and fatigued. "Faith is fine."

Neither Ida nor any of the others from Hope Springs who had gathered at the county hospital spoke. Sean wasn't sure he wanted to hear, either, but he croaked out the words they were all thinking. "And the baby?"

Sarah's hesitation spoke volumes. "He's...very tiny. Two pounds, two ounces."

Sean swallowed hard, trying to imagine how small that was. "But he...he can make it?"

He heard Ida choke back a sob and wrapped an arm around her shoulders.

"A baby this size... There are a lot of complications. We'll be transporting him to the neonatal intensive-care unit in Richmond as soon as we can arrange for the helicopter."

Sean wanted to force Sarah to say that the baby *could* live, that a miracle *could* be pulled out of the hat. But he was afraid if he pressed he would only force them all to admit something none of them felt ready to deal with.

So he kept his mouth shut. Too late, he thought. Too late for that lesson.

SEAN HEARD the steady thump of the chopper's blades when he stepped into the darkened hospital room. The baby was on his way to Richmond; someone would drive Faith the next day, after her release from the hospital.

He walked on tiptoe to her bedside. She barely rippled the surface of the sheets, she was that tiny.

Her eyes were closed, her soft hair fanned out around her pale face. There were deep hollows beneath her cheeks, shadows like bruises beneath her eyes. He ached to hold her, comfort her. But he knew that what he needed to do was get out of here before she awoke. He was the last person she needed to see.

Then she murmured something, so softly he thought she must be talking in her sleep.

She turned toward him, her eyes still closed, and said, "I burned your cookies."

Her voice was slurred with drugs and exhaustion. Sean's heart wrenched in his chest. He thought if he couldn't touch her, he might just die.

"It's all right," he said. Even though what she said made no sense to him, he knew it must mean something to her. And she seemed to need his reassurance.

"Was going to apologize."

He had to lean close to hear her.

"Got mad. Sorry I got—" she seemed ready to doze off "—mad."

He couldn't help himself. He cupped the side of her face with his hand. Had she been this frail when he saw her earlier in the day? How had he missed that?

"It's not your fault, Faith."

She smiled and leaned into his hand, her eyes still closed. Sean thought his heart might leap out of his chest.

Then he realized that as soon as she was fully alert, no longer drugged, she would remember who was to blame for all of this. She wouldn't want his comfort then.

The helicopter ambulance lifted off with a roaring whir. When the sound faded, Faith said, "Taking him to Richmond. Experts."

"That's right," Sean said, his throat suddenly thick. "They'll take good care of him."

She nodded. "Sarah said I can go tomorrow."

Then she began reaching for something.

"What is it, Faith? What do you need?"

"Hand," she said. "Hold your hand."

Squeezing his eyes shut against the tears, he took her hand in his and accepted the gift he felt he didn't deserve. She opened her eyes and he hoped she was woozy enough not to see the tear trickling out of the corner of his eye.

"When I go," she whispered, "will you go with me?"

FAITH LAY in the darkness waiting for daylight, impatient, even in her exhaustion, to follow her baby. Her poor tiny baby was in another town, and she hadn't even been allowed to hold him before they snatched him from her. Did he have ten fingers? Ten toes? A heart and lungs strong enough to see him through? She didn't know. And he was so far away.

A part of her flesh had been torn away, and the wound was too deep and painful to bear.

She had slept for a while, eased into unconsciousness by drugs. When she awoke, she saw a shadowy form sprawled in a recliner at the foot of her bed.

She studied the form in the light that filtered in from the hall.

Sean.

The thought had comforted her enough to allow her another hour of sleep before anxiety set up permanent shop in her muzzy mind.

She was fully awake now, fighting not to visit the dark recesses of her consciousness where fear was already constructing dire outcomes for her baby. Her heart flinched away from her bleak imaginings. She couldn't go there. She wasn't strong enough, yet she wasn't strong enough to stay away, either.

Faith wondered if she had really asked Sean to come with her to Richmond or if that had been one of the many dreams troubling her sleep. She couldn't be sure. But the fact that he was here, stretched out in that instrument of torture the hospital called a chair, took the edge off her fear. Sean would help her. Sean would be at her side. Sean wouldn't let anything bad happen.

She knew deep down that Sean had no control over what happened to her baby. But her confidence in him felt like the only concrete thing she had to cling to. So she held on for dear life.

IF FAITH HAD THOUGHT the weeks confined to her bed a kind of cruel and unusual purgatory, the days and weeks that followed became the depths of her own personal hell.

The neonatal intensive-care unit at Children's Medical Center—a part of the Medical College of Virginia Hospitals in Richmond—became her home, its doctors and nurses her sisters and mothers. Day in and day out she sat in the bright family room with daytime television as a backdrop and the pounding of her heart marking each minute until the hour she could visit Patrick. She knew this area of downtown Richmond near the Confederate White House as well as she knew Hope Springs.

Then, for an hour each morning and each afternoon, she was allowed to put on a hospital gown and mask so she could stand beside the isolette and stare at the tiny scrap of life fighting for his chance.

For the first week all she'd been able to do was stand there and cry.

Patrick had lost three ounces in those first few days. Typical, they told her, because a newborn this tiny had to fight so hard to survive. Tiny and shriveled, he looked more like a withered old man than the plump, precious baby she had dreamed of. He was hooked up to tubes and wires and machines, some to feed him, some to breathe for him, some to make sure the nurses who watched over him could monitor every heartbeat, every brain wave. He didn't seem to hear her voice. He didn't yet know her touch. He concentrated solely on survival, and Sarah had told her he'd already beaten the odds by hanging on for two weeks.

All Faith wanted to do was hold him. All she *could* do was stand by and watch, helpless but not yet hopeless.

Then the hour would be up and the nurses would gently, compassionately usher her out of NICU and back into the family room.

She made that long walk back to the family room now, bone tired, her eyes so heavy she could barely keep them open because whenever she tried to close them and sleep, her racing mind kept her awake. She stood in the doorway when she arrived at the family room, taking in one of those sights that never ceased to amaze her.

Sometimes it was Ida and Melvin. Sometimes Donna and her husband. Or a gaggle of women from the church, arriving with books and magazines and a bag of her favorite hard candies from Hey, Sweetie. Most of the time, however, it was Chuck and Sean. Sean and Chuck. Her two knights, who seemed to have made peace with each other for the sake of their frazzled damsel in distress.

This morning they sat hunched over a table, staring at a chessboard, neither of them moving. They studied their moves and Faith studied them.

Chuck was sturdy and upbeat, always ready with a knuckle under her chin and the predictable admonition, "Chin up." He came whenever he could get away from the store, and promised to take care of things at the house. He brought her a ripe tomato from her garden one day, but Faith hadn't had the stomach for it.

The one who drew her eye was Sean. Sean looked haggard. His last haircut was only a distant memory. His tan had faded to hospital pallor. And he had become Faith's anchor.

She walked over and sat in a chair between them. "How is he?" Sean asked, as he always did.

"A little better, maybe," she replied, as she always did.

No one else had seen Patrick, and she couldn't bring herself to let them know how desperate it seemed to her each time she laid eyes on her tiny son. She always tried to smile and she didn't tell them about the precious ounces he had lost.

But when Sean looked into her eyes, she thought he knew without being told. She averted her eyes. "Who's winning?"

"Me," the two men said in unison.

Faith looked up in time to see them exchange a wry grin. "I suppose you're both cheating, too."

Chuck glanced at his watch. "I'm afraid I'm not smart enough to figure out how to cheat at chess. Maybe you'd better take over for me so I can get to the store in time to open up."

With a hug she thanked him for coming and was soon alone with Sean.

"Take a walk?" he asked. "It's pretty out this morning. Not such a blast furnace."

She glanced in the direction of the NICU and shook her head. "Not yet."

"You can't stay here twenty-four hours a day, Faith." But he said it without chiding, as if he understood her compulsion to do precisely that.

"Maybe later."

"How about this. I'll stay. And you at least go out and breathe some fresh air."

She agreed, but only because she could see that it meant so much to him to do something for her.

Once outside she might as well have been staring

at the walls of the family room. She walked down the block and back at the quickest pace she could force out of her tired legs and took the elevator back upstairs. Sean shook his head.

"That must be a record time for a city block," he said. "Nobody's giving out medals, you know."

"I know it's hard for you to understand, but I have to be here."

Now Sean looked away, but not before she caught the bleak look that crept into his eyes. She kept thinking there was more to Sean's presence here than she understood, but each time she pressed him, she reached the same conclusion. He felt guilty.

And he loved her.

He hadn't said as much again. Who could blame him after the way she'd behaved the last time, and then all that had happened as a result? But she remembered his words and felt instinctively that he still carried those feelings in his heart.

Sometimes she wanted to tell him that she loved him, too. But she couldn't, not under this shadow. Besides, her superstitious heart told her she needed to save every ounce of her love for Patrick. If a mother's love could save a child, she wouldn't cheat him out of one bit of hers.

"Why don't I get us some breakfast?" he asked.

She agreed as before, because he seemed to need to help. When he returned she did the best she could with the biscuit, egg, bacon and coffee he brought.

"Patrick could eat more than that," he said when she pushed the tray away.

She wished. "I have my girlish figure to get back," she said.

"Your clothes already hang on you."

It was true. She had lost most of the weight she'd gained. Soon, she thought, there would be no sign she'd ever been pregnant.

She feared that day. Feared she might be left with nothing, no reminders, no baby. Only emptiness.

Sometimes that fear seemed more real than the present moment.

Before she could stop them, tears were streaming down her face. Sean set down his coffee and gathered her into his arms. He didn't say a word, just held her and rocked her until the tears had run their course.

"Thank you," she said, sitting there with her cheek still snuggled against his chest.

"Thank *you*," he said, although she couldn't imagine why.

SEAN HAD BELIEVED he was ready for this moment. But he looked down at the tiny pale creature named Patrick and thought he might have to turn and run.

The only thing that kept him rooted to his spot beside the isolette was the cold hand that gripped his. Faith had asked him to be here. He would do that or die trying.

"Hi, little one," she said, her voice soft with yearning. "How are you this morning?"

Sean listened as she chatted with her son, trying desperately to pretend they weren't surrounded by the incessant beeps of monitors and the hush of nurses' crepe-soled shoes. He had to force himself to look down at the sleeping baby, force himself not to question how this infant could ever survive, much less thrive.

He thought of the tiny baseball shirt he still had, the one he'd imagined slipping over the head of Faith's newborn baby. What a joke. This little fellow could be lost and never found in the shirt. He hadn't realized until this moment how desperate the situation was. He wished he hadn't come. But Faith had asked him, had arranged it with the doctor even though Sean wasn't a relative. He'd wanted to be here for her, thrilled to be asked. His wife had never asked, never accepted when he offered help and support of any kind. He thought of the way she'd turned away from him in her hospital bed that last time, refusing his touch, refusing to talk, jerking away from his kiss. Her rejection had hurt almost as much as the loss of their baby. So all the times that Faith accepted his help, he'd healed a little bit more.

But now this. He wasn't sure he could handle it.

"He's gained another ounce." The nurse sounded so cheerful, so enthused over the progress, that she might as well have said he'd been born reading and writing. Sean had had too much hope too many times to allow himself any this time, not with the stark reality lying in a high-tech isolette in front of him.

Faith looked up at Sean, her eyes glowing. "Isn't that wonderful? That brings him up to two pounds, six ounces."

Sean wanted to cry but didn't dare. He smiled into the eyes of the woman he loved yet couldn't protect. "That's a lot of progress."

She seemed satisfied with that and looked back down at her son. "Patrick, I brought someone to meet you. Patrick Aidan O'Dare, this is Sean..."

She paused and looked at him questioningly. "What is your middle name, Counselor?"

Sean hesitated. "You don't want to know."

"Oh, come on. How bad can it be?"

"Patrick."

"He's not going to get you off the hook."

"No, I mean, that's it. Patrick. Sean Patrick Davenport."

She stared. "You're kidding."

He shook his head.

"Well, this is certainly strange," she said. "It was Pop's name, you know."

He nodded.

"Well, Patrick Aidan O'Dare, meet Sean Patrick Davenport. No relation."

Sean swallowed the lump in his throat, willed to silence the part of him that desperately wanted to be something more than "no relation" to this little fellow. "Hi, Patrick Aidan O'Dare."

The baby lay still, not moving. Even the rise and fall of his chest, regulated by the respirator, was barely perceptible.

"He's going to live, you know."

Sean had never heard such conviction in his life. He wanted to avoid her eyes, but he couldn't figure out how without his reason for doing so being painfully obvious. He mustered all the confidence he could and looked at her. Her eyes prayed for his belief.

"He's his mother's son, isn't he?"

Again she seemed satisfied with his words. She smiled and linked her arm through his. "Exactly."

And Sean had to admit, if sheer determination could make the difference in one so young, Patrick's mother's fighting spirit might be all the baby boy needed.

THE EVENTS of recent weeks had taught Kelsy something very important, she thought as she got ready for bed.

Life is uncertain, and at one time or another the worst *will* happen. You can't hide from it. You can't run from it.

Faith's problems proved that. But what she could also see, and Faith apparently couldn't yet, was that you could make things worse by letting your fear get in the way of accepting the gifts that life did put in your path.

Kelsy caressed the swollen belly beneath her nightshirt and thought about the months she had refused to see the gift in her pregnancy. Thank goodness she had learned better. It wouldn't be long before she would hold her baby in her arms, something Faith no doubt longed for with everything in her heart.

Tears welled in Kelsy's eyes. She had much to be grateful for and she'd almost missed it. Because of her fear.

The way Faith was missing out on the gift of Sean's love.

Seized by a determination not to miss out on any

more of life's gifts, Kelsy picked up the telephone and started dialing. She'd never called Japan before, and it took hours to find the right number. But when she finally located the right hotel in the right city, the voice on the other end sounded as close as the next room.

He sounded pleased to hear from her. She hoped that was so. Her heart was pounding.

"Steve, I've got something real important to tell you and..." *No more stalling.* "We're going to be parents."

THEY LET FAITH hold her baby for the first time since he was born. But it wasn't the experience she expected. He didn't nuzzle against her the way babies always did. He didn't seem to know, as babies instinctively did, that this was his mother's touch.

She felt empty inside. She wanted to cry. He was so fragile, and the bond between them even more so, it appeared.

One of the nurses put a gentle hand on her shoulder. "Time for him to go back to bed."

Faith nodded, even though she wanted to hold her baby until he knew her. When he was lying on the sterile white sheet once again, she kissed the tips of her fingers, touched her son's cheek and whispered, "See you soon, Patrick."

As she left the unit, she could think of only one thing. Finding Sean. He would listen to her. His presence would make this easier. Thank God for Sean. She needed him. Faith hated admitting that, but she couldn't deny it any longer. He had become her strength, her courage; he helped her keep going when one more day seemed impossible. She sensed how hard this was for him, too, but that didn't prevent him from being there for her. Sometimes, with him at her side, she thought that having a partner might be better than single parenthood, after all. Especially a partner like Sean.

They'd been here five weeks today. Patrick's weight was just one scant ounce shy of three pounds. The doctor said they might start him on tube feedings once he hit three pounds. They had to be careful, the doctor said, because sometimes babies like Patrick lost weight again when they were taken off the IVs.

And Faith's milk had dried up. She wouldn't be able to nurse. She felt robbed, and there was no one to share that bitter feeling with. Sometimes she thought Sean would understand, but it wasn't something you shared with a man.

Unless that man was the father of your baby. Faith had to remind herself sometimes that wasn't the case with Sean. No matter how it was beginning to feel.

She heard his voice as she walked into the family room, but didn't see him. She looked around and was about to go down the next corridor in search of him when she heard another voice coming from the same direction as Sean's.

"Walter doesn't know I'm here."

It was a woman's voice and that, combined with the mention of Walter's name, made Faith stop in the doorway.

"Why did you come? Why do this to yourself?"

That was Sean. The tenderness in his tone gave Faith a moment of uneasiness.

"I had to see…to make it real, I guess. And he wanted me to adopt…"

The last words were muffled. Faith imagined the woman burying her face in Sean's chest, as she herself had done so many times. She leaned against the door frame for support.

"I asked him to leave," the woman said. "I should have done it years ago."

"We should have done a lot of things," Sean replied. "Both of us."

"I know. I should have… It should have been you and me, Sean, all these years."

Sean must have made some kind of nonverbal response, because the woman continued. "You know I'm right."

"Ah, Bev…"

His sigh was audible, even from where Faith stood. Sean and Walter's wife. Faith put a hand to her forehead to stop it from spinning.

"It's not too late, Sean. It's never too late."

Faith ran. Down the stairs and out the front door. She stood in the blinding sunshine, feeling unsteady. But there was nothing to hold on to.

CHAPTER SEVENTEEN

A HALF HOUR LATER Faith was sitting on a bench in front of the hospital when she recognized the woman coming out the front door. Beverly Brickerson. The elegant woman from the photographs that, months ago, had been burned into her memory.

The woman Walter had also deceived. And apparently the woman who now wanted Sean, who felt she'd been entitled to him all along.

Faith was calm again. But it was a deadly calm, the kind you call up when you know you have something dreadful to face and can't afford to fall apart. The calm she'd felt when her father died, when she'd let her feelings go on hold for the duration of the rituals surrounding death.

Beverly Brickerson was even more beautiful in person than in her photograph. She was tall and slender and lovely, the kind of woman who graced fashion magazines and movie screens. Faith knew, as every average American woman knew, that she was no match for a woman like that. But it had never mattered before. She'd always been content to be herself.

But at this moment she felt the abject hopelessness of having to compete with such a woman.

She felt the loss already.

Angry at herself, angry at this woman for disrupting what she had allowed to become another comfortable fairy tale, Faith stood as Beverly passed and said, "I'm Faith O'Dare."

She saw the way Beverly's lips tightened, saw a haunted look flash across her face. The woman nodded. "Then you know I'm Beverly Brickerson."

"Yes. I know." Plenty of things crossed Faith's mind, but as she looked into the elegant woman's face, she realized that the haunted look hadn't been a flash, after all. It lived in those eyes, a permanent resident that might never be evicted. Guilt pooled around Faith's heart for the part she'd played in that, no matter how unintentionally, no matter how innocently she'd been drawn into the deceit. Suddenly there was only one thing to say.

"I'm sorry," she said. "Sorry for my part in damaging your marriage."

Beverly smiled wanly. "I know where the blame lies. But thank you for..."

She couldn't seem to finish, and shrugged.

"I should have known," Faith said. "But I honestly didn't."

"I should have known, too. Years ago. But I didn't, either. Walter is very good at making us believe what he wants us to believe."

Faith nodded.

"He's... It's catching up with him, in case you haven't heard. One of his...friends was a client. The Virginia Bar frowns on that kind of thing, and she's filed a complaint. He could lose his license." There

was dignity in the squaring of Beverly's shoulders
and the tilt of her chin, despite the emotional burden
she obviously carried. "He'd already lost his family,
but I don't think that bothered him nearly as much
as the possibility of getting kicked out of his family's
firm."

Faith couldn't imagine living through the revelation of a lifetime of deception as this woman had. At
least the damage to Faith had been short-term, tran-
sitory. She had already healed. How long, she wondered, would that process take for Beverly and her
daughters? She found herself admiring the woman
and growing determined to show as much strength
and grace herself. "Will you be okay?"

"Oh, yes." Beverly nodded. "And you... I hope
you will, too. I'm sorry about your baby. And I hope
I haven't upset you by coming here. I...well, the
truth is, I felt the need to see Sean."

Now Faith's inner turmoil returned. Maybe she
was wrong to begrudge this woman whatever comfort she might find, even in Sean's arms. Turbulent
emotions still ruled Faith's heart—anger, pain, betrayal—but she forced herself to sound calm and un-
emotional. "Of course. I understand."

"Do you? Someday you should ask him why he
cares so much about your son. You're lucky to have
him as a friend. He's been a good friend to me over
the years and...I don't know, I just felt that seeing
him would make things better."

Faith wanted to ask if seeing him had, indeed,
made things better. She wanted to ask what kind of

friend Sean had been to Beverly. But she could see
the answers in Beverly's eyes.

She spoke through dry lips. "I'm glad we had the
chance to speak."

"So am I. And I want to wish you luck
with...everything."

"And you, too," Faith said, wondering how sincere her own wish was. Wondering how she would
get by without Sean, but knowing she would have to
find out. Pop wasn't the only one whose words of
wisdom proved right more often than not. Ida was
right, too, it seemed. *Learn to live without a man,
dolly. You can't count on one being around just because you need one.*

SEAN LOOKED GUILTY when Faith walked back into
the family room. She wished she hadn't been so
hasty about running out on the rest of the conversation between him and Beverly. She deserved to hear
it all. The whole truth would be easier to bear than
shadowy half-truths.

"You talked to Beverly," he said before she could
figure out what to say. "I saw you from the window."

"The two of you are close."

He looked uncomfortable. Faith sat across from
him. Her stomach felt queasy. Her heart pounded
against her rib cage; surely he could see it, hear it.

"We've known each other a long time. I told you
that."

"I somehow thought you were Walter's old friend.
Not hers."

His cheeks colored and Faith's heart plummeted.

"I guess I was in love with her. Before she met Walter."

The ground seemed to shift under her. She didn't stop to think about the implication that Walter had moved in on his best friend's girl. "And after? Were you in love with her after she met Walter?"

Sean stood and paced to the window. To hide his face? Faith wondered. To cover his reaction? She gripped the arms of the chair. He wasn't even denying it. She felt her calm evaporate, her strength diminish. "Maybe you'd better leave, Sean."

He whirled to face her. "Faith, you don't understand. There's—"

All the bitterness of being betrayed surged to the surface, leaving her with no hint of the grace and calm Beverly had inspired in her. She had only her own quick temper to see her through.

"I don't want to understand, Sean." She hurled the words at him. "I don't want a bunch of explanations or excuses. I've heard enough of those to last a lifetime."

He stood there with a stony expression on his face. "I'm not offering any excuses. I'm offering support and love. But it's clear you don't want that, either. You've been turning that down for months."

She opened her mouth to protest, but he paid her no mind.

"So if you're ever willing to accept what I do have to offer, you know where to find me."

"Sean, I..."

But he didn't slow down on his way out. Faith

took two steps in his direction and told herself it was for the best. She didn't know what to believe or how to feel. And it was better all around if Sean Davenport left and never looked back.

Nevertheless, she felt bereft of the final shred of comfort in her life.

KELSY PACED, waiting less for the next contraction than for Donna to return with some word about Steve.

He was supposed to have been here by now. As soon as the tournament in Japan was over, he'd said last week, he would catch the next plane for the States. *I have to be there for the big day. I don't want to miss a thing.* Hearing those words from him had lifted a burden from her heart, and she'd replayed them in her mind over and over again these past few days.

Then came the Braxton-Hicks contractions, followed by news of the earthquake that had hobbled air transportation out of Japan. Kelsy's baby had proved itself to be as impatient as its mom, and Steve was still stuck in Tokyo.

And now here she was in the delivery room at the county hospital, counting the minutes between contractions and knowing she was in this by herself, after all.

The door opened and Donna came in.

"How's it going?"

"Mother Nature has a cruel streak, that's how it's going. What did you find out?"

Donna shook her head. "No news. Walker Shearin

at the *Courier* said the Tokyo airport is reportedly open. But Fudgie's son is over there and he said nobody's getting out for at least another week.''

Kelsy felt the sting of unwelcome tears. "If you were Fudgie's son, you'd be looking for excuses not to come home, too.''

I just want to be there for the big day. Ha!

"You know you aren't getting any more mellow as the big moment approaches, don't you?''

"I have no intention of coming through this a saint,'' Kelsy said, feeling the beginnings of the next contraction. She gripped the edge of the birthing chair. "One saint at Times Square is going to be plenty.''

The two women exchanged a glance. They'd agreed that Faith was showing more fortitude in her ordeal in Richmond than either of them possessed. Attempts to feed Patrick were meeting with little success—they'd returned to special IV feedings called hyperalimentation. He'd lost two ounces and had a couple of bouts with irregular heart rhythm. Faith was worn-out dealing with everything alone.

Kelsy rode out the contraction, grunting a profanity. As the pain subsided, she welcomed Donna's strong hands on her shoulders, kneading away the tension. She eased back into normal breathing.

"We're sure it's not time for the drugs yet?''

"Patience, my dear.''

Kelsy made a sour face and resumed her pacing, which Donna had assured her would speed up the labor. As much as she wanted Steve to be here for the birth, she wanted this over with more.

"Maybe if he hears things aren't going well, he'll come back," Donna said.

Kelsy didn't have to ask who her friend was talking about. They had discussed the rift between Faith and Sean endlessly over the past few weeks, wondering what had caused it, what would heal it. Faith wouldn't discuss the situation with anyone who visited her in Richmond. Sean wasn't talking, either. And it was a toss-up who looked more tight-lipped and grim. It was clear to everyone that the two needed each other, but each seemed determined to outstubborn the other.

"It's worth a try," Kelsy said.

"Want me to go call?"

Kelsy brightened. "Yeah. Why don't you. And while you're at it..."

"I'll check the airlines."

The call to Sean went unanswered, but Donna had good news from the airlines when she returned. The flight from Tokyo had landed in Los Angeles earlier in the day.

"And there are two flights from Los Angeles to Richmond—one gets in two hours from now."

Two hours. Could she hold out long enough for Steve to get here? That was assuming Steve made the first flight out of Tokyo. "And the other one?"

"Well...it should have arrived two hours ago. So..."

Kelsy stopped pacing. She needed to slow things down. She tried explaining things to her baby in hopes of gaining a little cooperation. But nothing worked. When Doc Sarah came in a half hour later, Kelsy was fully dilated.

"Let's see if we can't get this little one into the world," Sarah said with her most reassuring smile.

"Now?"

"No time like the present."

"Couldn't we wait? Just an hour or two?"

Sarah patted her hand. "It isn't up to us, Kels."

So it was that Kelsy found herself pushing into a contraction when Steve burst through the birthing-room door.

"Am I too late?"

That was the moment Brooke Maria chose to make her entrance into the world. The first sound she might have heard, if she'd been paying attention, was her mother's cry of delight. The next, as she lay on her mother's tummy and squalled to protest against the noise and the light and the cold, might have been the preacher that her father brought with him, asking if anyone present knew of a reason this couple should not be joined in holy matrimony.

Brooke Maria grew silent at that moment, just in time for her parents to say, "I do."

PATRICK SEEMED RESTLESS and fretful, and Faith longed to soothe him. She imagined cushioning him against her breasts, brushing her lips over his little bare head and crooning mother-talk in his ear.

But it wouldn't happen today.

Today would be another hopeless-feeling day like all the others had been since Sean had left. And today, as always, Faith didn't see how she could get through another one.

She was ready to drop physically, ready to break emotionally. But she knew there was no one to catch her, no one to put her back together. So she kept going.

Oh, Hope Springs remained faithful to her. Someone came every day, to spell her so she could get some sleep, to visit her with news. She knew about Donna's plans to renew her wedding vows as soon as the baby was born and she could once again fit into her original wedding gown. The Catholic church would be keeping an eye on that one, in Ida's opinion, because getting Donna back down to a size ten would surely take a miracle. Faith had heard about Kelsy's later-than-last-minute wedding in the birthing room at the county hospital. She didn't even have the energy to wish she'd been there for all the excitement.

But she did experience a pang of regret that everyone else seemed to be having their happy endings. And here she still sat in the middle of a nightmare.

A nightmare made worse by her own fears, her own jealousy, her own hardheaded refusal to see the truth. She thought about Sean all the time. Sometimes he was the only thing she thought about besides her baby. She added up the evidence of his feelings for her, his feelings for her baby. She carefully reviewed everything he had done for her and the loyalty that rang out in every action he had ever taken.

But she had been too willing to convict him of the crimes committed by another.

And she was serving the sentence.

She thought of calling him. She dialed the number twice, but hung up before it started to ring. When she got home—when she and Patrick got home—she could try to make amends. Until then, Sean didn't deserve to get dragged back into her problems.

Faith sighed, and as always, touched the tips of her fingers first to her lips, then to her son's cheek.

"See you soon, Patrick," she whispered, then repeated her other ritual each time her hour in the unit was up. She imagined herself placing Patrick right into God's hands and leaving him there. The image comforted her until she could see her baby again. With a break in her voice, she said, "Keep fighting, son."

Then she turned and headed for the door. She hadn't slept well the night before on the narrow couch in the family room. Maybe she could get a nap now. Maybe—

The shrill bleat of one of the monitor alarms caught her up short as the door closed behind her. Heart leaping into her throat, she whirled to see which infant was experiencing difficulties, fearing as she had a hundred times that it would be Patrick.

She watched in horror as the nurses dashed to the isolette she had just left. They crowded around, working frantically. Faith froze, unable to move except for a hand that reached out in futility.

She heard the words "cardiac arrest" and cried out for help.

But the one she cried out for didn't hear and wouldn't hear. For she had run him off. And now she had no one to lean on while her son waged a battle he had little hope of winning.

CHAPTER EIGHTEEN

SEAN HEARD the frustration in the real-estate agent's voice. "I can't hold on to this house forever, you know. Someone's going to snap it up."

To illustrate, Bama snapped her pudgy fingers, attracting the attention of several other shoppers in the grocery store.

Sean nodded. "I'll decide soon."

"Good. I have a couple coming in from Baltimore next week and the old Harrilson place is perfect for them."

Sean promised to give her a decision by the end of the week, but as he walked back to Melvin's he wasn't sure how he was going to reach that decision. How could he decide whether or not to buy the cottage for his mother when he wavered every day about whether to remain in Hope Springs himself? He'd even backed out of a deal to sell his condo in Richmond. It still sat there, half-empty, waiting for him to make up his mind. Funny, he'd even started thinking of the big house on the corner as Melvin's again. And the real-estate agent wasn't the only one pressuring Sean for a decision.

"Son, if you're not going to stay, I'll need to know soon," Melvin had said on the porch the night before. "I'm a bit past my prime and I'd like a few years of retirement before I go plead my case with St. Peter."

Sean also promised Melvin a decision about remaining in Hope Springs. But the truth was he felt totally incapable of making up his mind right now. Were things really over with Faith, or could he afford to wait out this crisis and try again? Should he go back to Richmond and forget about Hope Springs, or stay here and trust that he could still throttle life out of dreams that seemed deader every day?

Everything hinged on Faith.

He climbed the front steps, weary with the effort to make sense out of his life. He had a will to draft. Maybe he could handle that and get something productive out of the day.

Melvin was waiting for him at the door, his complexion gray, his eyes watery and red. "It's the baby."

Sean felt the chill of dread. He breathed a feeble protest against whatever was coming. "No."

"His lungs collapsed. And—" Melvin drew a trembling hand to his forehead "—I...I'm not sure... Something about cardiac arrest."

The two of them were in Sean's car headed for Richmond within five minutes. The drive was interminable and silent. Whenever Sean glanced in Melvin's direction, the old man's eyes were closed and his lips were moving in silent prayer.

Sean pulled up to the front door of the hospital, ignoring the security people who shouted threats to tow his car away. Sean ran for the stairs, too impatient even to wait for the elevator. Maybe Melvin would park the car. Maybe they would have it towed. Either way, Sean didn't give a damn.

Faith wasn't in the family room, and Sean was about to head for NICU when one of the other mothers caught him by the sleeve. Her expression was condemning.

"Where have you been? That woman needs you."

"Where is she?"

"She saw the doctor a bit ago, but I haven't seen her since. I wouldn't be surprised if they've had to put her in a bed of her own. She's past going."

Sean knew the words were an accusation, but he didn't have time for his guilt. "The baby? How's Patrick?"

The woman took a deep breath. "I heard the doctor say they drew off the fluids in his chest cavity when his lungs collapsed. But it's touch-and-go."

Feeling drugged by the fear that flowed through him, Sean dashed to NICU and pounded on the door until one of the nurses recognized him and reluctantly let him in.

Sean peered into the isolette, yearning to find Faith but knowing he had to reassure himself about Patrick first. His first view of Patrick, the baby boy he'd come to think of as his own, gave him little hope. Tears he had been afraid to shed welled in his eyes, spilling down his cheeks.

FAITH STAYED on her knees in the hospital's dimly lit chapel, afraid to get up, afraid to stop praying. If she did, she might find herself unable to hang on.

The doctors had revived Patrick quickly. They'd put that tube into his lungs. Time would tell, they said. Forty-eight hours. And at the end of that time, they said, if he hadn't improved considerably, it might be time to consider how much more they could help her son.

Faith knew what that meant. They might tell her it was time to let him go, time to allow him to give up his struggle peacefully.

Fresh tears flowed as she thought of it. She wanted to place the outcome in God's hands, to tell God to do whatever was right. But she was afraid of God's decision and prayed, instead, that her son be given one more ounce of courage, one more ounce of strength and determination to survive.

"Please, God, he's all I've got. Please don't take him. Please."

By the time she dried this latest round of tears, it was time for another visit. She got up, stretching her stiff legs and wiping her wet and swollen eyes. It occurred to her that she should have voiced at least one little prayer for her own strength to go on.

She took the elevator upstairs, knowing as the doors swished open that she would hate the smell of hospitals for the rest of her life. She wished she had stopped for a cup of coffee; she desperately needed something to help her keep going. She promised herself a cup as soon as they ran her out of NICU.

She was startled when she looked through the door of the unit to see a man leaning over Patrick's isolette. Another specialist? Another crisis? Then she recognized the shoulders and back, the too-long, unruly hair. She stepped into the unit, but hung back when she heard Sean's voice. He was talking to her son.

"So I need you to hang in there, champ," he was saying, and she heard tears in his voice. "It's going to break my heart if anything happens to you. Because I've got these dreams, you see."

Faith always believed the last round of tears had to be all her body was capable of manufacturing. But her eyes always surprised her. More always fell, as they did now. Hearing the man she loved speak of dreams when she had run out herself gave her something to hang on to, once again.

"I can see you catching balls in a few years. Climbing trees. Riding a bike. I've got a puppy in mind, too, and a tree house. Don't you want to hang around for that?"

Faith could see all those things, too, and it tore at her heart to realize that Sean shared those dreams for her son.

"God didn't bring you this far to drop you, Patrick. So you hang in there. For your mom. She needs you. And I do, too. I can't stand to see one more dream die."

A little sob escaped Faith, and Sean turned. His cheeks were also wet with tears.

"I need *you,* too," Faith said, her voice shaking.

"I'm here," Sean said.

Suddenly Faith was in his arms, and she knew that God had answered her one unuttered prayer for the strength to keep going.

Now if he would only answer the other.

FAITH WAS SLEEPING, her face buried in Sean's shoulder, her feet curled up under her on the couch in the family room, when the doctor tapped her on the shoulder. Wakefulness and alarm flooded her simultaneously.

"He's fine," the doctor said. "He seems to be out of immediate danger."

"Thank God," Melvin said. He looked rumpled, as if he, too, had been dozing in a hospital chair.

Still, as Faith listened to the rest of the doctor's report, she couldn't release the tension that had kept her moving the past forty-eight hours. The burden had not yet been lifted and she knew it. Her life still revolved around this hospital, this room, that little isolette down the hall where her baby was being kept alive by a network of wires and electronic boxes.

But at least they weren't telling her it was time to unplug those wires, turn off those electronic boxes. At least today there was still hope.

And today, again, there was Sean.

After the doctor left, after they saw Patrick once more, Melvin talked her into going with Sean to his condo for some sleep.

"You need the rest," he said with fatherly concern. "You won't do Patrick any good if you end up in a hospital bed."

She knew he was right, so she allowed him to stay at the hospital while Sean took her to his condo and tucked her into bed. As he fussed over her, she murmured, "Thank you for coming back."

He smiled and kissed her forehead. "Thank you for not minding."

"I was wrong to send you away. I'm sorry." She was drifting off, but she had to get the words out before she slept.

"It doesn't matter now. Sleep."

"Hold me."

The last thing she felt was Sean snuggling in beside her, holding her close. She felt safe. Nothing bad could happen now.

SHE AWOKE feeling more rested than she had since Patrick was born. The solid warmth at her back—and in her heart—was Sean.

He stirred against her, and once more she felt the hopes and dreams he had awakened within her when he spoke to her son at the hospital. She touched the side of his face, traced his jaw down to his strong square chin. Without opening his eyes, he grasped her fingers gently in one hand and held them to his lips.

"I love you, Sean," she whispered.

He opened his eyes, and she seemed to see a world of love and security unfolding before her.

"Enough to let go of yesterday?" he asked.

"Enough to believe in tomorrow," she said.

He kissed her then, a long slow kiss that held promise after promise. She lay in his arms and felt so strong, so healed, as if the power of love could defeat any ill, right any wrong. That might not be so, she supposed, but she did feel its effects coursing through her blood right now. She took comfort in Sean's solidity and decided to trust both the comfort and his strength.

"I'm sorry," she said.

He kissed the corner of her eye and gathered her closer into the circle of his arms. "You said that last night. You didn't need to then, either."

"Yes, I did. I'd convinced myself that my fear was justified."

"There's no reason to be afraid of Beverly," he said. "We're close, but that's all. I was in love with her in college, but only for about twenty minutes."

Faith hesitated, then realized everything needed to be said. "Until Walter."

"Faith—"

"We don't need to hide from it anymore. All of it needs to be said if we're ever going to be free of it."

After a few minutes she felt him relax, felt the tension go out of him as he apparently made a decision.

"Yeah," he said. "Until Walter. I guess I should have known then that Brick wasn't exactly good-friend material. But I thought I wanted what he had, and he offered a way to get it. He had family connections, power, social standing—everything I had convinced myself was important."

"But it isn't."

"No," he said. "It definitely isn't."

She didn't have to ask what was important to him now. Every action she had seen him take these past months answered that question. People were important to him. Integrity and compassion and lending a helping hand. She was important to him. And Patrick. His actions had proved that. And she'd heard him say those words to her son.

"Beverly said I should ask you why you care so much what happens to Patrick."

He went very still, and she wished she was looking into his eyes.

"That's *my* fear, I suppose."

"*Your* fear?"

"Your pregnancy terrified me from the beginning. I was so afraid something would go wrong. And when it did...well, it was history repeating itself. I began to think it was me, that I must be the problem."

She pulled out of his embrace now, so she could prop herself on one arm and look into his eyes. She saw once again the unexplained shadow she had seen there before. "What do you mean, Sean?"

"My ex-wife, she was pregnant—" he paused and Faith could almost feel him gathering strength "—four times."

The words jarred Faith, as did the bleakness on his face.

"And she miscarried four times."

"Oh, Sean—"

"It was hard the first time. Devastating. We'd bought all this stuff...for the baby. And each time it got harder. People, friends, expect you to go on as if nothing happened because nobody else had even seen any signs that Rachel was pregnant. Nobody could understand how much you grieve."

But Faith understood from the way his voice cracked and broke over the words, the memories.

"Every time it happened Rachel put a little more distance between us. I tried so hard to be there for her, to reach her. But each time the wall got a little higher. Finally…"

Faith put her arms around his chest, sorry for all the times she had shut him out, rejected his help. "I'm sorry."

"That's over. But…"

"But Patrick has brought it all back for you."

"I never realized how much I was counting on him. How much hope I had for him."

A thought occurred to her, another one she wanted to turn away from. But she knew, once again, that there could be no hiding from anything. "Is that why you love me? Because I could give you the baby you lost so many times?"

"No. That's not even why I love Patrick."

"It's not?"

"No. I love Patrick because he's yours. And I love you because you're strong and spirited and you look trouble in the eye and dare it to take you on."

She stirred, uneasy and restless with his praise, but he shushed her and continued.

"I love you because you don't hold grudges and you don't wallow in self-pity. I love you because you stand on your own two feet—and you're willing to do it barefoot in the dirt."

Puzzled, she looked up at him and smiled in response to the smile on his lips. "What?"

"I've seen you like that twice now, first thing in the morning, walking out to your garden with a coffee mug in your hand and no shoes on your feet."

And she saw something in his eyes when he spoke, something like wonder, and it filled her heart all over again. She swallowed back the powerful emotions and said, "Counselor, does that somehow allude to your need to keep me barefoot and pregnant?"

He laughed softly. "We can negotiate all the fine points. I'm willing to settle for barefoot at the moment."

"I should know better than to negotiate with an attorney."

"I've never seen you lose any major points."

She laughed.

"Will you marry me, Faith? Will you let me be the father to your baby?"

A shadow descended over the moment. How desperately she wanted to say yes and have it be so. But she couldn't know. And she couldn't imagine how it would affect them if the last part of that proposal wasn't possible. "I... Ask me later?"

"I will. Believe me, I will."

SEAN PRAYED a lot in the month that followed. He prayed for Faith and he prayed for Patrick, and he was astonished when his prayers began to be answered, slowly, steadily.

His relationship with Faith deepened. Her fear of their relationship was replaced by calm certainty, and he found himself losing his need to take care of every little crisis in her life.

But the most amazing miracle was Patrick. After the crisis of his collapsed lungs, he seemed to grow more determined to survive. He gained weight. He began to nurse. His skin grew pink and the grip of his tiny fingers grew strong. And one day he weighed in at four pounds, twelve ounces, and the doctors announced that he could go home.

Everyone in the neonatal intensive-care ward cheered. Faith cried. Sean cried. And most everyone from NICU trickled downstairs to the chapel for the wedding.

"Here?" Sean asked. "You're sure you want to do it here?"

Faith nodded. "Right here. Because this is where I found my dreams again. I heard them in your voice one day."

The bride wore a denim skirt, and instead of a bouquet, she carried a baby in her arms. Her eyes filled with tears as they spoke the words that made the three of them a family. Sean's mother and nurses and orderlies and the hospital chaplain waved them off as they left, not for a honeymoon, but for home.

"I can't wait to get there," Faith said from the back seat, where she sat to keep a close eye on Patrick.

Sean thought of Hope Springs and the life that waited there. "Me, too."

Hope Springs was glad to see them, as well. When they crossed the city limits—past the sign that read You'll Need No Other Medicine but Hope—and turned onto Ridge Lane, a huge banner had been strung across the street.

Welcome home, Patrick, Faith and Sean.

People waved from the sidewalk. Others were waiting at the house with food and hugs.

And for the first time in his life, Sean knew he was home.

EPILOGUE

SOME PEOPLE in Hope Springs thought that when Faith O'Dare Davenport came home with her new baby and her new husband that the baby boom at Times Square Crafts was over.

Instead, they found, it was just beginning.

Fourteen-pound Ghengis Khan wasn't happy about it, for when the following spring rolled around, he found that his position as divine master of the front porch had been usurped by thirty-four pounds and nine ounces of crying babies.

Brooke Maria showed up first in a crib that had come all the way from Japan. The crib sat on the porch most of the day so Kelsy could keep an eye on her from inside the store, so people could run up and take a peek. She had red hair and pink cheeks and she cried all the time. Khan moved farther away on the porch swing, but the crying still disturbed his rest. And a good attack cat needed his rest.

Aretha came next. A chubby-faced, smiling baby, she gurgled more than she cried, but that didn't make life any easier for Khan. It also increased traffic on the porch, because anyone who wasn't interested in seeing the two new babies wanted to find out first-hand how Donna had managed to get into her original wedding dress so quickly. Khan took himself to the far railing, which was not as comfortable as the porch swing. He even fell off once, although he instantly pretended the tumble was his idea.

The final straw was Patrick. He wasn't the cutest of the three—in fact, he looked downright scrawny next to Maria and Aretha. But the people in town kept calling him a miracle baby. Sean had to come at least twice a day to coo at him, and everybody fretted and fussed over him. Faith accepted all their attention calmly and told them Patrick was going to be a fine strong boy.

Khan wasn't so sure.

Khan wasn't sure he wanted to wait around to find out. He'd gone on a reconnaissance mission around town the night before and was considering taking up residence on the front porch where Sean practiced law. The traffic there was more to his liking—less hectic, less noisy.

Then he heard someone ask Faith, "He's still so tiny. How do you keep from worrying about him?"

And Faith walked over to the railing, scratched Khan between the ears and said, "Why, Khan looks out for him for me. Don't you, old boy?"

From that moment Khan took up residence on the top step and kept a careful eye on everyone who came by for a look at the Times Square baby boom. Traffic didn't die off, but Khan felt satisfied that he was keeping everything under strict control.

*   *   *   *   *

Continue your love affair with Hope Springs
in October 1998.

*The second book in this exciting trilogy
promises even more surprises!*

Catch more great

# HARLEQUIN™ Movies

featured on the movie channel tmc

Premiering March 14th
Treacherous Beauties
starring Emma Samms and
Bruce Greenwood based on the
novel by Cheryl Emerson

Don't miss next month's movie!
Hard to Forget
based on the novel by bestselling
Harlequin Superromance® author
Evelyn A. Crowe, premiering
April 11th!

If you are not currently a subscriber to
The Movie Channel, simply call your
local cable or satellite provider for more
details. Call today, and don't miss out
on the romance!

the movie channel tmc

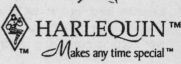HARLEQUIN™
Makes any time special™

100% pure movies.
100% pure fun.

Harlequin, Joey Device, Makes any time special and Superromance are trademarks of
Harlequin Enterprises Limited. The Movie Channel is a service mark of Showtime Networks, Inc.,
a Viacom Company.

An Alliance Television Production

Detective Jackie Kaminsky is back—and this
time *First Impressions* aren't adding up…

Second Thoughts

Jackie Kaminsky had seen enough break and enters to know
that intruders usually took something. This one left a calling
card and a threat to return. The next visit was from a killer.
Jackie had a list of suspects, but as they became victims, too,
she found herself thinking twice about *everything* she
thought she knew—professionally and personally.…

**"Detective Jackie Kaminsky leads a cast
of finely drawn characters."
—*Publishers Weekly***

MARGOT DALTON

Available in March 1998 wherever books are sold.

**The Brightest Stars
in Fiction.™**

Look us up on-line at: http://www.romance.net   MMD421

BESTSELLING AUTHORS
IN THE SPOTLIGHT

.WE'RE SHINING THE SPOTLIGHT
ON SIX OF OUR STARS!

**Harlequin and Silhouette have selected stories
from several of their bestselling authors to give
you six sensational reads. These star-powered
romances are bound to please!**

THERE'S A PRICE TO PAY FOR STARDOM…
AND IT'S LOW

$1.99 U.S.
$2.50 CAN.
Special
Offer

As a special offer, these six outstanding
books are available from Harlequin and
Silhouette for only $1.99 in the U.S. and
$2.50 in Canada. Watch for these titles:

At the Midnight Hour—**Alicia Scott**
Joshua and the Cowgirl—**Sherryl Woods**
Another Whirlwind Courtship—**Barbara Boswell**
Madeleine's Cowboy—**Kristine Rolofson**
Her Sister's Baby—**Janice Kay Johnson**
One and One Makes Three—**Muriel Jensen**

Available in March 1998
at your favorite retail outlet.

PBAIS

FATHER: UNKNOWN (#784)
by Tara Taylor Quinn

Her name is Anna. And she's pregnant.

That's all she knows, all the doctors can tell her. Anna's been in a subway accident, and when she regains consciousness, she has no memory of who she is or where she came from. She has no idea who the father of her baby might be.

Jason Whitaker sees her on the TV news…and recognizes her. She's Anna Hayden. The woman he still loves. The woman who rejected him *three* months before—and is now pregnant.

Two months pregnant.

Watch for *FATHER: UNKNOWN* April 1998 wherever Harlequin books are sold.

Look us up on-line at: http://www.romance.net

HS9ML784

FIVE STARS
MEAN SUCCESS

If you see the "5 Star Club" flash on a book, it means we're introducing you to one of our most STELLAR authors!

Every one of our Harlequin and Silhouette authors who has sold over 5 MILLION BOOKS has been selected for our "5 Star Club."

We've created the club so you won't miss any of our bestsellers. So, each month we'll be highlighting every original book within Harlequin and Silhouette written by our bestselling authors.

NOW THERE'S NO WAY ON EARTH OUR STARS WON'T BE SEEN!

OVER
5 MILLION
BOOKS SOLD
SPECIAL OFFER INSIDE

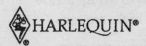 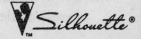

**Look for these titles—
available at your favorite retail outlet!**

January 1998
Renegade Son by Lisa Jackson
Danielle Summers had problems: a rebellious child
and unscrupulous enemies. In addition, her Montana
ranch was slowly being sabotaged. And then there was
Chase McEnroe—who admired her land and desired her
body. But Danielle feared he would invade more than just
her property—he'd trespass on her heart.

February 1998
The Heart's Yearning by Ginna Gray
Fourteen years ago Laura gave her baby up for adoption,
and not one day had passed that she didn't think about
him and agonize over her choice—so she finally followed
her heart to Texas to see her child. But the plan to watch
her son from afar doesn't quite happen that way, once the
boy's sexy—*single*—father takes a decided interest in *her*.

March 1998
First Things Last by Dixie Browning
One look into Chandler Harrington's dark eyes and
Belinda Massey could refuse the Virginia millionaire nothing.
So how could the no-nonsense nanny believe the rumors that
he had kidnapped his nephew—an adorable, healthy little boy
who crawled as easily into her heart as he did into her lap?

**BORN IN THE USA: Love, marriage—
and the pursuit of family!**

 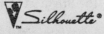

Look us up on-line at: http://www.romance.net

BUSA4

Available in March
from *New York Times* bestselling author

ELIZABETH LOWELL

Carlson Raven had no choice but to rescue Janna Morgan—
the beautiful, courageous woman who struggled against the
stormy sea. When he pulled her from the choppy waters and
revived her with the heat of his body, his yearning was as
unexpected as it was enduring.

But Carlson was as untamed and enigmatic as the sea he
loved. Would Janna be the woman to capture his wild and
lonely heart?

LOVE SONG FOR A RAVEN

Available in March 1998
wherever books are sold.

MIRA BOOKS **The Brightest Stars in Women's Fiction.**™

Look us up on-line at: http://www.romance.net   MEL422